It was time to dance

The wine had infused Sara's veins with a delicious warmth, and she liked the admiration in Julian's eyes. She was ready to feel his arms around her, to feel his body near.

The combo was good, the music smooth and suited for ballroom dancing. They danced well together—on and on, with little talking, just taking pleasure in being close. It seemed the most natural thing in the world to be dancing the evening away in this man's strong arms.

When the musicians took a break, Sara felt a bit dazed, as if she had awakened from a long sleep. But that was Sleeping Beauty. *Let's not confuse our fairy tales,* she reminded herself. Tonight she was Cinderella, and all this wonder would dissolve at midnight. She wanted to spend the night with this man. But what did one say in such a situation to an eleven-year-old daughter and a fourteen-year-old son? *Momie wants to have sex with a man, so I won't be home tonight.*

Dear Reader,

She's the one who rocked you to sleep, bandaged your scrapes with TLC and made your house a home. Mom. This month Anne Henry celebrates Mother's Day and those special women in our lives with *Cinderella Mom,* May's Calendar of Romance title.

In A Calendar of Romance you can experience all the passion and excitement of falling in love during each month's special holiday. Join us next month when Barbara Bretton honors every little girl's hero—her father—in #441 *Daddy's Girl.*

We hope you're enjoying all the Calendar of Romance titles, coming to you one per month, all year, only in American Romance. We'd love to hear from you.

Happy Mother's Day to all our moms!

Debra Matteucci
Senior Editor & Editorial Coordinator
Harlequin Books
300 East 42nd St., 6th floor
New York, NY 10017

ANNE HENRY

CINDERELLA MOM

Harlequin Books

TORONTO • NEW YORK • LONDON
AMSTERDAM • PARIS • SYDNEY • HAMBURG
STOCKHOLM • ATHENS • TOKYO • MILAN
MADRID • WARSAW • BUDAPEST • AUCKLAND

Published May 1992

ISBN 0-373-16437-8

CINDERELLA MOM

Chapter One

As Julian's rented Pontiac began the long gradual climb up Signal Hill, he braced himself for the view at the crest. He felt an overwhelming urge to make a U-turn and head back down the hill, away from the town of Murray, away from the past.

When he left Murray, Oklahoma, over twenty years ago, he swore he would never return. He disliked the tyrant aunt who had raised him, disliked the lackluster town, disliked the people who lived there.

He tightened his hands on the steering wheel as he topped the hill, preparing himself.

And suddenly there it was. *Murray.* His childhood home.

The "skyline" still consisted of the water tower, the grain elevator and the white steeple of the Baptist church. The whole town—its business district and surrounding rows of houses occupying no more than twenty-or-so square blocks—was just a dot on the prairie.

There were more trees than he remembered. From this distance the town looked harmless enough. Quaint even. Like a Grandma Moses painting.

The road sloped gently downward—a great coast on a bicycle, Julian remembered. That was how he spent much of his spare time—riding up and down blacktop roads on an old Swinn he'd bought at a junk sale and jerry-rigged into working condition.

A supermarket and a John Deere agency had been built on the edge of town. Julian was surprised. He couldn't imagine why corporate bosses would waste their money and effort on a backwater town like Murray.

Julian turned left onto Main Street and felt as if he had gone through a time warp. Dusty, drab little Murray hadn't changed much in two decades. Cars and pickups still parked in the middle of the wide street—more pickups than cars—and not very many of either.

But as Julian took a closer look, he realized that the post-World War II facades had been removed from many of the buildings, revealing the vintage brick exteriors underneath. The effect was rather charming, like the pictures he'd seen of Oklahoma towns in the twenties and thirties.

Someone had tied a red bandanna around the neck of the bronze statue of a World War I soldier who presided over the intersection of Main and Central. The town never got around to erecting memorials to those who had died in subsequent wars and simply added their names to the ''Honor Roll'' plaque.

Julian waited for a yellow hound to amble his way to the shady side of the street. The fabric shop was now a liquor store, and the space once occupied by a pool hall was now a bakery. But the barbershop and old-fashioned drugstore were still there, next to Marvella's House of Beauty. And the B & J Cafe was still catercorner from the bank.

The bank looked less pretentious than Julian remembered. He had spent many a Saturday morning washing the financial institution's large plate glass windows. The bank still kept its windows spotless, Julian noted, but the clock that had chimed away the hours of his childhood was no longer working.

The second block of Main Street had not fared so well and had more storefronts boarded up than not. The feed store had enlarged, however, with a garden center now occupying the lot next door.

The water tower at the end of Main still challenged ambitious graffiti writers. Ed proclaimed his love for Sue in large red letters. And the Murray Broncs were either number one or some foolish fan had engaged in a little wishful thinking.

Julian left his car parked in the middle of the street between an ancient Ford pickup with a gun rack behind the seat and a shiny Greer County sheriff's car, and headed for the B & J Cafe.

When he walked in the door, heads turned and conversation paused while the customers—all men—in the cafe gave him a quiet perusal.

Julian had left for the airport this morning directly from a breakfast meeting with the hospital medical staff and was still wearing his uniform. He realized he must be a curiosity in a town that seldom saw strangers and the only uniforms were worn by law-enforcement officers.

A few of the men nodded a greeting in his direction, none with any recognition on their faces. They returned to their afternoon coffee break but continued to steal curious glances in Julian's direction.

"Now, who do you suppose that is?" one of the men half-whispered.

"Army," a man in a barber's smock whispered back. "A major. Don't recognize his brass. It's not artillery or infantry."

Julian wasn't surprised that no one recognized him. When he left Murray, he had been a shy, scrawny seventeen-year-old with a broken front tooth and sun-bleached hair that his aunt cut with a pair of sewing shears rather than allow him to spend money on anything as frivolous as a barbershop haircut. Now Julian was six feet tall with a muscular build. His broken tooth had long since been capped, and his dark hair had a neat, military cut.

Julian took a corner booth and surveyed the men while he waited for the waitress. He recognized Mr. Shoemaker, the banker, and old Dr. Victor, who had once set his broken arm. The uniformed deputy sheriff and the barber were both unfamiliar. Judging by the businesses left on Main Street, Julian decided the other men would be the proprietors of the feed and liquor stores.

The menu on the chalkboard was the same as always: hamburgers, cheeseburgers, chili, fried chicken, chicken-fried steak or fried catfish. Potatoes came french fried, hash brown or mashed with gravy. The national battle against cholesterol apparently had not reached Murray.

The waitress was pretty. The other men in the cafe thought so, too. They kidded with her as she refilled their cups. "Say, Sara honey, which of us good-looking hunks of American manhood do you think is the sexiest?" the deputy asked with an exaggerated wink to his cohorts.

"Why, Lonnie, you all make me swoon so I can hardly pour this coffee. Just look how my hand is shaking," she said as she refilled their cups, her pouring hand as steady as any surgeon's.

Sara. Julian liked that. And her style.

Sara put the coffeepot back on its hot plate. As she approached the corner booth, she smiled and pulled an order pad from her pocket.

"What can I do for you?"

She had a nice smile. And shiny brown hair. She wasn't as young as Julian first thought. Past thirty. He tried to think if he'd known any girls named Sara from his Murray years.

"Do Bea and Jim Cate still own the cafe?" he asked.

"They sure do. For thirty-two years now. You know them?"

"Yeah. I was the town window washer for several years," Julian said, tilting his head toward the windows across the front of the cafe. "The charge for my services was one whole dollar, but if I did a good job, Bea would give me a piece of her famous apple pie."

Sara smiled again. Wonderful teeth. Wonderful skin. Even in her simple waitress's uniform, she was so lovely he wanted to stare.

"They've gone shopping in Oklahoma City, but if you'll tell me your name, I'll sure let them know you dropped by."

"Yes. Tell them Julian Campbell said hello. I'll try to come back by before I leave town."

"Well, Julian Campbell, do you want a piece of Bea's famous apple pie warm with ice cream or warm with Cheddar cheese?"

"Cheese, please, and a cup of coffee."

When she returned with the pie and coffee, Sara asked, "So, you grew up here in Murray?"

Julian nodded. The word *unfortunately* formed in his mind, but he didn't say it out loud. "How about yourself? You from around here?"

"No. I'm from Oklahoma City. But I married a Murray boy. Jim and Bea's son actually."

"Big Ben Cate?"

Her face lit up. "Why yes! Did you know him, too?"

"Everyone in town knew Ben. He was the local football hero."

"And who were you?" Sara asked with another smile.

Julian laughed. "Just the kid who washed windows. One year, I played a rented clarinet in the marching band— badly."

"I played clarinet in high school, too. Haven't touched one since," Sara said over her shoulder as she hurried to the cash register so Mr. Shoemaker could pay his bill. The other men followed the banker to the cash register, leaving an assortment of change scattered about the two tables.

"Don't spend it all in one place, honey," the deputy said with a lingering pat on Sara's shoulder. Judging from the belly hanging over his trousers, the deputy looked as if he stopped by for pie frequently.

Julian watched Sara clean off the tables and allowed himself to regret the gold wedding band on her finger.

In spite of the ring's presence, he waited for one last refill of his coffee cup. He didn't really want any more coffee, but he would like to see her smile one more time.

Interesting. He hadn't had more than passing interest in female smiles for some time. He was beginning to wonder if he ever would.

Thank you, Sara Cate. At least I know I'm still alive.

JULIAN USED TO THINK it was funny that the town's one attorney was named Mason. Murray's attorney was Percy Mason, however, instead of Perry.

"Percy Mason, Attorney-at-Law," the second-floor window above the feed store said. As a boy, Julian had never been able to figure out what it was that made Mr. Mason an attorney. There was no courtroom in Murray. No judge. Little crime. Divorce was rare. Did Percy Mason just sit around all day making out people's wills?

Actually, a will was why Julian was climbing the steep wooden steps to the lawyer's second-floor office. Aunt Rachel's will.

Mason, snowy-haired and plump, sat behind a very large desk covered with an amazing clutter of folders and papers. Evidently he had elected to take a nap on the couch under the window rather than join the other businessmen for a coffee break at the B & J. The right side of his face still bore sleep creases. His wonderful hair was pressed flat on the right side.

"Ah, Major Campbell, welcome back to Murray," Mason said, half-rising from his chair and extending his hand. "Have a good trip?"

"Yes. But it was difficult getting away on such short notice, and I just have a few days' leave. I hope that any business I need to tend to won't take too long."

"Well, you'd have had more notice if I'd known where to contact you. Had to track you down through the Department of Army. Your aunt's services are in the morning at the Methodist church. I took the liberty of ordering some flowers in your name. We'll need to drive over to the county courthouse Monday morning, so you can pick out a tombstone while we're in Mangum."

"Methodist Church? Aunt Rachel was a Baptist."

"Well, she and the Baptist minister had a falling out a number of years back. Rachel Warren wasn't the forgiving sort, you know."

"Yes, I know. Which brings up my first question. Why in the hell did she leave that farm to me? My aunt and I didn't part on the best of terms."

"Yes. I remember. Well, she didn't exactly leave the place to you, Major. She died intestate—which is legal talk for 'without a will.' Since you are her next of kin—her only kin, as far as I can determine—you win by default, so to speak. But dying intestate makes things a bit more complicated legally. The probate court has to declare you her sole and legal heir before the property can be dispensed. We'll have to provide documentation. Tidying things up takes a bit longer."

"Without a will?" Julian had to laugh. "Well, that explains it. I couldn't figure out why she'd make such a gesture after years of silence."

"Actually, she had been thinking about making out a will for some time and maybe putting you in it. But she wanted to attach all these strings. To inherit the farm, you'd have to come back here and live—and take care of all her animals. But I told her she couldn't run the farm from the grave. She was also thinking about leaving the place to the Baptists if they'd fire Brother Robinson—and take care of her animals. I told her she couldn't run the Baptist church from the grave, either. I suggested she bequeath her property to some worthy charitable organization, maybe one that looked after homeless animals. But she didn't trust charities. And while all this considering was going on, she went to bed last Monday night and never woke up. The mail carrier figured something was wrong. It was almost noon when he brought the mail, and the goat hadn't been milked. Which reminds me. Your first problem is the animals."

Julian remembered his aunt's penchant for animals. She would take in stray cats and dogs and fuss over them like babies. But she had no softness, no affection at all, for the stray nephew who showed up at her door.

"How many animals?" he asked.

"God only knows. She's had cats, dogs, a pair of goats, chickens, geese, a horse. A regular zoo. The Cate kids have been taking care of them until you got here."

"Maybe they'd like to take them all home with them," Julian said hopefully.

"I wouldn't count on that. It takes a lot of money to feed a menagerie like that. Rachel spent more feeding animals than feeding herself."

"What about the place itself? She owned it free and clear, as I recall."

"Not anymore. She had to take out a mortgage a few years ago to pay her back taxes."

"I want to sell the place, of course. Will that be difficult?" Julian asked.

"Maybe so. Maybe not. Times are hard, as you can see by the empty buildings on Main Street. There are lots of repossessed farms in the county that lending institutions are practically giving away. And not too many takers, at that. It's hard these days to make a living from the land. But Rachel's place has the pecan orchard, a nice pond, forty acres under cultivation and another forty under lease for pasture. Fences were getting bad, though. And the house needs paint. But if you're willing to price it right and carry the buyer's note, you should be able to realize something from the sale."

"Did she have any other assets?" Julian asked.

"Small savings account. A few bonds. I've prepared an itemized list here of everything I've found, including the farm machinery, but not including the contents of the house. Now, why don't you have a look around, see what of her things you want to keep. We can talk about it more on the way to Mangum Monday."

"Fine. One more thing. What about a place for me to stay? I didn't see that old motel out on the highway. Is there another one around?"

"'Fraid not. That old tourist court burned down a few years back. But you do own a house." Mr. Mason said, handing Julian a ring of keys. "One of these should get you in the door. I think you know the way."

Julian left in a daze. Probate court. Taxes. Realtors. Tombstones. *Animals*. And he thought he'd come down here, sign a couple of papers and be done with it! Now it looked as though this would not be his last trip to Murray after all.

As he walked toward his car, he glanced at the B & J. He'd come back later for dinner. Maybe lovely Sara would still be there. Too bad she was married. If and when he started going out with women again, he wanted to find someone like her—a woman close enough to his own age to be a companion and friend, a woman who had grown up listening to the same music he had and lived through the same history.

He wondered if the Cate children who'd been taking care of the animals were Sara's. Probably so.

Big Ben Cate's kids. If they were anything like their father, they would excel in sports and be the darlings of the whole town.

If Julian could have traded places with anyone, it would have been Ben Cate. He had been the most popular boy in school. Everyone looked up to him and admired him—including Julian. Not that they were friends or anything like that. Julian didn't really have any friends. He was Old Lady Warren's orphan boy. Different. The only kid in school without parents. And Bea Cate used to say he was skinny enough to go through a picket fence sideways. A skinny nobody.

But Ben Cate always smiled and said hello when they passed in the hall at school. Sometimes he'd stop and ask Julian how he did on a test or if he was going to the game. A few times, they studied algebra together. Ben called Julian by his name and not "Julie," a nickname that he had been given in grade school. He hated the name. But everyone in town called him that—except the teachers and Ben Cate. Even Ben's mother called him "Julie Boy." As for Aunt Rachel, she hadn't called him much of anything. "Boy," mostly. *Unload that firewood by dinner, boy. Can't you work any faster than that, boy?*

If he ever saw Ben again, Julian would like to shake his hand. When Ben was around he hadn't felt invisible.

Without really intending to, Julian found himself heading back to the B & J. He could order a Coke this time.

Sara wasn't there.

A plumper, older Bea came bustling out of the kitchen. "So there's the mysterious man in uniform," she said. "I swan, Julie Boy, you went and grew up and got yourself double-dipped in the handsome tank."

Julian was surprised when Bea enveloped him in her arms and kissed him on the cheek.

Then she stepped back to give him a once-over. "I couldn't believe it when Sara described this gorgeous, uniformed man named Julian Campbell. I told her the only Julian Campbell I knew was a skinny little kid that would come up to her nose."

Julian had to smile. He was so bound and determined to think ill of Murray that he had forgotten some nice people lived here. He had not only liked Ben Cate, but he had liked Ben's family. The Cates were decent people.

Bea had felt sorry for him. Julian had often seen a look of pity on her face. And she used to make excuses for Rachel. "Your aunt just doesn't understand about kids. But she's an honest, God-fearing woman who took you in when she didn't have to. Don't you forget that when you get to feeling sorry for yourself. You could be living in an orphanage."

Julian used to wonder if he wouldn't prefer an orphanage to Murray. How could any place be worse than Murray? How could anyone be meaner than Aunt Rachel?

"Jim and I were real sorry to hear about your aunt," Bea said, propelling him to a counter stool and pouring him a cup of coffee.

"A shame you and Rachel couldn't have seen each other again and make up before she died," Bea continued, pushing the sugar server in his direction.

"I would have come. All she had to do was ask."

"That's what I told her. She was as stubborn as a hard-of-hearing mule with rheumatism, that aunt of yours. She said you did the leaving—you had to do the coming back."

"You know why I left?" Julian asked.

Bea nodded. "She apologized for that."

"No, she didn't. She begrudgingly admitted she had been wrong. I hadn't taken money from her billfold after all. That's hardly the same."

"But to run off without a goodbye..."

"The time had come for me to leave, and I didn't want to hear how ungrateful I was."

Julian's stomach was churning with the old hurts. He was sorry he had come back. They didn't need him to bury that mean old woman. And her farm could blow away for all he cared.

Bea touched his arm. "You staying out at her place?"

"I don't seem to have much choice in the matter. Holiday Inn seems to have bypassed Murray. You know, it's hard for me to understand why any of you stay in a place like this."

"Why, it's home," Bea said simply. "Jim and I grew up in this little town. We raised our boy here, and we're helping to raise our grandkids here. When we die, we'll be put to rest among the ones we love. For me, Murray is the dearest place on earth."

"Was Murray dear to Aunt Rachel?"

"I don't know, Julie Boy. Your aunt—something happened to her a long time ago that robbed away her heart and left her empty and afraid. I think she wanted to love you, but she didn't know how. Maybe her being hard on you and making you work was her way of saying she cared."

Julian doubted the truth of Bea's words and declined to comment. Instead he asked, "Are your grandkids the ones who have been taking care of Rachel's animals?"

Bea nodded. "Quite a collection Rachel accumulated. She wasn't afraid of animals like she was of people. The kids have been looking after things since the mailman found her on Tuesday."

"Ben's kids?"

"Yeah. Sara and Ben's. Boy and a girl. Wonderful kids. I don't know what Jim and I would do without them. I love 'em so much it scares me. And Sara. That's one mighty sweet girl our Ben married. She's like my own daughter."

"Pretty, too," Julian observed, taking a last sip of coffee and picking up his cap.

"We won't be at the memorial service in the morning," Bea said apologetically. "I feel real bad about it, but we've been promising the kids for months that they could enter the fishing derby over at Canton Lake. In fact, they're probably waiting on me now with the camper loaded and ready," she said with a glance at her watch.

"Don't give it a thought," Julian said. "I'd rather go fishing myself. And I don't even like to fish."

"I tell you what. You come over to the house for dinner Monday evening. I want Jim to see how well you turned out. And maybe we can help you decide what to do with all those animals. I'll personally volunteer to wring the rooster's neck. That's the noisiest dang bird west of the Mississippi. Course I'd have to stew him. He'd be too tough to fry."

"I hope I'm on my way back to North Carolina by Monday evening," Julian said. "I need to be at work on Tuesday."

Bea hesitated. "Sunday evening, then. We'll get home in plenty of time. You come on Sunday. And bring your appetite."

SARA SMILED when she looked at what Mary Sue had packed for the camping trip. Her daughter had forgotten her pajamas and toothbrush but had a suitcase full of books, games and two stuffed animals.

Sara didn't check Barry's duffel bag. At fourteen, he was insisting on more independence and privacy. The duffel bag was an old one of Ben's from his high school days, the faded emblem of the Murray High Broncs on its side.

She carried the children's bags out to the camping trailer. The adults planned to have everything ready to roll by the time the children got home from their after-school ball practice. Barry played baseball, Mary Sue softball.

The trailer was already loaded to the gills with lawn furniture, a folding table, charcoal grill, boxes of groceries, Japanese lanterns to string around the campsite, an electric bug killer. It looked as if they were preparing for an expedition to the Sudan rather than a two-night trip to Canton Lake.

Bea always insisted on taking too much stuff, and Jim just smiled indulgently, saying she'd take the kitchen sink if she could figure out how to unscrew it. And instead of usual camping fare, Bea cooked for days ahead of time preparing pot roasts, casseroles, frying chicken, baking an assortment of desserts. She even made mashed potatoes on camping trips! If Sara were in charge of the food, they'd be roasting hot dogs and eating sandwiches.

Sara got impatient with the whole camping and fishing scene. She didn't like the hassle of packing and unpacking the camper. She didn't enjoy showering in public bathhouses. And she didn't care much for fishing. But the children loved everything about such adventures, even sleeping stacked in the cramped camping trailer. If Sara offered to stay home and manage the cafe or work in the garden, she got a round of protests. Her children and their grandparents wanted her to share the fun. So, like always, Sara was a good sport.

Sometimes she still found herself marveling at how a girl who had never been on a horse, never planted a garden or canned vegetables, never held a hoe or picked caterpillars off tomato vines ended up living on a farm and raising two country children.

But she liked most things about country living. The sunsets. Fresh air. Gardening. Horseback riding. A sense of community. Peacefulness. She seldom thought to lock the car or the front door. No one did. And she could allow her children more freedom than she ever would have dared elsewhere. Bea and Jim had been right about that. They said that growing up country would be the best gift she could give her children.

She wondered if Rachel Warren's nephew felt the same way about country life. Maybe he and his family would move to Murray and live in Rachel's house. It would be nice to have a woman friend her own age close by to visit with over coffee.

Julian Campbell seemed like a nice man. Very nice. He had a sincere smile. But sad eyes.

Sara liked the way he *didn't* call her "honey" and flirt like the other men. She got tired of all that flirting. Why couldn't those men just call her by her name and talk to her about the weather and sports and what they read in the paper as they did with other men?

JULIAN FELT AS IF he should be riding his old Swinn instead of driving a car out to Rachel's.

The house and barn he had personally painted two different times looked as though they hadn't been painted since. The lawn and shrubs he'd tended for so many years were overgrown. The fruit trees by the barn had split, with branches resting on the ground. The pecan orchard was choked with underbrush. The fences he had endlessly mended were in disrepair. The driveway he'd kept graveled was washed and rutted. In spite of himself, it made Julian sad to see the place so run-down.

As soon as he stopped the car, two huge yellow Labrador retrievers came loping up to the car, tails wagging. "How you guys doing?" Julian said, scratching their heads. Two other dogs quickly joined them—a three-legged yellow hound and a yappy spotted terrier. Two very large geese flapped their wings and honked indignantly but kept a respectful distance. A cat came out of the barn. Two other cats were enjoying the last rays of the afternoon sun on the back step of the house and lifted their heads for a languid glance in Julian's direction. Another cat peered at him from the roof of the shed.

The four dogs accompanied him as he took a look around the premises. In a paddock by the barn were two goats, a donkey and the world's most sway-backed mare. The elderly mare looked up from her grazing and ambled over to the fence.

Timidly, Julian reached out to stroke her neck. He'd never been comfortable around horses, but the old girl didn't seem to mind being touched. He tried scratching her velvety nose.

"You couldn't possibly be good for anything. Rachel must have saved you from the dog food factory, old girl," Julian told the horse. She responded by rubbing her nose against his arm in a not-so-subtle hint that it could use a little more scratching.

The eggs had been gathered in the hen house. The rooster was strutting about, keeping his distance and a wary eye on Julian.

Julian was surprised to find the house unlocked. But then this was Murray. Hardly a high-crime area.

Julian opened the door, squared his shoulders and went inside. The kitchen was not as large as he remembered. The linoleum that he'd installed was worn through in the traffic areas. But otherwise the room was the same. Tidy. No frills. Pots hanging over the stove. The same well-worn wooden table where he and Rachel had eaten their silent meals.

He glanced into the small parlor with its stiff furniture and lace doilies. In the years he had lived in the house, the parlor was used only when the preacher came to call. The other callers Rachel would infrequently entertain sat at the big, round kitchen table.

Rachel's bed was unmade—a jarring note in the tidy house. She had died in that bed just four nights before, the same bed in which she had been born. Rachel had lived her entire life within these walls. To Julian's knowledge, she had never traveled any farther than Oklahoma City.

Julian stood staring at the bed, trying to feel sadness or some sort of good feeling for the woman who had died there. But he felt only emptiness. He and Rachel had failed each other.

He was shocked to see his tiny bedroom behind the kitchen exactly as he had left it. "My God," Julian said out loud. His airplane models were still on the shelves alongside his books. On the bedside table was the same old-fashioned wind-up alarm clock. The bed was even covered with the same quilt.

Why? Had she just never bothered to get rid of his things? Did she think that he was coming back?

Then he felt tears coming to his eyes—not for Rachel, but for the lonely little orphan boy who had lived in this room. "Damn you, old woman! Why weren't you nicer to that poor little kid?"

Julian brought his bag in out of the car. The hound followed him into the house. The other dogs seemed content to wait on the porch. The dog curled up on a blanket in the corner of the kitchen. Apparently the three-legged dog was the only one who had been granted house privileges.

After unpacking his bag, he changed his clothes and went back outside to see about the animals. A note in a childish hand was tacked to the barn explaining what to feed each animal and instructing him to milk the nanny goat morning and evening. A postscript warned him that the donkey bit. The note was signed Mary Sue Cate.

The rooster was braver now and pecked at Julian's legs as he threw out feed. "You better watch out, old man. I've had one offer today to turn you into rooster stew."

He discovered that he could still milk a goat. Rachel had always believed that goat milk was better for the digestion than cow's. The nanny was reasonably cooperative during the process but kicked over the pail. Julian shrugged. He didn't want the milk anyway. Just the smell of goat cheese over the years had brought back unpleasant memories.

He went to the B & J for dinner. A dour-looking woman named Martha served him chicken-fried steak. The Cates usually didn't come in evenings, she explained. Julian and an old farmer in overalls were the only customers. The farmer was hard of hearing, and Martha communicated mostly with nods and grunts. Julian ate his meal in silence.

A surprising number of people came to Rachel's funeral. A funeral-goer herself, Rachel had always been in attendance when townfolk passed on, wearing her black funeral dress and black hat with the tired cloth flowers. Their kin owed her.

No one cried. That fact seemed sadder than her passing.

After the service, the ladies of the Methodist church brought lunch out to the farm. The minister and a dozen or so of the folks who'd attended the funeral dropped by to eat ham and pie and comment on how natural Rachel had looked. Everyone agreed that when their time was up, they wanted to go as peacefully as his aunt.

Julian wandered into Rachel's bedroom with a vague notion of going through her personal effects. He pulled open a bureau drawer and stared down at carefully folded underclothes. Later, he decided.

He poked around the barn some, the four dogs trailing after him. He gathered eggs, raked out the hen house, fixed the hinge on the barn door. Before long, he found himself mending fences. He could almost hear his aunt's words. *Don't wait until I tell you to fix it, boy. You got eyes. Do what needs doing.*

After he milked Nanny and fed the animals, he warmed some of the funeral food for dinner and settled down for an evening of television.

Rachel's ancient black-and-white television only got four channels, badly. But he stared at the flickering screen until the test pattern came on. Then he retired for another restless night, sleeping on the cot of his childhood.

Out of sheer boredom, he spent Sunday mowing and trimming. He was ready for some human company and relief from the funeral leftovers by the time Sunday evening rolled around.

The Cate farm adjoined Rachel's but it was still a half mile or more, front door to front door. Julian drove, feeling once again as though he should be riding a bicycle.

He was surprised and pleased when Sara opened the door, looking prettier than before in a denim dress and western belt. She gave him one of those wonderful Sara smiles as they shook hands.

Behind her in the living room, two children were watching television. Julian wondered if their father was here, too.

"Kids, come here and meet an old friend of your father's," Sara called.

Both youngsters had inherited their father's blond hair. The girl was about ten or eleven and already showed promise of being as pretty as her mother. The boy was older, his shoulders starting to broaden, a line of fuzz visible above his upper lip.

"These are my children, Mary Sue and Barry," Sara said proudly. "Children, this is Major Campbell."

Mary Sue stepped forward with a shy smile and shook his hand first. Barry followed suit. "When did you know my dad?" he asked.

"In high school," Julian explained.

"Did you play football?" Barry asked eagerly.

"No, but I saw your dad play many times, including the game when he made a game-winning, seventy-yard run against Verden for the state 1-A Championship."

"Cool!" Barry said. "They got a plaque for him over in the high school. And even retired his number."

"As well they should have. He was a great one. Is your dad going to be here tonight? I'd sure like to see him again."

Julian knew immediately he had said something wrong. Mary Sue and Barry looked at their mother with puzzled expressions. Sara looked embarrassed, flustered.

"I'm sorry," she said. "I thought you knew. Ben's dead. He was killed almost three years ago in a tractor accident."

Chapter Two

Ben Cate dead!

Julian found it hard to believe. Ben had been bigger than life. He was the sort of young man people were weaving legends about while he was still living them. Ben had had everything—including the lovely young wife and two embarrassed children standing in front of him.

Julian felt confused and very sorry. Ben Cate had been kind to him at a time in his life when he desperately needed kindness.

"No, I didn't know he was dead," Julian said softly. "My aunt and I—well, we didn't stay in touch. I'm sorry. He was a terrific guy. I know you're all very proud of him."

"Yes, we are," Sara said. She put her arms around her children's shoulders. Her son was almost as tall as she was. "We miss him every day, don't we kids?"

Mary Sue and Barry nodded, both looking down at the floor. It was an uncomfortable moment. Julian would have gladly backed out the front door and returned to Rachel's house for more leftovers.

"Why don't you kids go finish watching your program," Sara suggested. "Major Campbell and I will go say hello to Grandma and Grandpa."

Julian followed her down the hall into the kitchen. Bea was frying fish. Jim was making a salad.

While his wife was getting plumper, Jim had gotten leaner, his skin more leathery. The smile lines around his mouth had become creases.

"Nice to see you, Julie," Jim said with a hearty handshake. "I hear you've done all right by yourself. An officer in the Army. Your aunt was mighty proud of you."

"She was? I wasn't aware that she even knew I was in the Army."

"Course she did. Your wife wrote to her every Christmas."

Brenda wrote to his aunt? That was news to Julian. But it was the sort of thing Brenda would do. Brenda was a stickler for thank-you notes and greeting cards. And she thought he was mean never to write that poor old woman in Oklahoma. "That 'poor old woman' never terrorized you with a broom, or you wouldn't feel sorry for her," Julian had insisted.

"Julian didn't know that Ben was dead," Sara told her in-laws as she tied an apron around her waist.

A veil of sadness fell across the two old faces.

"I'm sorry," Julian said. "Ben was a fine person."

Bea and Jim nodded. Yes, their Ben had been fine.

"I don't know what I would have done without Bea and Jim," Sara said. "Since Ben died, they've been like my own parents. The children and I live here with them."

"Ah, honey, you are our own," Jim said, kissing his daughter-in-law's cheek. "You and those kids have given Bea and me a new lease on life."

Jim explained to Julian that when Sara and the children came to live with them, he and Bea started closing the B & J on weekends and hired Martha so the family could eat at home in the evenings instead of grabbing a hamburger at the cafe.

"We practically raised Ben at the B & J," Jim explained, "and we decided we weren't going to do that to our grand-children. We wanted them to eat family meals at home in the evening and go on family fishing trips on weekends."

Julian sat on the kitchen stool, sipping a beer and feeling very much the outsider as he watched Sara help Bea and Jim with the final preparations for dinner. He offered to help, but Bea said, "You just sit there and rest yourself. When we drove in earlier, we noticed all that hard work you've been putting in over at Rachel's farm. Place is looking much better. Rachel had gotten too old to do much and used what income she had to feed animals instead of paying a hired hand."

The three adult Cates worked together well. Bea was in charge, but Sara and Jim carried out their roles efficiently as potatoes got fried, corn on the cob roasted, squash stewed, corn bread baked. Jim kept going out the back door to check the barbecue grill. Sara opened a jar of home-made pickles and another of strawberry preserves. Julian was flattered that they were going to all this trouble for his benefit. But then this was Murray. Visitors didn't come very often, he supposed.

Finally, the food was cooked and piled into serving dishes, but the meal was delayed a bit while Jim and the children made final preparations on some secret in the dining room. Sounds of chairs being pulled about and giggling came from behind the closed double doors.

Finally, the doors swung open, revealing a room deco-rated for a party.

A banner was hung across one wall. "Happy Mother's Day, Grandma and Mom!" Balloons and streamers hung down from the light fixture. Gift-wrapped packages waited on the sideboard.

Mother's Day! Julian's heart sank. No wonder, Bea had originally invited him for Monday night. They hadn't gone to all this trouble for him. It was a family celebration. He shouldn't be here at all.

"It's nice to have an old friend of Ben's here to share our little tribute to the two greatest ladies in the world," Jim said graciously.

Julian wanted to protest. He wasn't really Ben's friend. If Ben were still alive, he'd probably have to stop and think even to remember Julian Campbell at all.

Jim said grace and began serving from two platters—one laden with fried fish, the other piled high with barbecued ribs. "Venison," Jim explained as he put some ribs on Julian's plate. "I bagged this guy last fall. You like to hunt?"

"Actually, I've never been hunting," Julian explained.

"Not in your whole life?" Barry asked incredulously. "Me and Grandpa hunt all the time. My dad was the best shot in the whole state. I got all of his trophies and medals to prove it."

"Grandpa and I," Sara corrected. "Major Campbell didn't have anyone to hunt with when he was growing up."

"I've got my own rifle," Mary Sue said. "I can shoot as good as Barry."

Barry shot his sister an irritated look but didn't dispute her words.

"Tell us about your wife," Bea said. "You got children?"

"No children. And no wife. Not anymore."

"Oh?" Bea said.

"My wife and I are getting a divorce."

"I see," Bea said, in a tone that obviously said she didn't *see* at all. The word "divorce" still hinted of scandal in a town like Murray and was referred to in hushed tones. It was something nice folks didn't do.

"What do you do in the Army?" Barry asked.

"I run a hospital," Julian answered.

"You mean you don't drive tanks or fly planes or anything like that?" Barry demanded.

"I'm afraid not," Julian said. "I work in an office and shuffle papers, write memos, make sure other people are getting their work done."

"Our daddy flew an airplane," Mary Sue said.

"He did some crop dusting on the side—to help make ends meet," Sara explained.

"Well, that's certainly more exciting than running a hospital, isn't it?" Julian asked Mary Sue.

Barry and Mary Sue both nodded, agreeing with him wholeheartedly. "He could play the guitar, too," Mary Sue said.

Julian discovered that he didn't like venison. It had a strange, wild taste he found unpleasant. The fish was tasty, but he had lost his appetite. He tried to act interested in his food and in the conversation that continued to revolve around the exploits of Big Ben Cate—all-state football *and* baseball player, sharpshooter, church deacon, musician, calf roper.

"It was Ben's idea to plant peanuts. Now we have almost as much land in peanuts as wheat," Jim said proudly. "If he'd lived, he'd have turned into a better farmer than his old man."

Several times Sara tried to change the conversation, asking Julian how long he'd been in North Carolina, how many years he'd been in the service, how he'd managed to put himself through college. He gave her perfunctory answers. She was just being polite.

Julian remembered to tell the children he had opened a charge account at the feed store, and asked them if they would continue caring for the animals—for pay, of course. And for every animal they gave away, there would be a five-dollar bonus.

"My hospital is facing a general inspection. As soon as I get that over with, I'll come back and clear up my aunt's estate," he promised. "We'll add up the bonuses then."

Julian tried to leave before the opening of presents, but Sara and Bea both insisted he stay for coffee and dessert, which apparently came after presents.

Mary Sue turned out the lights and carried in a cake with candles, singing "Happy Mother's Day to You."

"I think you should get candles and wishes on Mother's Day, too," Mary Sue said eagerly.

Bea and Sara agreed and blew out the candles in unison.

"I made the cake by myself," Mary Sue said. "Grandpa just helped me measure."

First, Bea unwrapped a quilted vest that Sara had made. Then a handsome photograph album from Jim and the children. Several of the pages had already been filled with photos and clippings from Ben's high school football days. And then Mary Sue and Barry proudly carried in a framed, poster-size enlargement of one of the pictures—Ben in his jersey, smiling at the camera.

Bea sniffled a bit. "Wasn't he just the handsomest boy you ever did see?" she asked as she embraced her husband. "And I've been meaning to put all those clippings in an album for the longest time," Bea said, with hugs and kisses all around. "What a nice surprise!" She handed it to Julian so he could have a look. Julian hoped his smile didn't look too frozen as he turned the pages.

The children's school pictures had been framed for their mother. And they presented their grandmother and mother both with a box of bath powder.

Then Mary Sue read poems she had written—first for Bea and then for Sara. The best mother and grandmother in the world.

And finally Jim stood and lifted his water glass in a toast. "There wasn't anything my mother wouldn't have done for her kids. My son Ben had the same kind of mother. And it fills this old farmer's heart with joy to see that my grandkids do, too."

Julian dutifully raised his glass. After the toast, there was another round of hugging and kissing. So much love.

Julian felt like a voyeur. An outsider. A little boy with his face pressed against the toy-store window.

Mother's Day.

He remembered making a card for his mother at school. "Happy Mother's Day" laboriously written in large first-grade letters. His mother had taped it up on the front of the refrigerator and said it was the most beautiful Mother's Day card she had ever seen.

Julian had forgotten about that card. It had had his school picture on the inside along with the outline of his hand.

Sara walked him out to the car. "I'm sorry," she said. "They do talk about topics other than Ben."

"I know they do. You've got nice kids, nice in-laws. Nice memories."

"Yes, I'm very lucky. You don't have any of those things, do you?"

"Actually, being with your family tonight helped bring back a nice memory of my own mother. She died so long ago, I have very few memories of her. For most of my childhood, it was just me and Aunt Rachel. And those

memories are painful. I've had some good years with my
wife, but after two people part, one tends to go back and
filter all those memories through a new perspective, and
they get skewed in the process. You decide you couldn't have
been happy after all, or the marriage would have lasted forever.''

The moonlight made her hair darker, her skin whiter. The
moon goddess. An apparition. Not real at all.

"I'm sorry Ben is dead,'' Julian went on. He wanted to
take her hand but didn't dare. "Truly I am. I know he was
a wonderful father and husband, and you must miss him
dreadfully. But I also feel very confused.''

"How's that?'' she asked.

The soft evening breeze teased at her hair and brought the
scent of her perfume to Julian's nostrils. He took a deep
breath, silently praying that the right words would come.

"I always thought Ben Cate was the nicest kid in this
town,'' he began. "I respected him and was jealous of him
at the same time. I would have given anything to be like him.
To run down the field with the football. To have everyone
know who I was and like me. And when I found out the
other day that you were married to him, all those old feelings came back. I was glad you were married to someone as
fine as Ben, but I was sorry you were taken. Real sorry. In
the space of one short smile, you made me realize that I still
wanted to find a special someone in my life.

"For a long time, I hoped that special someone was the
woman I had married. Brenda and I worked at it, but it was
never really there for us. And that special someone wasn't
going to be you because you were Ben Cate's wife. But suddenly, sitting there in the B & J Cafe in Murray, Oklahoma,
I knew that woman was out there some place. I actually
walked out of the B & J feeling better than I had in a long
time.''

Sara was leaning on the fence, her face in profile. The sweetness of that profile made him ache.

"And now I find out that Ben is dead," he continued. "I find myself grieving more for him than for the woman who raised me. He had so much to live for. Such a damned rotten break for him, for you and those kids, for Bea and Jim! So unfair. But at the same time, I want to see you again. I want to find out about you, find out if we might someday care about each other in a special way. But feeling that way makes me feel like a grave robber."

SARA WENT BACK into the house in a daze. The dining room table had been cleared. Sounds of Bea cleaning up came from the kitchen. Jim was in the living room helping the kids with their homework.

Sara ducked into her bedroom to compose herself before joining Bea in the kitchen.

She sat on the bed and put her hands against her cheeks. Her face felt hot, her hands cold. In spite of a broad-brimmed hat and number-15 sunscreen, she'd gotten too much sun over at Canton. The reflection off the water was more treacherous than the sun itself.

Or was it Major Julian Campbell who made her skin burn?

She had been widowed for almost three years, but tonight was the first time that a man had paid her court. She couldn't believe that he was saying what he was saying. She wanted him to stop and, at the same time, wanted him to go on. She didn't know whether to run in the house or throw herself into his arms.

As it was, she acted like a prudish goon. He offered to delay his departure until Tuesday. But she told him she had to go to a PTA meeting tomorrow night, when she didn't have to do any such thing.

She had been embarrassed and afraid. She wasn't sure what "seeing" her again meant. Did that mean having dinner at the B & J? Did it mean driving to Mangum for a movie? Did it mean a drive in the moonlight? A kiss? Something else?

Sara stared in the dresser mirror at her flushed face.

She wasn't up to this. She had hardly dated at all before she met Ben. She was barely eighteen years old when she'd met him at an amateur rodeo. She was there with a girlfriend, who was barrel racing at the same event. Ben was entered in calf roping and bronc riding. He didn't win, but he was the handsomest boy there. Sara had planned to get home early but changed her mind and went along with her girlfriend and a group of the youthful performers for a late-night dinner and some dancing.

Ben was a year older, already out of high school. His folks had wanted him to go to college, but he was restless. He would have liked to become a professional rodeo cowboy but felt he wasn't good enough to make a living at it. When he was offered a job by a company that supplied stock to rodeos, he accepted. He would travel about the country, hauling bulls and broncs to rodeos, taking care of and handling the animals while they were there. He'd get to see the country and make good money, he explained to Sara.

Ben drove into Oklahoma City three times to see her before he left the state and headed for the West coast. Two weeks later, he sent her a plane ticket to Los Angeles and a proposal of marriage.

She had married Ben almost without a courtship and wasn't adept at small talk and flirting. Now, sixteen years later, she was thirty-four years old and felt adolescent and stupid. She was both sorry and relieved that she had told Julian no.

She went into the bathroom for a drink of water and two aspirin. Maybe they would calm her. The flush was gone from her face, but now she looked pale.

Why did you have to go and get yourself killed, Ben Cate? she thought as she added some blush to her cheeks. *I don't know what I'm supposed to do now. I don't know how to live the rest of my life.*

When Ben's proposal of marriage arrived, her mother had insisted Sara wait until after she graduated to get married. And what about her plans for college? But Sara could not possibly have waited. Ben might change his mind. She was in love.

"Honey, you can't possibly be in love with a man you don't even know," her mother had insisted.

Her mother was right. And while Sara never got used to the life on the road, her girlish crush turned into genuine love for her handsome cowboy husband. And with love came fear as she watched him risk his life every day, handling animals chosen because they were the strongest and meanest that could be found. The animals had wild eyes and killer instincts. But Ben shrugged off the bruises and even a few broken bones. The vagabond life suited him. The rodeo cowboys were his kind of folks.

When it was time for Barry to start school, she begged Ben to quit and find some other line of work. Anything. She'd rather he clean streets than end up maimed or crippled or dead. But Ben sent Barry back to his parents in Murray to start school and kept on traveling. Those were hard times for Sara. She cried at night for her son and resented Ben for keeping her from him.

And then Ben was gored in the leg by a Brahma bull. The injury left him with a permanent limp. Finally, he was ready to go home.

Ben used the money they had saved to make a down payment on a farm near Murray. With his crippled leg, farm work was difficult—even driving the tractor.

It was the tractor that killed him. He was cultivating a hillside and must have turned too sharply. When they found him, the tractor was on its side, Ben under it.

Ben had bought the farm when oil and land were high in the state. When the bottom fell out of the oil industry, land went down, too. A lot. And the price of cattle. After selling the farm and paying the mortgage, she didn't have enough to pay off other debts. Bea and Jim paid the rest and invited Sara and her children to live with them.

Whenever Sara got depressed, she reminded herself how lucky she and her children were to have Bea and Jim. *Damned lucky.*

Sounds from the kitchen interrupted her musing. With a deep breath, Sara headed down the hall.

She worked hard at keeping her expression a careful neutral as she strolled into the kitchen. But Bea was looking at her funny.

Sara turned the water on too hard and sprayed the front of her apron. She adjusted the tap and began rinsing off the plates.

"Wonder why the major and his wife are divorcing?" Bea asked.

"Some marriages just don't work out," Sara said. Her voice sounded funny, as though she was talking into a well.

"Seems to me, a roving eye is what ends most marriages," Bea said. "And it's usually the man doing the roving."

"I don't know why Julian Campbell is divorced, and you don't either," Sara challenged. "And I think it is none of our business."

"I'm going to put that album on the coffee table," Bea said. "And hang Ben's picture over the bookcase."

"It's just a blown-up snapshot, Bea. It wouldn't look right in your pretty living room."

But it was Bea's living room. Bea's kitchen. Bea's house. Sara had no more status in this house than her two children.

The things she had longed for all the years she and the children followed Ben on the rodeo circuit Sara still longed for. Close friends. A home of her own. Going to college.

With one exception, all the women her age in Murray had husbands and houses. She'd gotten to know some of them better than others, but her single state separated her. She didn't go to couples' events at the church. She didn't go to square dances at the community building. At school functions, she was the only parent without a spouse.

Sometimes Sara wondered if she wouldn't prefer to have the old travel trailer back rather than to live in another woman's house and be a guest in her kitchen—even if the kitchen was spacious and well equipped and the woman was very dear to her.

Actually, another trailer was what Sara wanted—not a travel trailer like the one she and Ben pulled behind the truck as they went from rodeo to rodeo. But a house trailer permanently installed in the grove of blackjack oak behind Bea and Jim's. Then she could have a home of her very own, and her children could continue having all the benefits of small town life and a daily association with loving grandparents.

So, Sara accepted her in-laws' charity and tried to save. She smiled at B & J customers she didn't care for so they would remember to tip her. Most of her bedroom was taken up by a quilting frame, on which she made quilts that she sold through a store in Santa Fe. She mended her old clothes so she could buy new ones for her children. Actually Bea would have bought all their clothes, but Sara drew the line at this. She had to hang on to some semblance of independence and pride.

As for continuing her education, Sara seldom thought about that anymore. She hadn't the time or money.

Bea and Jim assured her that she didn't need to worry about the future. They would take care of everything while they were alive and trust funds established by their wills would provide for Sara and the children after they were gone.

Sometimes Sara grew weary of gratefulness.

Tonight was one of those times. She didn't want to be in Bea's kitchen. She hadn't wanted to spend the weekend fishing. She had no control over her own life.

Her children were well adjusted and happy, but Sara was lonely and restless. The town's only eligible males were either seventeen or seventy. She had no social life. No home of her own. And she was tired of being grateful to Bea and Jim. Never once, however, did she doubt her decision to make Murray her permanent home. All she had to do was look at her children's healthy bodies and happy faces and know she had made the right decision.

Sara looked out the window over the sink, across the east pasture to Rachel's farm. The pole light was on in the yard making an island of light in the darkness. Sara couldn't tell if there was a light on in the house.

Was he in bed? Was he thinking about her? Why hadn't she told him yes? One evening with a nice man didn't have to mean anything.

And he was nice. Sensitive. Not all bravado like so many men. Not afraid to reveal his emotions.

For a minute, she had thought he was going to touch her. Not embrace her or anything like that. But his hand was poised, as if he was going to touch her cheek or hair.

That would have been nice.

Just a touch.

A crash brought her abruptly out of her reverie. A plate had slipped from her hands and shattered in the sink—one of the plates from the special-occasion china that had once belonged to Bea's mother.

Bea came rushing over to stare at the damage.

"Oh, Bea, I'm so sorry. I'll buy you another one."

"That pattern hasn't been made in years," Bea said. "Lordy, girl, you're as flighty as a long-tailed cat in a room full of rocking chairs. What did that man say to you out there that's got you so riled up?"

"He likes me," Sara admitted. She could feel the telltale flush returning to her face. "He wants to see me again."

"Is that so?" Bea said, picking up the pieces of her precious china. "He finds out you're the widow of a friend one minute and goes after you the next. Not in very good taste, if you ask me."

"I didn't," Sara said, untying her apron.

"Didn't what?"

"Ask you. I didn't ask you what you thought. I was just answering your question. Now, if you'll excuse me, I need to see how the children are doing with their homework."

JULIAN SAT in the darkness on the back step, staring across the field at the Cates' house. Billy, the three-legged dog, had come to sit with him and have his head scratched.

After Sara had declined his invitation, she had all but run back in the house, saying she had to help Bea with the dishes.

The light had long since gone out in the Cate kitchen. Only one light still burned in the house. He wondered if it was in Sara's room.

What a tasteless oaf he had been—asking Sara out when he'd only just found out her husband was dead. What a stupid thing to do!

He wondered if she really had a PTA meeting tomorrow night or if she was just being polite.

Even if there was a PTA meeting, it wouldn't last all evening. There would still be time to...

To do what? Julian wondered. Where did mature people go on dates in Murray?

The supermarket might have movie rentals. But they'd have to watch it at Bea and Jim's. There sure wasn't a VCR connected to Rachel's antique television.

And what to do on a date was an academic question anyway. Sara obviously did not want to see him tomorrow evening—before, during or after the real or fictitious PTA meeting.

It was just as well, he told himself. Sara was lovely, but he could see that an involvement with her would be an involvement with the whole Cate family. And how could he hope to compete with their idolized Ben?

Her kids were definitely unimpressed with him, Julian realized. They thought he was a wimp. Sara probably did, too. Maybe he was.

He wondered if Murray had a convenience store where he could buy a six pack of beer. Probably not.

God, he hated this town.

Chapter Three

Julian had been to the Mangum courthouse once before—when his Aunt Rachel had been formally declared his legal guardian. The proceedings had been in the same room—a large, cluttered judge's office on the second floor. A different judge was behind the desk, but the room with its high ceiling and heavy, dark furniture looked the same.

His aunt had bought him a pair of tan slacks, a white shirt and new shoes for the occasion.

While the judge and his aunt talked, Julian had watched a fat pigeon out the open window as it sat on the ledge preening its feathers, thinking he'd finally found something in Oklahoma that was the same as in Chicago. Pigeons used to sit on the ledge outside the window of his and his mother's tiny apartment, eating the bread crusts he'd put out for them.

The judge read a letter from Julian's mother about how she didn't know where the boy's father was and she wanted her sister to have the boy. The judge signed some papers and pushed them across the desk to Rachel. Then he had turned to Julian. "Do you understand what is happening here today, Julian Campbell?"

"Yes, sir."

"Tell me."

"Aunt Rachel will be in charge of me."

"That's right. She has agreed to raise you. Now, she gets no money for this. Your mother didn't have any money to leave for your upbringing. But Miss Warren will feed you and take care of you and give you a home. In return, you must be a good boy and mind her and never make her sorry that she agreed to take you in. Do you understand that, boy?"

"Yes, sir."

"And you're going to do your schoolwork and your chores when she says? And never talk back to her?"

"Yes, sir. I promised my mom before I left Chicago."

"Good. You're a lucky boy, Julian, to have a good woman like your Aunt Rachel willing to take you in. Some orphaned children aren't that lucky."

Orphan. That's what he was now. His mother had lived long enough to know that he arrived in Oklahoma safely. He had talked to her on the telephone. Her voice was so weak he could hardly understand her. Then another phone call came a few days later from a social worker. Aunt Rachel called it "passing on," but Julian knew she meant that his mother was dead. "It's all right for you to go to your room and cry," she had told him.

After they finished with the judge, Rachel took Julian across the street and bought him a lemonade. He had wanted a fountain Coke, like his mother used to buy him at Woolworth's lunch counter, but Rachel said that soda pop was just colored sugar water and a waste of money. Julian had already figured out what Rachel thought about wasting money. He had put a nickel on the railroad track that crossed the south end of Main Street and earned a stern lecture from her on the value of money. She had not let him keep the squashed coin. There would be no rewards for foolish behavior.

Rachel had nothing to drink herself. "You are my only kin, boy," she had said as he sipped the lemonade through a straw. "Your mother and I had an older brother, but he's dead now, too, and he never married. I'll do the best I can with you but don't expect me to be like your ma. You only get one ma in this life."

Julian realized that buying a drink at a soda fountain was Rachel's way of making the day a special occasion. She was his guardian. It was official now; she had a piece of paper to prove it.

Even then, Julian knew she didn't really want him. But she was doing a good thing by taking him in. He had wanted to say something nice to her but all he could think of was to thank her for the lemonade.

That same old drugstore was still across the street. He and Percy Mason had had fifteen minutes to spare before their appointment with the judge, so they had gone inside. Mason ordered a cup of coffee. Julian had an old-fashioned fountain Coke, the best drink that had ever been invented.

As a boy, he had given his window washing money to Rachel, which she would use to buy his school clothes and books. But sometimes his customers would give him a tip, and he'd join the after-school crowd at Murray's one drugstore. Julian would sit on one of the high stools at the counter, sipping a Coke through a straw, trying to make the drink last as long as possible, feeling almost as though he belonged.

After he ran away from Murray, Julian had no money for soft drinks. Every dime became precious. But when he'd finally finished educating himself and had launched his military career, he drank soft drinks all the time. Even for breakfast. To this day, whenever Julian had a soft drink, he took a perverse pleasure in the act. *See there, Rachel Warren. I can do whatever I want.*

The probate proceedings were brief. Julian left copies of his birth certificate and a sworn deposition that, to the best of his knowledge, he was the nephew and only heir of Rachel Elizabeth Warren.

The clerk said when a date was set for a probate hearing, he would be notified and a notice would be published in the county paper.

After they left the courthouse, Mason drove Julian to a realtor's office. The real estate agent—a ruddy-faced man named Hennessey—took a listing on the farm but told Julian that while he shouldn't spend a lot of money fixing up the place, he should at least paint and make it look as nice as possible.

"I'll stop by and have a look, then leave a list of suggested improvements and repairs with Mr. Mason," Mr. Hennessey said. "But I can tell you now that the farm should look well-tended. Air out the house and clean out the closets. Replace low-wattage light bulbs with bright ones— and see that the curtains are clean and starched. That kind of thing sounds petty, but it goes a long way in making a house look like someplace someone might want to live."

From the realtor's office, Mason took Julian to the monument company. Julian selected an austere headstone that would bear only Rachel's name and the dates of her birth and death.

The stonecutter tried to talk Julian into something less plain, with some flowers perhaps, or with the words "Beloved Aunt" under Rachel's name, but Julian declined. Then as they were leaving, he saw a stone designed for an infant, with a lamb carved on it. Julian went back to the stonecutter. "Make one with an animal of some sort."

"I only do lambs and birds," the man said.

"A bird then," Julian said.

It was lunchtime when they arrived back in Murray. Julian declined Mason's invitation to have lunch with him at the B & J. Sara might be there. He wouldn't feel comfortable seeing her after their awkward parting last night. Once again, he mentally kicked himself for mishandling the entire encounter. And wondering all over again if there was any point in trying another time with her when he came back. Maybe by then, she'd be willing to give him a second chance.

Julian had several hours before he needed to leave for Oklahoma City to catch his evening flight to North Carolina.

He changed clothes and opened a can of soup for lunch. Then he puttered around—filling the watering trough, burning some trash, throwing away odds and ends of rusty machine parts from the shed behind the barn. He tried to look at the farm as a prospective buyer would and wasn't impressed. Such a plain little place. Not even a front porch on the house or a weather vane on the barn. The pastures looked as if they hadn't been fertilized in years. The pecan trees were suffering from some blight and needed serious pruning. The dirt dam on the pond was eroding and needed the attention of a bulldozer. Julian had planned to sell the farm as it was. Maybe he still should. Except the realtor wasn't sure he could.

He could hire some work done, Julian supposed, but that would be expensive. He would like to be able to pay off the mortgage and have a little nest egg left over. Otherwise, he might as well just turn it over to the bank that held the mortgage.

What made more sense was for him to spend a couple of weeks of painting, weeding, trimming, grading, mending. He'd put down new linoleum in the kitchen, new screens on the windows, new boards in the porch steps.

The Cate children came by after lunch to make sure he was still leaving this evening.

"Grandma says we can have the chickens if Grandpa will fence a place far away from the house and we promise to take good care of them," Mary Sue said excitedly. She even clapped her hands.

"We can even have the rooster," Barry said, "but Grandma said she reserves the right to wring his neck if he wakes her up in the morning. She said the five-dollar bonus will have to be for the whole flock. We can't expect you to pay us sixty dollars for taking twelve scrawny chickens off your hands. She said the whole lot of them wouldn't bring half that at the supermarket."

"Tell your grandmother that I said it's a small price to pay, but if she feels real bad about it, she can bake me an apple pie. And tell your grandfather there's some chicken wire stored in the shed. I'll help him build a chicken yard when I get back here."

"When are you coming back?" Barry asked.

"I don't know. It might be a month or two. Can you two manage?"

They nodded. Cute kids. Brown and lean and healthy looking. Blond hair bleached almost white by the sun. Barry was in that gangly adolescent stage but already showing signs of the handsome young man he would become. Mary Sue still had a little girl sweetness about her face.

"How come you and my dad were friends if you didn't go out for any sports and didn't go hunting or riding?" Barry asked.

"We were friends at school. I was good at algebra, and we studied together some. My last year here, he nominated me for homeroom parliamentarian. And everyone voted for me because of him. The parliamentarian didn't do anything, but it made me feel good. It was a nice thing for him to do."

"Did you have a girlfriend?" Mary Sue asked.

"Not in high school. I was short and bashful. No one except your dad ever paid much attention to me."

"No, I mean later," Mary Sue persisted. "After you got married. My grandma says you must have run around on your wife if she's divorced you."

Thanks a lot, Bea, Julian thought. "No. I didn't have a girlfriend," he explained. "I think my wife just got tired of moving all the time. When you're in the Army, you do a lot of that. And she missed her family."

The Cate youngsters and four dogs followed him around for a while, asking more questions about their father. Barry helped him saw off dead limbs from the pecan trees and tack down the loose screening on the screen door.

"Well, I need to get changed and be on my way," Julian said finally. "Be sure to scratch that old mare's nose whenever you come over. Ordinarily, I steer clear of animals bigger than I am, but she's a nice old girl."

"Her name is Phyllis," Mary Sue said. "She's twenty-six. Miss Rachel said that's like being over a hundred if she were a person."

"Well, she looks every year of it," Julian said with a laugh. "Did you kids know my aunt Rachel very well?"

"Sure," Barry said. "She let us keep half the eggs we gathered. And paid us to help her with the chores. We hoed her garden and washed windows. In the winter, when the pipes froze, we carried water for the animals."

"And you got along with her?"

Barry shrugged. "I guess. She grumbled if one of us didn't gather the eggs right after school. But she was old. My greatgrandpa over in Blair—he grumbled all the time, too. If I said it's a nice day, he said we needed rain. If it rained, it was bad for his joints."

"I felt sorry for Miss Rachel 'cause she was alone," Mary Sue said. "You should have come to see her once in a while." The little girl looked up at him with large, accusing eyes.

"I suppose. But my aunt and I didn't get along, and I ran away when I was seventeen. I always thought she'd have chased me off with her broom if I ever darkened her doorstep again."

Barry laughed. "Yeah, she was always telling us she'd take the broom to us if we didn't do things right—jus' like Grandma tells us she's going to hang us upside down until all the stubbornness runs out."

"And you weren't afraid of Rachel?" Julian asked.

"Naw," Mary Sue said. "She was just weird. She'd act mean sometimes, and other times she'd give us milk and cookies."

"My grandpa said to tell you that Miss Rachel still had your grandfather's Winchester in case you need a good rifle," Barry said.

"I'd forgotten about that old rifle," Julian said. "She used it sometimes to shoot at coyotes who came too close to her chickens. I'll probably sell it. I haven't shot a gun since my ROTC days in college, and I did it then only because it was required."

"Doesn't the Army make you stay in practice?" Barry asked incredulously.

"No. Not guys like me. The only guns we have in hospitals are grease guns for the mechanical equipment."

"I've already bagged my first deer," Barry said.

"I can shoot, too," Mary Sue bragged, "as good as Barry. I can ride as good as him, too, but he's a better calf roper. We got our own horses. Do you like to ride?"

Julian hesitated, then admitted he'd never even been on a horse. The children exchanged looks. *A full-grown man who'd never been on a horse!*

He paid the children what he owed them to date and went inside to change for his trip. Sara Cate's children were about as impressed with him as she was, he decided. Pencil pushers didn't carry much weight in a town like Murray where the measure of a man was based on how tough he was. And Julian Campbell didn't shoot guns, ride horses, play football or even drive a truck. He didn't build barns or dynamite dams. He was scared to death of snakes, and the only exercise he got came from jogging. And he would be willing to wager that not a single person in Murray jogged.

Julian was leaving for the airport when Sara came trotting up the drive on a gray horse. He stopped the car and got out.

She didn't get off the horse. "I lied about the PTA meeting," she said down to him. Her horse lowered its head and tugged at the high grass along the drive. "I'm not sure why," Sara went on. "I was embarrassed, I guess. You're the first man who's asked me on a date in a lot of years. But when you come back, I'd be pleased to go out with you if you were of a mind to ask."

"I appreciate your telling me," Julian said, shading his eyes with his hand, as he looked up at her.

Her hair was windblown, her skin tan. A navy bandanna was tied around her neck. She was wearing faded jeans and a plaid shirt with the sleeves rolled up. Her feet were in scuffed cowboy boots. With the Oklahoma sky big and blue behind her, she looked like an advertisement for clean air and country living.

"Well, you think you'll be?" she asked, fanning horse flies away from the horse's neck.

"Be what?" Julian asked.

"Of a mind to ask me out?"

"Oh yes. I'm sure I will be."

She smiled. "Bye, now. Have a good flight."

He wanted to reach out and touch her, even if only the toe of her boot, but he settled for a wave. She turned the horse, slapped its rump and galloped down the lane. Fast. He wondered what Sara would think when she found out he couldn't ride a horse.

BEA WALKED OUT to the barn while Sara was unsaddling Hank. "Have a good ride?" she asked, offering the gelding a handful of oats.

Sara nodded as she wiped down Hank's sweaty flanks. She could tell by the tone of her mother-in-law's voice that the question was a leading one.

"I saw you heading over to the Warren place," Bea said, tucking her hands under her apron.

"Is that a question or an accusation?" Sara asked, moving around to the other side of the horse.

Bea took a deep breath. "I'm sorry. I guess it did sound that way. I was just wondering why you would do that. Go over there to see a man you hardly know."

"I went to tell him goodbye and to tell him that the next time he comes I'd like to go out with him. You know, on a date."

"Aren't you a little old for 'dates'?"

"Is that what you think?" Sara asked as she pulled the water hose over to fill Hank's bucket. "That I should never again in my life enjoy the company of a man?"

"No, I reckon not. I suppose you get lonely without Ben. It's only natural. You're still young. But you have a special responsibility because of those two children to make sure any man you hook up with is the right sort and will do right by you and yours."

"Are you saying Julian isn't that sort of man?"

"I don't know. I'm always suspicious of divorced men. Nine times out of ten they're scoundrels. And Julian Campbell doesn't like our town, our way of life. He couldn't wait to leave here and took the first excuse he could find to run off from his aunt. Rachel Warren was a hard woman, I'll admit, but he owed her more than a goodbye note on the kitchen table. Barry and Mary Sue need a man who likes country living and will raise them like their daddy would have. Otherwise, I think you should live with your memories."

Sara dumped a measure of oats into Hank's trough. The horse neighed his appreciation and began munching away contentedly. Sara closed the stall door and leaned against it, facing her waiting mother-in-law.

"Bea, if Ben hadn't gotten hurt, I don't know if he ever would have come back here to Murray. He had turned into a real gypsy. He liked rolling down the highway. He liked to hang out with other men who felt the same. He loved our children, but he wasn't a particularly good father."

Bea started to interrupt, but Sara held up her hand. "No, hear me out," she demanded. "Ben was willing for us to be separated from Barry when he got old enough for school rather than settle down, and I almost left him because of it. Now, don't get me wrong. I loved Ben Cate and still miss him every day of my life. I'd give anything if he were still alive. But he wasn't perfect. And sometimes I think you're doing those children a disservice letting them believe that he was. He's not the saintly hero you're making him out to be."

Bea's mouth was an angry narrow line as she turned heel and marched back to her kitchen.

Sara went into the stall to lean her face against Hank's neck and take comfort in his solid warmth, in the horsey, living smell of him. "I wish we had a place of our own,

Hank. But then, you are really Jim's horse, aren't you? I
don't have a horse or a house or anything to call my own
except those two kids, and I wonder about them sometimes."

But already, Sara was feeling guilty. Where would she and
the kids be if it weren't for Bea and Jim? They didn't want
her to move out. They wanted her and the kids to stay with
them forever. That's what the kids wanted, too.

Everyone is happy but me, Sara thought. And if changing her life meant making the others unhappy, she wouldn't
feel right about it.

In the kitchen, Sara scrubbed her hands and began chopping the ingredients for the salad. The same ingredients
every night—iceberg lettuce, tomatoes, carrots and celery.
The dressing was always French. But if Sara did the gro-
cery shopping and brought home a head of romaine or leaf
lettuce, no one ate it. When she insisted on baking a chicken
instead of frying it, the children said they liked Grandma's
way better. When she made rice to serve with the roast one
Sunday, everyone wanted to know where the mashed potatoes were. When she marinated the pot roast and cooked it
on the grill, instead of roasting it with potatoes and carrots
as always, Jim said it was "interesting."

Now, she mostly did only what Bea directed her to do. It
was easier that way. The kitchen was Bea's domain, and
Sara was there by invitation only. She didn't even think
about it much anymore. Except tonight, she chopped the
carrots and celery with more vengeance than usual. Bea kept
looking over at her, annoyed by the noise she was making.

Oblivious to the tension between the two women, Jim and
the children chattered and laughed during dinner. Jim said
that no one cooked a pot roast as good as Bea. He always
said that. And it was probably true. But Sara didn't eat any.
She didn't eat any of Bea's fresh peach pie either. Proba-

bly, she was just being contrary. She loved warm peach pie with a scoop of ice cream. Bea would say she was cutting off her nose to spite her face.

THE DRIVE FROM MURRAY to Oklahoma City was a pretty one with an open, rolling landscape punctuated by meandering streams lined with native oak and elm trees. Cattle country mostly. Some wheat.

The sky was bluer here. The sunsets prettier. The air fresher. But Julian never had understood why people would willingly choose the life of drudgery and isolation that working the land brought. He preferred the orderly life of a military base with white-painted curbs, manicured grounds and the flag lowered every evening at precisely five o'clock. There, life did not depend on the whims of nature. The salary was reasonably good, and it came every month. And when he retired, he'd have an income for life. Most of those who stayed with the land ended up like Rachel, too old to make repairs and work the fields, too poor to hire help, living out the last days of their lives on a run-down old place with only a bunch of animals for company.

Of course, Rachel had established a relationship with Barry and Mary Sue. That surprised Julian. They weren't afraid of her. Either Rachel hadn't been as ferocious as she used to be, or those two youngsters were a lot more fearless than he had been at their age.

He wondered what they would think when he showed up to take their mother out. He already knew Bea wasn't going to like it. A divorced man wasn't good enough for Ben's widow.

The image of Sara looking down at him from horseback was one Julian would not soon forget. *Would he be of a mind to ask her out?* His mind was going to have a hard time thinking of anything else. He was both thrilled and full of trepidation.

He found Sara lovely, charming, honest, desirable. But she was tied to the town of Murray and to Bea and Jim Cate as surely as she been sentenced there by a judge.

Was there any point in courting a woman like that? Not that he was ready to go out and buy an engagement ring. He wasn't completely divorced yet, for one thing. Although he had lived apart from his wife for over a year and the papers had been filed, the divorce would not be final until the waiting period required by Florida law had been fulfilled. But that was all just a technicality. And a first date could be a timid first step—two people checking each other out. When they said good-night, it could mean goodbye. Or it could lead to a second and third date, to a relationship, an engagement, marriage.

People who went on dates were generally looking for someone. Otherwise they'd spend time with friends and family and not subject themselves to the risky, nerve-racking business of dating.

That's why people tended to date the type of person who would fit into their life. He reasoned that a man who hated dogs, for example, probably shouldn't ask out a woman who raised show dogs. And a former country boy had no business falling in love with a country girl when he abhorred the thought of ever again living in a rural community.

Julian was never going to move back to Murray. And he couldn't imagine Sara as an Army wife and her two children as Army "brats." Army families couldn't get attached to places. They saw their relatives infrequently. They didn't keep chickens. And home was where the Army sent them and their furniture. In Julian's case, home could be wherever the Army maintained a hospital for its personnel—which was just about everywhere.

Julian was dedicated to the Army. He had gone to school on an ROTC scholarship. The Army had sent him back to school to get his master's degree in hospital administration. An Army career had given him the dignity and security he needed after growing up a poor orphan boy with seemingly no prospect of a better life.

It was more than repaying an obligation. Julian wore his uniform with pride. And he liked hospital administration.

A hospital was a small city unto itself. Along with medical and nursing staffs, Julian's job dealt with cooks, gardeners, guards, electricians, secretaries, telephone operators, janitors, plumbers and a variety of other maintenance and technical support personnel. Every day was different and exciting. And like most people who work in health care, he knew what he did was important.

Julian arrived at Oklahoma City's Will Rogers Airport in plenty of time to return the rented car and buy the latest mystery by his favorite author.

But during the first leg of the flight, he had a difficult time concentrating on the story. Ironically, the book was set in a small Texas town that reminded him very much of Murray and the people he had just left.

Finally he closed the book and his eyes. He dozed for a time, but his mind kept taking him back to the quiet little town of his boyhood, to the pretty woman with the lovely smile.

Where would he take Sara on their date?

That thought kept him occupied for some time. For good idea or not, he would have at least that one date. He wanted for them to dress up. To go someplace romantic. To see candlelight reflecting in her eyes. To feel her in his arms while they danced to soft music.

The flight out of St. Louis was delayed, the late-night drive from the Raleigh-Durham airport seemed endless. When he finally inserted the key in the lock of his Fort Bragg apartment, it was almost two a.m. He put his suitcase down and looked around, seeing his Spartan residence anew. Rachel's house was plain, but there was a homeyness about it that was lacking in his bachelor officer's quarters with its bare walls and quartermaster-issue furniture.

The apartment was in a 1930-vintage building and had high ceilings, a fireplace, nice wooden floors. But the furniture consisted only of necessities. Footsteps echoed on the rugless floors. With no lamps, the only lighting came from harsh overhead fixtures.

After the decision to divorce, his wife had taken most of the furniture and decorative objects. He had always thought of everything as hers anyway. She had selected most of it. Paid for a lot of it. She had decided how it would be arranged. And her tastes were more pretentious than his. He had never felt comfortable stretching out on a sofa covered with crushed velvet.

Now, he didn't even have a sofa—only side chairs and a couple of end tables. One end table held a portable television, the other a telephone. Why had he been living like this for over a year? Julian wondered. Had he just not noticed or was he punishing himself for not working harder at marriage?

Tomorrow, he vowed, he was going to buy a sofa and some lamps and a rug. And a picture to hang over the sofa.

No, not tomorrow. He had a very full day. He might have to wait until the weekend, but he was definitely going shopping.

Maybe he wouldn't sell his grandfather's rifle. He could hang it over the mantel. After all, it was a family heirloom.

His bed was little more than a cot. Maybe he'd buy a real bed, too. And suddenly he could hardly wait for the weekend. He was going to acquire possessions! He was going to turn his barren apartment into a home. He was going to start living again.

So, why the change, old boy? he asked himself. Had a visit to his boyhood home for the funeral of his old nemesis, Aunt Rachel, changed him that much?

No, not altogether. A lovely lady with shiny hair and a beautiful mouth was more responsible for these new feelings.

And he was going to see her again!

Even if nothing came of seeing lovely Sara again, her smile had awakened something inside of him. He had forgotten that life was more than a habit.

Life was to be enjoyed.

Chapter Four

Summertime in Murray revolved around the schedules of the community's various ball teams—softball teams for the girls, women and men; baseball for the boys. The adults played in church leagues, the youngsters on teams sponsored by various business and civic groups.

Parents, grandparents, neighbors and interested Murray citizens would bring their lawn chairs and coolers full of soft drinks to Murray's ballpark to cheer for their favorite team. And once or twice a week, fans would drive to games in Anadarko, Chickasha, Lookeba, Apache, Cement, Corn or any of a number of western Oklahoma towns.

For Sara, evenings at the ball games were most satisfying, sitting next to Bea and Jim, sipping a tall plastic glass of iced tea, visiting with the other parents and spectators, watching Mary Sue play first base or Barry pitch. Her children were talented players, but even if they weren't, she would have been there at every game.

She could never take her children away from this, Sara thought as she leaned back in her aluminum chaise and enjoyed the cooler evening temperature after the blazing heat of the day.

Mary Sue was coming up to bat. Sara put down her glass of tea and sat up straight, her pulse quickening.

Mary Sue wasted a strike on a high ball. She got a piece of the next pitch, hitting a high foul behind the row of spectators along the third-base line. On the next pitch, Mary Sue connected solidly and hit a line drive between second and third base. Immediately, Sara was on her feet, cheering, Jim and Bea beside her. Mary Sue slid safely into first base, dusted herself off and turned to wave at her cheering section.

Ben should be here, Sara thought. He should be watching his children grow and change. He should be seeing how much his parents loved their grandchildren. He should be keeping her from loneliness.

But at least Ben had gotten them all back to Murray where their family seemed to belong. And because of that, their children were growing up strong and safe and healthy, spending their summers fishing, playing ball and riding their horses or bikes. Sara seldom gave a thought to anything worse than skinned knees befalling her children. Everyone in town kept an eye on everyone else's children.

She was really quite lucky, she reminded herself. She could be living in a run-down apartment someplace, trying to hold down two jobs, seeing her children only long enough to tuck them in bed at night.

Not having her own kitchen was a small price to pay for her children's happiness and security. That was true before Major Julian Campbell came to town. It was true now.

In a way, Sara wished that Julian had never come. Then she wouldn't be sitting here at her daughter's ball game, surrounded by people who knew and cared about her and her children, yet feeling so lonely she ached.

Sara was wise enough, however, to know it wasn't the man himself she ached for. Julian Campbell seemed nice enough, but she really didn't know him. He might be selfish or dishonest. He might not care a thing about kids' summer ball.

But Julian had looked at her in a special way and made her feel womanly and alive and desirable. Made her bed seem empty when she thought she was accustomed to sleeping alone. Made her long for someone she could really talk to and laugh with. She wanted to hold hands again. To dance again. To kiss again. To be frivolous once in a while and not always have to be the serious, dutiful mother.

She wanted to love again while she was still young. And she wanted a love that would endure forever.

Silly girl. Why not wish for a million dollars while she was at it?

But for a thirty-four-year-old widow living in a rural Oklahoma town with her two young children, winning a million dollars in a lottery almost seemed more likely than falling in love again.

She was isolated in her young widowhood. And being financially dependent on her in-laws seemed even to rob her of adult status. Bea and Jim treated her more like Mary Sue and Barry's older sister than like their mother.

Sara didn't earn a salary at the cafe. The five Cates lived more off the profits of the B & J than their farm, so working there was a family responsibility. Sara's only cash came from tips and selling her quilts, and she could only make a couple of quilts a year no matter how far into the night she worked. She paid for her children's clothes and school supplies and provided their allowance. She saved what was left and had accumulated a small nest egg that Bea and Jim didn't know about. Her mobile home money.

But she was a long way from buying a mobile home. And would probably never stop being dependent on her in-laws. Sara realized that Bea and Jim expected her and the children to stay with them forever. Instead of settling into a boring, uneventful old age, their house was full of life, their days full of activity. And they loved it! But sometimes Sara thought she would smother under all that kindness. Even now, Bea had taken her iced tea glass from her hand and was packing it with fresh ice. Sara watched her mother-in-law refill the glass with tea, add a lemon wedge, wrap a fresh napkin around the side and hand it back with an accompanying cookie.

Sara didn't want more iced tea. She didn't want the cookie. But it was easier to take them than to turn them down. Bea needed to be fussing over someone at all times.

Mary Sue's team was in the field now. She was crouching on the base line, glove ready and waiting. Sara remembered from her own playing days how that felt—to be half-hoping and half-fearing the batter would hit one her way. Maybe Mary Sue would be the hero of the game, but maybe she'd make an error and be the goat.

The only safe way was not to play at all. And thank God that Mary Sue was willing to risk losing so she could play the game.

And what about Mary Sue's mother? Was she willing to enter into the first inning of a relationship or was she going to forfeit the game?

Sara wanted to see Julian. That much was certain. It was a bit frightening just how much she wanted to see him, how much she thought about him. She even held imaginary conversations with him in her head, telling him things about herself, asking him things about his life, his marriage. Sara had an incredible curiosity about his first wife. Was she beautiful? Did Julian think of her still? When would his divorce be final? Did he even want it to be?

And Sara imagined herself with Julian in dozens of situations—having dinner, doing the dishes, taking a walk, riding in a car, planting a garden. And making love. Sometimes a potent mental image would flash across her mind, and she would lose herself in it. Customers had to repeat their orders. Television programs got tuned out. Even her children's banter. She couldn't repeat two words they had said.

"I didn't ask you for a glass of milk," Barry would say, his tone puzzled. "I can get my own milk. I asked if I could have an advance on my allowance."

"Grandma says you're getting kind of addle-brained," Mary Sue had said. "Can't you take a pill for that?"

But even if Julian Campbell turned out to be the kindest, most romantic, gentlest man in the world, Sara could not imagine a relationship with him working. She and her children wouldn't be living in a tiny travel trailer as they had all those years on the road with Ben, but they would be moving around, never knowing what the next year would bring, never putting down roots, never making permanent friends.

After the game, the Cates joined several other families in the picnic area that adjoined the ball complex for a covered-dish supper.

The park was new, the result of a great deal of community effort and was now the source of a great deal of community pride—Murray's first real park. It didn't have a lake like Chickasha's park. It wasn't built on a river bank like the one in Anadarko. Its only trees were saplings. But someday they would grow large and make this park shady and beautiful.

I'll be old then, Sara thought, already feeling as if the years were running past her. She would have a quiet life in Murray, raising her children and would someday bring her grandchildren to this park to have a picnic in the shade of fine tall trees.

So, what's the matter with that? she asked herself. *Not a bad life at all.*

Bea, as usual, brought pies. It was expected of her. Sara had made potato salad the way her mother used to make it—with bacon and poppy seeds.

Dot Brubaker's more ordinary potato salad went first. Only a few people politely helped themselves to Sara's concoction.

"What are those little black things?" Barry asked.

MORE THAN A MONTH PASSED before Julian could make his return to Murray. By that time, Percy Mason had forwarded the realtor's list of improvements he should make on the farm before it was put on the market. Julian continued to wonder if he would be throwing away his time and money fixing up the farm for sale.

He could sign away the farm and never go back to Murray. Mason assured him he would not be damaging his credit rating by doing so. The mortgage was a debt of Rachel's estate and not Julian's personally.

But Julian wanted to go back. He wanted to see Sara again, and the farm gave him an excuse.

And oddly enough, spending two weeks of manual labor—even in the unrelenting Oklahoma sunshine—sounded like a nice respite from meetings and memos.

He wanted to call Sara and tell her he was coming, but maybe she would think that was unnecessary. After all, she could look across the west pasture and see if he had arrived. Or maybe he was just too nervous to call her. How would he identify himself? *Julian? Julian Campbell? Major Julian Campbell, Rachel Warren's nephew?* And what would he say after the obvious? *I think about you all the time. I think I'm falling in love with you.*

He got the phone number from information, and even dialed it once, but he didn't complete the call.

One of the post-op nurses was from Oklahoma City. Julian felt himself blushing when he asked her to name the most romantic restaurant in central Oklahoma. Without hesitation, she said the Eagle's Nest in north Oklahoma City and gave a glowing description. "And who is the lucky lady?" she asked.

"A nice widow lady from Murray who might think it was silly to drive all the way to Oklahoma City for dinner," he explained.

"Oh, I expect she'll like it just fine," the nurse said.

IT WAS LATE on a Thursday evening in mid June when Julian once again pulled into the rutted driveway of his aunt's farm. The dogs came running from the barn, barking frantically as they ran alongside the car. He stopped short of the house, studying it in the light of the headlights, trying to decide if he felt better about this homecoming than he had a month ago. Buster, one of the Labs, put his feet on the side of the car and stuck his head inside the window to be petted.

Why had Rachel stayed on after her father died, he wondered as he scratched the dog's head. She could have sold the farm and moved away.

But she had never known any other life and the unknown can be frightening, he supposed. She hadn't had Career Management in the Pentagon arranging her life for her, sending her all over the world. Julian's courage had always come in the form of military orders. Rachel had had no such impetus in her life.

And he remembered what Bea had said about the town. For Bea and Jim Cate, Murray was the dearest place on earth. Maybe Rachel felt that way, too. Julian had lived many places but never considered any of them dear.

Had there ever been a special man in Rachel's life, he wondered—a man who might have taken her someplace, showed her a bit of the world? But it was hard to imagine the Rachel Warren he knew ever being young and in love.

Billy, the three-legged dog, followed him into the house, the other three heading back to the barn. In the old days, Rachel would have been sitting at the kitchen table, waiting for him while she darned socks or read magazines. Sometimes she would have the radio on. Other times she would be playing a stack of sappy old records. World War II-era stuff.

She would pour him a glass of milk and put two cookies on a plate—and wait until he finished, then wash the glass and plate. If they talked at all, it would be about the weather or she might ask him who won the football game. She never asked if he had a good time, if he had friends, how the band's halftime performance went. And he never asked her what she thought about as she sat there in the same chair, night after night.

He had forgotten about those old phonograph records. "Don't Sit Under the Apple Tree With Anyone Else But Me." "Swinging on a Star." "I'll Be Seeing You In All the Old Familiar Places." The music of her youth. She played it a lot.

Standing there in his dead aunt's kitchen, Julian realized something for the first time. The music must have brought back memories for her. That's why she played it. And suddenly he felt like crying. He had never really known her at all. Nor she him. They were two lonely strangers living under the same roof.

He walked over and touched the back of her chair. What had she been remembering, he wondered, when the music played?

A tap at the back door brought him back to the present. It was Sara, smiling through the screen door. Julian felt a rush of sheer joy at the sight of her.

"I heard the dogs," she explained.

"Yes, I'm sure everyone in the county did. Come in. How are you?"

"Fine. I brought you a pie."

"Good old Bea," Julian said warmly. "That's awfully nice of her."

"*I* made this one. Percy told us you were coming in this evening."

"I'm sorry. The word 'pie' just makes me think of Bea."

"I know. She's famous for them. Ben used to brag about them all the time. 'Just wait until you taste my mom's apple pie,' he'd say. Only problem was, he was usually eating one of mine at the time."

How lovely she was, Julian thought. He wanted to stare at her, to memorize her—the curve of her smooth tan cheek, the fullness of her perfect lips, the slight indentation in her chin. He wondered what it would be like to touch her hair, to press his lips in the hollow at the base of her throat.

"It's fresh cherry," she said, putting the pie on the table.

"You must miss Ben a lot," he said. "I guess it's pretty rough for you, being left alone with two kids."

"Yes, it's been hard without Ben, but I'm not alone. Bea and Jim have been wonderful. Without them, I'm not sure what I would have done. We were heavily in debt, Ben and I. And he had no life insurance. I had to sell our truck to pay for his funeral."

"Can you stay?" Julian asked, pulling out a chair. "I'll make some coffee to have with the pie."

She smiled. "I thought you'd never ask."

Later, Julian tried to remember what they talked about as he bustled about the kitchen, making coffee, gathering up plates, silverware and napkins, searching for the sugar bowl. Something about tornado season. And how Rachel's old rooster was driving Bea crazy. His flight probably. But mostly he remembered moving around the room immersed in a sea of pleasure. He felt as though he'd been drinking vintage wine. The worn-out old kitchen looked quaint rather than shabby. Even the night sounds coming through the screen door took on a haunting beauty—the chirping of the crickets, the hooting of an occasional owl, the far-off howl of a coyote.

Although he complimented her pie profusely, he hardly noticed its taste. He didn't know if the coffee was weak or strong. He didn't care.

Her eyes sparkled when she talked about her children.

She put her fingers to her mouth when she was trying to think of something.

She had a good laugh. Hearty. Genuine.

Her wrists were delicate.

Her fingernails were clipped short and buffed shiny.

Her hair was shiny. Her eyes. Her gold earrings. Her teeth. All shiny. A radiant woman.

He wondered if he was going to have to sit on his hands to keep from touching her. Just her hand. Just a finger.

She still wore a wedding band. Gold. Ben Cate's wife. How could he ever hope to compare with Ben Cate's muscles, Ben Cate's good looks? Girls used to follow him with their gaze as he strolled down the hallway at the high school. He had a smile that belonged on a billboard.

Julian told her about the restaurant in Oklahoma City. The Eagle's Nest. A very special place, he'd been told.

She frowned. And the warm, soft-focus mood vanished. "Have you been there?" he asked. "Don't you like it?"

"No. Quite honestly, I haven't been out to dinner other than MacDonald's in Chickasha or the cafeteria in Norman for a long time. Is this an elegant place?"

"Yes, apparently it's quite elegant. With a dance combo. Candlelight. Waiters in white jackets. The works. I'd really like to take you someplace special. Is that okay? I even brought my dress uniform to wear."

She hesitated. And chewed on her lower lip.

Julian wondered if it was the dancing that bothered her. Maybe she didn't dance.

Or did the thought of going out of town with him make her nervous?

"We can be back here by midnight," he assured her.

She nodded. Not enthusiastically.

"Saturday night okay?"

She nodded again. And smiled. "I'm sure it will be lovely."

He walked her out to Jim's pickup truck. The moon was almost full in a cloudless sky. The air smelled like moist earth and freshly cut hay. "Thanks for coming over," he told her. "And for the pie. I've never been welcomed home quite so nicely."

"Does the farm feel like home?" she asked.

"No, not really. What I should have said was 'welcomed back.' This isn't home."

"It could be a nice place," she observed. "I've always thought the house needed a front porch—with a porch swing. And cedar trees lining the lane. A shade tree out back."

"I'll leave all that to the next occupants," he said. "All I want to do is patch things up and sell it."

"Well, good night now," Sara said, her hand on the door handle of the truck.

"Would you mind terribly if I kissed you?" he asked.

She didn't answer but slid her arms around his neck and pressed her lips against his. Briefly.

He pulled her back and kissed her again, parting her lips with his tongue. *Oh yes,* he thought. *Finally.* The feel of her was sweet beyond belief. He pulled her even closer. So slim. Subtle. Her lips so soft and yielding. The wetness of their kiss intoxicating, making him want more, making him want all of her.

She was the first to pull away. She put a hand to her breast. "My," she said breathlessly. "I wondered what it would feel like to kiss you. Well, now I know."

SARA CLIMBED BEHIND the wheel of the truck and couldn't remember what to do next. *Oh yes. The key. Start the ignition.*

Her automatic pilot took over and somehow she managed to execute a U-turn and point the truck down the driveway.

She had forgotten that a kiss could be so personal, so passionate.

"Wow!" she said out loud. And laughed. Then she said it again. "Wow! I want to do that again, Sara old girl."

And soon. Saturday night they'd go out on a real date.

Then—suddenly—she didn't feel quite so nice.

What the hell was she supposed to wear to a restaurant like that? Formally-clad waiters. Fine wine. Candlelight. She'd look and feel like a country bumpkin. It made her stomach hurt to think about it. She didn't have a fancy dress. She didn't have fancy shoes. Or an evening bag.

Why hadn't she just told him? *I'm sorry, but if you go out with me, it will have to be someplace plain.*

Mentally, Sara went through her meager wardrobe. She had several white-nylon waitress uniforms for work. She had jeans for around the house. Some skirts and blouses for

PTA and potluck suppers at the church community hall.
And a couple of serious dresses for church and funerals. Not
a dancing dress in the bunch.

She tried to think of someone she could borrow from. But
most of the dancing couples she knew either went two-
stepping over at the Western bar in Chickasha or square
danced at the American Legion hall in Hobart.

JIM AND THE CHILDREN had already gone to bed. Bea was
sitting in the living room. The television was playing, but
Sara had the distinct impression that Bea had not been
watching it.

One thing about her mother-in-law, one always knew exactly how she felt about things. And now, Bea was disap-
proving. Her pursed lips said it. The tilt of her chin. The way
she had her hands tightly folded in her lap.

"So, that's why you baked a pie," she said, turning off
the television.

"I baked two pies—one for us and one to take over to
welcome Julian back."

"Fresh cherry is better with almond extract," Bea said.

"I prefer fresh lemon juice."

"Taking a man a pie," Bea said, her chin sticking out like
the bill of an angry old goose. "How obvious can you be?"

"Oh, I suppose I could have put up a big sign in the front
yard," Sara said.

"Don't you sass me, young lady."

"Bea, I am not a 'young lady.' I am not your daughter. I
am not going to stand for you treating me like I am a
naughty teenager. I took a pie to a man. A nice man. I like
him. I wanted to do something to show that I liked him—
just like you would do if you were in my shoes. Jim always
said he knew you were the woman for him the first time he
tasted your apple pie."

"If I were in your shoes, I wouldn't be damaging my reputation by going alone to a man's house late at night."

"I am thirty-four years old! What am I supposed to be saving this reputation for? So I can die a frustrated old widow lady who hasn't been with a man in forty years?"

"What if the children's friends tease them because their mother is chasing after a man?"

"Single people do chase after each other. And the mother of the children in question happens to be a single woman. Julian Campbell is a single man—or at least he will be soon."

"A *divorced* man!" Bea corrected.

"Yes, divorced people are single. What are you afraid of, Bea?"

Bea stared at Sara, then closed her eyes and sagged back in her chair. "I'm afraid of you leaving Jim and me alone. Don't you know how important our little family is to us? Don't you know how happy we've been having you here? I liked to died when Ben got killed. I thought Jim was going to die, too. It was like the sun went out. But those children have given us a new lease on life. We love 'em so much and want what's best for them."

"I do, too, Bea. And maybe this is the best place for them. I'm the one who has to decide, however. Sometimes I think you forget that they are my children."

"No, honey, I don't. But just make sure you are deciding what is best for them and not what you happen to want at the moment."

Bea had a point, Sara acknowledged as she headed down the hall to her children's rooms. Her first responsibility was to Mary Sue and Barry.

Mary Sue no longer slept with a doll. It still seemed strange. Sara leaned over to kiss her daughter's soft, damp cheek. Precious little girl.

Sara opened the window to let some air in the stuffy room. Bea had some notion that night air wasn't good for people. They did this little battle back and forth all the time, with Sara opening and Bea closing windows.

Barry had opened his own window and was propped up in bed reading. He had recently discovered Jack London and was consuming every book the man had written.

"Just ten more minutes," he begged. "I'm at a really good part."

"Then in the morning you'll be begging for ten more minutes of sleep," Sara said, gently taking the book away.

"You went over to see that Julian guy, didn't you?" he asked.

"Yeah. He's nice, don't you think?"

Barry shrugged. "I guess. He sure is different."

"In what way?" Sara asked, smoothing Barry's hair back from his forehead. So handsome, this boy of hers. And getting so big. But still her darlin' Barry.

"He doesn't *do* anything," Barry explained.

"Major Campbell helps run a very large hospital."

"You know what I mean—he doesn't do anything to brag about."

JULIAN CAME to the B & J for lunch the next day. Friday was always a busy day. Sara theorized that wives were shopping and cooking for the weekend and didn't want husbands home for lunch. Or maybe Friday lunch out was a celebration of week's end. But for whatever reason, almost every business person in town came for lunch on Friday, and the Cates knew to have plenty of food and extra apple pie.

It was hard for Sara to concentrate on her work with Julian there. She got orders wrong. And blushed a lot—not from her customers' constant flirting but from Julian's watching her as she hurried about and his ready smile every time she looked his way.

"Can we go to a movie or something tonight?" he asked as she placed an order of fried catfish in front of him.

"Not tonight," she said. "I've got some things I need to do."

"I've made our dinner reservation for tomorrow evening. We need to leave by six."

Sara nodded.

"Would you rather do something else?" he asked.

Sara looked over her shoulder. There were people waiting by the cash register to pay. She assured Julian that dinner at one of Oklahoma City's finest restaurants would be a wonderful treat and got back to work.

As soon as Bea relieved her at the cafe, Sara rushed home to change into a skirt and blouse, left a note for her children explaining her absence and headed for Norman.

The University of Oklahoma was in Norman, and although it wasn't a large city, it had a variety of dress shops and department stores to serve both the town and university communities. Sara tried the shopping mall first and wasn't even tempted to try anything on. Everything was either too expensive or too fussy or both.

In an elegant shop in the campus-corner area, she found the perfect little black dress with a jeweled belt. Understated and elegant. But when she checked the price tag she was shocked. Could college students really afford to pay prices like that?

"It would look great on you," the saleswoman said.

"It's beautiful," she said. "But I can't afford it or anything else I've seen. What I need is a fairy godmother, I guess."

"Sometimes I find things at the secondhand stores," the woman said, lowering her voice to a conspiratorial whisper.

Sara glanced at her watch and asked to use the phone.

Jim answered.

"I'm running late," Sara explained. "Will you put that casserole in the oven and pick Bea up at the cafe? Don't wait dinner for me."

She raced through the hospital auxiliary thrift shop and another operated by the Presbyterian church. As a last resort, she tried a secondhand clothing store on Main Street run by a local women's club. And there it was. Not a dress this time, but a navy faille evening suit with beaded lapels. Sara brushed the dust off the shoulders and took note of the designer label, the covered button holes, the silk lining, the hand beading. An outfit like this would cost a fortune new. Even its secondhand price tag was more than Sara wanted to pay.

The cut of the jacket was perfect. The way it hugged her waist then flared out in a peplum was incredibly flattering. The beading was just enough to be tasteful. The split in the back of the skirt was high enough to be just a bit provocative. And she could get by with her navy pumps.

She made an offer that was half of the price on the tag. The manager countered with a third off. Sara accepted.

She raced into J. C. Penney's to buy navy hose. And found a small satin evening bag on the sale table.

All totaled, for the suit, hose and bag, she had spent several months' worth of tips, and she'd probably never wear the evening outfit again. But she was thrilled with it. Now, she could look forward to her Saturday-night date with Julian.

A light was still on at the dry cleaners. Sara tapped on the door.

Mary Payne, the owner, peered around the blind and opened the door. Mary was the only other single mother in Murray, and the two women occasionally drove to Norman for a movie or a play at the university theater.

"Sorry, Mary. You've got one last customer," Sara said.

"I haven't ever seen this outfit before," Mary said as she made out the ticket. "What's the occasion?"

"I'm going to the city for dinner tomorrow night."

"Now, Sara, we don't clean on Saturday. You know that. We're open 'til noon for pickups only."

"Please, Mary. I'd really count it as a big favor."

"The Army guy?"

Sara felt herself grinning. She couldn't help it. "How in the world did you hear about him?"

"Honey, this *is* Murray. Everyone knows all about Rachel Warren's nephew. Bill Greer said the man couldn't take his eyes off of you when he came into the B & J. You like him, too, I take it?"

"Well, I've sure been thinking about him a lot. It's strange to be thinking about a man after so many years. And very distracting. I keep walking into rooms and forgetting why I'm there."

"Go for it, honey. And tell him to send a friend down here for me. I have a weakness for men in uniform."

"But what if you liked this uniformed man and he hated Murray?"

"I'd pack my bag."

"And your kids?"

Mary sighed. "Then I'd unpack my bag and go cook dinner. But it seems so unfair, Sara. I stayed here for my children's sake after Harry ran out, and my reward is I'll probably stay single the rest of my life."

Dinner was half over when Sara arrived home. "I bought a new outfit," she explained. "Actually, I bought an old one at a secondhand store, but it's the prettiest thing I've ever owned. Julian Campbell is taking me out to dinner tomorrow night at a wonderful restaurant in Oklahoma City.''

Her announcement was greeted with stony silence.

Chapter Five

Mary had Sara's "new" outfit ready by noon. "Is Rachel's nephew going to stay on out at her place?" she asked as she gave Sara her change.

"No. He still has a number of years of service left in the Army."

"So, will you be moving away? Bea and Jim must be fit to be tied. They are so crazy about those two younguns of yours."

"Mary, this is the first time I've ever gone out with the man. Let's not start ringing wedding bells."

"Well, this little suit is pretty enough to get married in — just in case. But you'd best talk him into becoming an Oklahoma farmer or buy a tombstone for Bea and Jim."

After lunch, Sara shortened the skirt to a more current length, washed her hair and manicured her nails. She felt like a high school girl, spending so much time getting ready for a date.

Mary Sue hung around, interested in the process. Never had her mother taken so much time putting on her makeup, fussing with her hair, fretting over a missing earring.

Sara wore cotton gloves to put on her panty hose. Years of pulling a quilting needle — or "between" — through layers of fabric had left the fingertips on her left hand roughened so they caught on stockings.

When Sara finally put on the navy suit, Mary Sue jumped up and down and clapped her hands. "Grandma, come look! Mom looks like Princess Di."

A glum-looking Bea came to the bedroom door, but her expression softened at the sight of her daughter-in-law. "Oh, my, Sara. You do look like a princess."

"I feel a little bit like one," Sara admitted. "It's nice."

Bea sighed. "Believe it or not, I remember feeling like that, having the mirror for a friend. Mary Sue, honey, run get grandma's diamond ear studs. Princesses need real jewels, don't you think?"

"Thanks, Bea," Sara said with a hug.

"Well, I don't like this Julian business one little bit. If I had my way, you'd stay home with us and watch a movie on television. But I don't blame you for wanting to be pretty for a man, to feel special. I guess you've been needin' some of that. And you're a good mother to those children. I know you won't do anything that isn't right for them."

The doorbell rang, and Sara jumped.

"Jim, get the door and offer Major Campbell something cold to drink."

Major Campbell. The last time he was here, Bea called him "Julie Boy."

Mary Sue returned with the earrings. She and Bea agreed they were the perfect touch. Barry was at the bedroom door now, staring. "What do you think, son?" Sara asked as she turned around to give Barry the full effect.

"You don't look like my mom," he said. "How come you never dressed up for Dad like that?"

"I did, honey. A lot. But that was before you were born. After you kids came, we didn't have the time or the money for dressing up. Now, don't I even get a hug for looking good?''

"Naw," Barry said, backing out the door. "I like you better in blue jeans.''

Julian was resplendent in a summer white dress uniform. Even Barry seemed impressed and wanted to know what the different ribbons and brass insignias stood for. But when Julian explained that the ribbons were for meritorious service and not for heroism, Barry headed out the back door, no longer interested.

Jim seemed a little awed by this uniformed version of the kid who used to clean windows down at the cafe. He wanted to know if Julian would ever be a general.

Julian explained that medical-support personnel seldom became generals. But there was a good chance he could retire at 30 years as a full colonel.

Bea contributed nothing to the conversation.

"Well," Julian said, interrupting an awkward period of protracted silence, "I guess this pretty lady and I had better be off. Thanks for the iced tea.''

Bea, Jim and Mary Sue followed them out the front door and stood on the porch as Sara and Julian walked down the long sidewalk to Julian's rented car. But there were no cheery goodbyes—only stony silence.

"That was a little thorny. What's going on? Are you breaking some sort of rule by going out tonight?" Julian asked.

"You might say that. I don't think they'd mind so much if you were a widowed farmer who lived next door. But they view you as a threat and would just as soon I didn't have anything to do with you. I'm sorry. Their apprehension is premature and embarrassing. They make me feel like I'm sixteen and going out with the town thug.''

He reached over and touched her hand. "You look beautiful—absolutely beautiful."

Sara smiled. And relaxed. Tonight, she was a princess and the uniformed man at her side was Prince Charming, and she was going to have an evening to remember regardless of how her family felt.

"I feel like Cinderella going to the ball," she said.

"Would you mind terribly if I stopped the car and kissed you?" he asked.

"Oh, I think that sounds like a lovely idea."

The road widened at the top of the hill, and Julian pulled over. Turning, he took her in his arms as though she were the most beautiful, fragile creature in the world—a kiss so sweet, it brought tears to Sara's eyes.

"I'm honored to be with you tonight, Sara Cate," he said.

"And I with you, Major Julian Campbell. Let's have ourselves a lovely time. A celebration, okay?"

"And what shall we celebrate?"

"Life."

And he kissed her again, not so delicately this time.

THE RESTAURANT TOOK her breath away. She may have grown up in Oklahoma City, but she had never dined at a place as elegant as the Eagle's Nest.

The restaurant occupied the top floor of a building in far northwest Oklahoma City and offered a fantastic panorama of the downtown and the surrounding countryside—from horizon to horizon.

As Sara looked around at the elegantly clad women seated at the tables or being led about the dance floor by their partners, she felt herself relaxing, even growing a bit smug. She looked as good as any of them. And no other woman had so impressive an escort.

Sara felt every head turn as they followed the maitre d' across the dance floor to their table. Everyone was thinking what a handsome couple they were, she realized. It made her walk tall and proud at Julian's side. "See the envy in all those women's eyes?" she asked.

"No, I was noticing the men. I don't think I've ever been with the best-looking woman in the place before. It's a feeling I could get used to."

The maitre d' pulled out a chair and seated Sara. With a flourish he opened the napkin, placed it on her lap and handed her the leather-bound menu.

Sara had to suppress a giggle. It was all too much fun. She suffered a momentary setback when the cocktail waitress came. *A cocktail?* God, she was years away from cocktails. It took her a second, but she managed to order a margarita. That's what she used to order back in the days when she and Ben were young and partied every weekend, before babies and money problems and fear.

"Would you like to dance?" Julian asked.

Sara started to say yes, then realized the combo was playing "Love Will Keep Us Together." She and Ben used to dance to that song. *Their* song. He would hold her close. They believed in its message.

"No, not right now," she answered. "After dinner, maybe. I haven't danced in so long. Maybe a drink will help me feel less inhibited."

The outer part of the restaurant rotated to provide an ever-changing view, and they watched a spectacular sunset glow with an incredible pallet of colors.

Sara pointed out some of the landmarks she recognized. Lake Hefner. Lake Overholser. The state capital complex. And to the south, a postcard view of downtown Oklahoma City's skyline.

"Murray's out there," she said, pointing to the south-west. "It's an hour and a half away and a world apart."

"Do you like living in that other world?" he asked.

"Sure. It's the right place for me to live because of my children," she said.

"Don't you think your children could be happy some-place else?" he asked. "Lots of well adjusted kids come from all manner of places, most of them not as small and out-of-the-way as Murray."

Sara waited for the cocktail waitress to serve their drinks before answering. "I know children can grow up healthy and happy almost anywhere," she said, "but I believe Murray is the best place for *my* children. They are sur-rounded by love and daily reminders of their father. Ben seems more real to them in the town where he grew up and is remembered well. I know their friends, their teachers—everyone in town, for that matter. I feel safe there. I don't worry about the future. For so many years, I didn't feel safe. I didn't know what would happen the next day, much less the next year. I didn't know how I was going to get my chil-dren raised. Now, I know."

"I suppose rural life has its advantages, but children lose something, too. Do you want your children to be citizens of the world or narrow-minded provincials?"

"Don't you talk about my people like that," Sara said hotly. "We citizens of Murray may not be sophisticated like you are, but we are good people. The world would be a bet-ter place if more of its citizens were like the folks who live in Murray."

Julian held up his hands in surrender. "Okay, so a high percentage of good people live in little towns. But what about you? Is living in Murray the best thing for you?"

"You haven't been listening to me," Sara said, not both-ering to conceal the irritation in her voice. "When a person has children, what is best for them *is* what is best for the parent. Children have to come first. Seeing my children have a good life is what's best for me."

"Do you really believe that being a good mother means putting your own life on hold? And what happens when Mary Sue and Barry grow up and move away? Are you going to live there with Bea and Jim forever?"

"I think I'd like to go to college then. The university is only about an hour's drive. I'd like to get a degree and teach school maybe—something more challenging than waiting tables."

"And you are willing to wait years before you do that? Why don't you and the children move to Norman now? You could work part-time and go to school part-time."

"I couldn't earn enough in a full-time job to support my children."

"And Bea and Jim wouldn't help you?"

"I already owe them too much. They paid off a lot of our debts after Ben died. And they've all but supported me and the kids since then. I'd love to pay them back someday, but probably I'll never be able to. Even if I could, I owe them a whole lot more than money. They took us in. Can you imagine how much that meant to me? They love us. We're a family—the Cate family. I don't pay rent. They buy the groceries. I try to do my part at the B & J and help with the housework. I gather you think I'm making some sort of awful sacrifice by living with them, but I'm not. I feel a little hemmed in at times, but on the balance I'm very fortunate. Now, if you don't mind, I'd like to stop talking about my life and enjoy being here in this beautiful place."

"One more question," Julian countered. "I think I'm falling in love with you, Sara. Yet, unless I'm mistaken, it sounds like you are unwilling to make any changes in your life. Is that right? Am I wasting all this emotion on a hopeless cause?''

"I don't know," she said softly. "Maybe so. I'm not ready to deal with that yet. All I want is tonight. I felt like I'd awakened inside of a fairy tale when we walked in this place. Don't spoil that feeling by getting serious."

"Okay," he agreed. "No more serious stuff. We will eat, drink and be merry." He lifted his glass. "Here's to tonight."

Sara touched her glass to his. "Tonight," she said with a smile. The drink was good. But she should have tried a new drink tonight. Margaritas made her think of Ben.

She watched while Julian quizzed the steward about the wine list. He could have been speaking another language with all that talk about bouquet and imported versus domestic. Sara wondered if she should tell him she wasn't much of a wine drinker. She'd hate for him to waste a lot of money on something she wasn't sophisticated enough to appreciate.

But Sara realized in a place like the Eagle's Nest, one drank wine, so she said nothing.

Julian and the steward finally decided on a wine Julian was unfamiliar with but the steward recommended highly. A red wine from Australia. Black Opal. Sara liked the name.

They interrupted their conversation to look at the menus, and in spite of the variety of entrees, Sara decided almost instantly. "Salmon!" she said. "I haven't had fresh salmon in years. And a Caesar salad. I haven't had one of those in years, either."

When the wine was served, Sara took a tiny first taste. Then a second. It was just as the steward described. Rich, full, important. "I think I just learned to like wine," she said. "This is heaven."

He smiled. "Yes, the world is just full of things waiting to be discovered."

"Don't, Julian. I know you think that people in little towns are limited. But everything is a trade-off, isn't it? You drink wonderful wine, and we drink pure, unpolluted well water. You have a more varied life, and we have glorious sunsets and the hoot of an owl on a summer's eve."

"Touché! Okay, I acknowledge there are good and bad things about our different life-styles."

"Just because I live in a little town doesn't mean I'm not interested in other places. I want to know about your life and all the places you've been."

Sara liked to watch him as he talked. Such an earnest man. He weighed his words carefully.

She wondered if men had any idea what women found sexy. They probably thought it was all a matter of muscles and thick heads of hair.

Julian's hands fascinated her. Large, strong hands with a sprinkling of black hair across the back. Well-groomed nails. She had imagined his hands cupping her breasts, arousing her body.

And his mouth. Such a mouth! Good, strong teeth. Wonderful, well-defined lips that could cover her own mouth and make her weak.

As for hair, his was receding a bit. She wondered if it bothered him. He wore his hair very short in the military fashion. She liked the neatness of it. No curls or swirls or sideburns. It made him seem all the more masculine.

He had a good body with broad shoulders and a slim, flat belly, lean buttocks and thighs that looked elegant in his dress uniform and sexy in jeans and a T-shirt.

She liked the way he cocked his head to one side when he listened to her. And he did listen to her. And respond thoughtfully. He was willing to have a conversation with her and not just kid around like the male customers in the B & J.

When she asked Julian about his goals, he said he wanted to continue in a very satisfying career, move up in rank and retire at 30 years with a pension that was three-quarters of his active-duty salary.

"And I'd like to find someone to share my life, someone who would enjoy traveling with me and is a good sport about government quarters and moving around a great deal," he added.

The waiter made the Caesar salad at the table with a great deal of flourish. Sara ate slowly, savoring every bite. She wondered if her children would ever learn to eat food like this. They were connoisseurs of country cooking but tended to turn their nose up at anything different.

The salmon was exquisite, the service perfect and each sip of wine tasted better than the one before. Sara enjoyed watching Julian talk and learning about his life as an Army officer. He had lived in Germany and the Philippines as well as numerous places in the United States.

"I'd like to go back to Germany," he told her. "In fact, I've requested it. When I was there before, I took classes in German and was just getting where I could really say something when we came home. My wife liked it, too. We traveled a lot in Europe. I think it was our happiest time. Then we were stationed at Fort Bragg. Brenda didn't like it there, or maybe it was she'd reached her limit of getting settled in yet another set of Army quarters. She had inherited some money and wanted a house on a golf course. I suggested she go find one, and she took me up on it—in Florida, near where she grew up. End of story."

"Except for the pain," Sara added.

"Yes, except for the pain. And the sense of failure. Maybe I should have resigned my commission and gone to

Florida with her. She gave me a chance to do that. And I thought about it—a lot. I love the ocean. I could have had a boat. I kept asking myself if it was just my fragile male ego getting in the way. Would I be bothered living in a house that not only belonged to my wife but was far grander than anything I ever could have given her? But Brenda couldn't have children and wasn't interested in adoption. And I think when it came right down to it, we were boring each other to death.''

"Do you miss her?''

"Sure. Don't you miss Ben?''

"Yes. Even tonight, a song the combo was playing made me think of him. *Our* song. And I felt sad. I either miss him, or I think of things about our marriage that weren't so good and feel guilty. Bea and Jim have chosen to remember only good things about Ben and rationalize away his faults. Losing all that money wasn't his fault. Taking unnecessary risks was brave. Raising his children camped out at rodeos was educational. The Ben they remember best was a football hero—a golden boy with the big smile who bragged about his mom's pie and liked hunting with his dad better than just about anything.''

They told the waiter to come back later with the dessert cart, and finally, it was time to dance. The wine had infused her veins with a delicious warmth, and she liked the admiration in Julian's eyes. She was ready to feel his arms around her, to feel his body near.

The combo was good, the music smooth and suited for ballroom dancing. Sara felt awkward at first, dancing with a man for the first time after so many years of not dancing at all, but after a few missteps she was able to stop thinking about her feet and relax.

Her mind added words to the music. Something about love lifting her higher and higher. *Not love,* she reminded herself. All she wanted to think about was tonight. Just tonight. Until Julian came along, her future had seemed as clear as glass. Now it was fogged. And she honestly couldn't deal with it. Not yet. Maybe never. But that didn't mean tonight couldn't be special.

Julian let go of her hand and circled her body with both of his arms. Sara's arms went automatically around his neck. She laid her head against his shoulder and let the music take her.

They danced well together—on and on, with little talking, just taking pleasure in being close. It seemed the most natural thing in the world to be dancing the evening away in this man's strong arms.

When the musicians took a break, Sara felt a bit dazed, as if she had awakened from a long sleep. But that was Sleeping Beauty. *Let's not confuse our fairy tales,* she reminded herself. Tonight she was Cinderella, and all this wonder would dissolve at midnight, but by golly, she was going to enjoy it until then.

They finished off the last of the wine just as the waiter rolled the dessert cart to their table. Julian selected a strawberry crepe. Sara asked for fresh raspberries with cream. And coffee.

"Such decadence," she said as she relished the berries. "The supermarket in Murray has them only once in a blue moon. In fact, this whole evening has been unreal. How does one get back to reality after all this?" she asked with a wave of her hand indicating the restaurant, the everchanging view, the music, the wine.

"For some people, this is the real world," Julian said. "And where you are living is someplace else."

"Maybe so, but I'll bet they don't appreciate coming here like I do. For me, being here is like being in a fairy tale."

When the band returned, the first number they played was a rumba. Sara wanted to sit it out, but Julian insisted. And in no time, she was dancing to a decidedly Latin beat.

"Where'd you learn to dance like this?" she asked.

"My wife taught me. We were pretty good."

"In that case, I guess I should take you to a cowboy bar some night and teach you two-steppin'," Sara challenged. "My husband taught me to do that. We, also, were pretty good."

After the rumba, the music once again went mellow. In spite of the crowded dance floor, Sara felt as though she and Julian were separated from the other dancers and enclosed in their own private cocoon that neither the world nor her worries could permeate. Only the music could. And it felt incredibly nice. She and Julian were one. The dancing provided a way for them to hold each other and almost make love without it really counting.

Time grew hazy. Sensations became distorted. Each note of music was more crystal clear than the one before. The warm, male aroma of the skin on Julian's throat had been nice before but was now intoxicating.

His touch grew so intensely pleasurable that Sara could think of little else. Soon she stopped trying and allowed her mind to float away from her. No small voices inside of her sounded warnings about the dangers of loving too soon and living for the moment. About parental responsibility and putting her children first. Conscious thought was abandoned, leaving her only with the ability to respond.

Changes stirred within her. Wonderful, exciting changes. She couldn't have stopped them if she wanted to.

They returned to their table for a brandy, but this time the wonderful floating feeling stayed with her. She held on to Julian's hand while she sipped the smooth brandy and savored the heat it brought to her insides. She felt as though she was going to explode with pleasure.

They returned to the dance floor for the combo's last set. The lights dimmed, and they dared to plaster their bodies more closely against one another. She felt him grow hard and wanting against her belly and felt herself open and waiting in return. It was almost too intense to bear.

At last, the music stopped. Arm in arm, they rode down on the elevator with two other couples, not saying anything, not looking at one another, a question hovering between them.

In the car, he kissed her again and again, deep kisses that spoke most eloquently of his longing. He ran his hands up and down her body, groaning with desire. "I want you so much, Sara. I haven't wanted like this in forever. I'd forgotten how it was to want a woman so."

"I want you, too," she admitted. "More than you'll ever know. But it's midnight, and I need to get home."

"Come home with me," he pleaded. "Stay the night with me."

"To do that, I would owe Bea a phone call and my children an explanation. I'm not ready to do either. Not yet."

"My God, Sara, don't you ever get to do what *you* want?"

"Yes. I came with you tonight. And that in itself wasn't an easy thing to accomplish. Let me have tonight as it is."

"Do you promise that another night you will stay with me?"

"No, I don't promise anything at all," Sara said. She felt like crying. He was ruining everything.

They were both quiet on the way home. Sara sat in the curve of his arm like a teenager on a date, but she didn't feel like a teenager. She felt like a very grown-up woman with a very delicate and adult problem to deal with. She wanted to spend the night with a man. What did one say in such a situation to an eleven-year-old daughter and a fourteen-year-old son? *Mommy wants to have sex with a man, so I won't be home tonight.*

IT WAS ALMOST TWO when they pulled in the driveway at Bea and Jim's. The porch light burned like an accusation.

"You're sure?" he asked one last time. "You could call and tell them we had car trouble and had to stay over in Oklahoma City. In a convent."

"I'm sure our presence has already been noted."

"So what's the deal? Are you supposed to remain celibate for the rest of your life? Since when does motherhood make that a requirement?"

"Please don't ruin the evening, Julian. It's been so wonderful. Let's end it on an up note, okay?"

"When will I see you?"

"Is tomorrow soon enough?"

"No. But I'll take it. How about breakfast?"

"Yes. I'll come over. We can have a late breakfast. Maybe I can talk the kids into coming. I'll tell them you have some questions about the animals."

She could tell by the look on his face that children wasn't what he had in mind. But having them there would put off any lovemaking. Sara needed time to think. She seemed about to enter into what was probably a short-term affair. And she wasn't sure that was a good idea.

"Okay," he said. "The kids and breakfast. Invite Bea and Jim, too. But tomorrow night, I'd prefer that you leave the family at home."

Sara could not resist one last kiss before getting out of the car. It turned into another and another. He unbuttoned her jacket and plunged his hand inside of her bra, kneading her breast, gently pinching her nipple. It felt glorious. Absolutely glorious.

They were just making matters worse, but she didn't want him to stop. Not ever.

He buried his face against her cleavage. If only she could take her bra off, he would have his mouth on her breasts. The very thought made her weak with longing, dizzy with wanting him. Almost ill.

Such longing. Such sweet, terrible longing.

JULIAN TRIED TO BE CALM as he drove home. *Damn.* He had gone and fallen in love with the wrong woman. He didn't need the complications. He didn't need the grief.

And he didn't need her bringing her children to breakfast!

God, that boy of hers obviously thought he was a wimp.

Her daughter looked at him as though he was some sort of alien being.

And Bea. Hell, Bea would gladly have run him off with a shotgun.

Julian realized he wasn't just courting a woman. He was going to have to court the whole damned family. And he didn't want to do that. He didn't want to make friends with a sullen adolescent boy, a wary little girl and a pair of irate in-laws. He didn't want to be embarrassed because he was afraid of horses and hated guns. He didn't want to have ties to this town. He hated the place. If he had any sense at all, he'd pack up and leave. *Now.* Before he got any more lovesick over a woman he probably couldn't have.

But he knew that if Sara brought a herd of wild horses and an army of hostile Cates with her in the morning, he'd still be glad to see her.

Questions about the animals. Yes, he needed to think of ways to get those kids to talk to him. To forget he was an ogre who wanted to steal their mother.

Maybe they'd like to help him paint the barn. He could pay them. Kids always liked to earn money.

And he'd offer to help Jim build that chicken coop. Hell, he'd even go hunting if he needed to. Ride a horse.

No, strike that one. No way was he going to ride a horse. He'd slay a dragon with his bare hands, but he wasn't going to make a fool of himself on a horse.

And then there was Bea. What was he supposed to do about Bea? Short of jumping off the water tower, he couldn't think of a thing he could do to make Bea happy.

Chapter Six

They came on *horseback* to his house for breakfast. Julian was stunned. Horses—before breakfast! He wondered if Sara was making some sort of statement or if Sunday-morning rides were standard fare for her and her children.

Julian could understand riding horses only if there was no other means to get from one place to the other. He understood that horses were a necessity until modern times. And that nowadays some folks considered riding the animals to be recreational. But Julian couldn't imagine getting up on top of a thousand-pound beast when there was a very real possibility of not only falling off and killing oneself but of getting kicked, bitten and saddle sore.

Oddly enough, however, the expressions on the faces of the three Cates as they galloped up the drive were quite joyful. He thought for a minute they were going to run into the fence, but all three riders drew their steeds up just short of disaster and nimbly dropped to the ground. *Amazing.*

Julian and the dogs trotted across the yard to greet their guests. Mary Sue actually planted a kiss on her horse's nose, then tied the reins to the fence, and rather than walk around the animal, ducked under its middle! Barry swatted the nose of his paint horse when the animal acted as if he was going to chew on his arm. "Cut it out, Spanky," he said.

"I was hoping Bea and Jim would come," Julian told Sara, which was sort of true. If he wasn't going to be alone with Sara, he might as well try to make points with the whole family.

"Grandma is mad 'cause we're missing church," Mary Sue said as she petted each dog in turn. "Mom asked her how come it's all right to miss church when we go fishing but not all right when we're invited to a neighbor's house for breakfast?"

Sara offered a lame smile over her daughter's head. "There are no family secrets with Mary Sue around. She keeps us open and honest, don't you, sugar?" she said as she stroked her daughter's blond ponytail.

"Looks like I owe you kids some extra money," Julian said. "I see that the geese, donkey and goats have left us."

"We put an ad in the Oklahoma City paper," Barry explained, keeping his distance. "Mom said you would pay us back. Some people who need goat milk for their baby took the goats. Two nuns from Oklahoma City took the geese and promised they weren't going to eat them. And a couple of old guys wanted the donkey for packing their camping gear when they go hunting. I think we've found homes for all the dogs in town—'cept Billy. No one wants a three-legged dog. Grandma says the cats go with the place, and that we should feed them until someone moves in. So, that leaves only old sway-backed Phyllis and Billy. Grandpa says we can't have them, but Mary Sue can talk him into anything."

"What I need now is to hire a couple of painters," Julian said. "Either of you kids interested?"

Mary Sue's face lit up. "Hire? You mean you'll pay us?"

Barry dug the toe of his boot in the dirt. "We got ball practice," he reminded his sister.

"Not in the mornings," she pointed out, "and not every day."

"You'd get tired of it after fifteen minutes, and I don't want to," Barry claimed.

"We can talk about it later," Sara interjected firmly. "I never thought I'd want to eat again after all that food last night, but I must confess I'm starved," she told Julian. "An early morning ride is good for the appetite, isn't it kids? And I can smell the coffee clear out here."

Once inside, Barry wanted to turn on the television, but Sara shook her head no. Sullenly, he sat at the table and ignored the glass of orange juice Julian put in front of him.

Sara poured herself a cup of coffee and sat by her son. But Mary Sue hovered at Julian's elbow.

"I've made pancake batter," Julian said, "but then I couldn't find the griddle, so I'll have to cook them one at a time in the skillet."

"Rachel kept it in the drawer under the oven," Mary Sue said.

Julian opened the drawer and, sure enough, there it was.

"I like to make pancakes the way my aunt did," Julian said. "She used graham flour and put a little allspice in the batter. And she made her own blueberry syrup from fresh blueberries. I don't know how to make the syrup, but I do use graham flour and allspice."

"She made strawberry syrup, too," Mary Sue said. "It was good, too."

"Sounds like you knew my aunt pretty well," Julian said.

"She was our neighbor," Mary Sue said with a shrug. "Grandma says it's important for folks to be good neighbors."

"Well, your grandma is exactly right," Julian said. "Would you separate the bacon for me and put it in the skillet?"

With Mary Sue helping, they soon had one platter full of bacon and another platter piled high with pancakes.

"Eat all the pancakes you want," Julian announced. "I've got more on the griddle."

"Aren't we going to say the blessing?" Mary Sue asked.

"Sure," Julian said. "Why don't you do the honors?"

Mary Sue looked at her mother, puzzled. "He means why don't you be the one to ask the blessing," Sara explained.

With the food properly blessed, everyone helped themselves—even Barry, although at first he took only one piece of bacon and one pancake. But he quietly had seconds and thirds.

"Do you like to cook?" Sara asked Julian.

"Yeah, it's a hobby of mine. Sometimes I'd cook one of my specialties for dinner parties. I make a mean curry and am quite good with ginger chicken."

"You mean the people at the party knew that you cooked?" Barry asked incredulously. Julian got his message. *Real men didn't cook.*

"I only like chicken fried," Mary Sue said. "And I've never had that curry stuff. My grandma is the best cook in the whole state. Grandpa says so all the time. She's even got ribbons from the state fair for her pies."

"I like to cook, too," Sara said. "When we were moving around a lot, I liked to try the food from different regions, but Bea does most of the cooking for us now."

With breakfast over, there didn't seem to be anything left for Julian to do but walk them out to their horses.

"Why don't you get on Spanky?" Barry challenged, offering Julian the reins.

"Thanks, but I'd rather not."

"How do you know you don't like horseback riding unless you try?" Barry challenged.

Julian hesitated.

"He's gentle as a kitten, aren't you Spanky boy," Barry said, patting his horse's neck. "You've just got to watch out for his biting, but other than that, he won't hurt you. You're not afraid, are you?"

"As a matter of fact, I am," Julian said. But he stepped forward anyway. He understood he was being put to a test. In the eyes of this boy, if he didn't get on the horse, he would be deemed a coward.

"I'll fix the stirrups," Barry said and deftly lengthened the straps. "Just put your left foot on the stirrup and swing your right leg over."

Awkwardly, Julian did as instructed.

"Now, just give him a little kick and make a kissing sound," Barry said.

Sara started to object, but as soon as Julian made the kissing sound, the horse took off at a swift trot with Julian bouncing around so dreadfully that he had to grab onto the saddle to keep from being unseated.

And as soon as he grabbed the saddle, the reins dropped to the ground. "Whoa!" he called out. "Whoa!"

But the horse kept right on going. Faster and faster. Julian was bouncing so hard, he felt as if his teeth would come loose.

Then he began swaying dangerously back and forth. He wasn't going to be able to hold on much longer.

But suddenly Sara was on her horse beside him, reaching for the dangling reins.

And Barry's horse stopped as abruptly as he started, with Julian almost catapulting out of the saddle over the horse's neck. Spanky lowered his head to graze in the grass by the fence.

Shakily, Julian made an ungraceful dismount.

Sara jumped down from her horse. "Are you all right?"

"Other than feeling very foolish, I'm fine."

"I'm so sorry," Sara said. "Barry did that on purpose. This is Ben's old cutting horse. He's been trained to take off in a flash when you kiss-kiss."

Sara grabbed both sets of reins and walked beside Julian with the horses following. The two children were shaking with laughter. Barry was laughing so hard, he grabbed hold of a fence post to keep from falling over.

"Young man, you stop that laughing right now and apologize to Major Campbell!" Sara said hotly.

"Ah, I didn't mean any harm," Barry said, still giggling. "It was a joke."

"He could have fallen off and been hurt. I want an apology, young man. Now!"

"Yeah, yeah. I'm sorry. I told Grandpa it would make you mad."

"Do you mean to tell me that your grandfather was in on this?" Sara demanded.

"Yeah. He said you'd think it was funny, but I didn't think so. You've been kind of cranky lately."

"Well, you were right. I don't think it's one bit funny. I'll deal with your grandfather shortly, but right now I want you to apologize again, and this time, sound like you mean it. *I am sorry, Major Campbell.*"

Barry repeated the words, then grabbed his horse's reins from his mother, scrambled into the saddle and offered a little exhibition in fancy riding as he kissed loudly and galloped the horse down the drive at breakneck speed.

"You sure looked funny," Mary Sue said to Julian with a giggle.

"It's not funny, Mary Sue, so wipe that smile off your face," Sara demanded.

Mary Sue tried to oblige but the giggles kept coming as she climbed on her own horse and took off after her brother.

"I guess I did look pretty funny, huh?" Julian asked, trying to lighten the moment.

"I'm so sorry," Sara said again. And Julian realized she was crying.

"Look, no one meant any harm. Boys are mischievous sometimes. He doesn't like me around, and it was his way of showing me for what I am—a real greenhorn."

"There's no excuse for him or his grandfather. And I want you to like them all," she said miserably, using her bandanna to wipe the tears away from her cheeks.

"I do," Julian said. "At least I don't dislike them. I understand. I'm an outsider. And a threat. If you and I care for each other enough, it could change their lives."

"I do care for you. A lot. But it's all so complicated. You don't like Murray, do you? Not even a little bit. But couldn't you keep the farm and come here for your vacations? Get used to the place in small increments? And maybe live here someday? Then we could..."

"Then we could what?"

"Nothing. I don't know why I'm talking like that. We really don't know each other."

"Yes, we do," Julian said, daring to take her hand. "We found out a lot about each other last night. We found out that we like each other's company a great deal. We found out that we like the feel of our bodies together. We found out that there's a lot of magic in the air when we're close."

She nodded. "Yes, we did do that. But maybe it was just the wine and the music. How do we know how we'll feel next month or next year?"

"No one knows that. Look, can we continue to spend time together while I'm here and then see how we feel? In the meantime, I can try to make friends with the kids and with Bea and Jim. And maybe before school starts, you and the kids can visit me in North Carolina. We can go to the beach and maybe visit some of the historic places they studied in school. They'd like that, wouldn't they?"

She nodded. "I think so."

They started walking down the driveway, hand in hand, Sara's horse and the four dogs following.

"Or maybe you don't want to have anything to do with a man who has to hold on to the saddle to stay on a horse," Julian said jokingly. "I must have been quite a sight."

"Don't make light of what happened. You could have been hurt," she reminded him.

"As it turned out, nothing was injured but my pride," he admitted. "I can't remember ever feeling so stupid. And afraid. My life was passing in front of my eyes. I thought, 'No, please don't let me die now that I've found Sara!' "

"You weren't thinking any such thing. I saw the look on your face. All you were thinking was 'Help!' "

"Well, I do thank you for saving my life. Somehow I feel like we got the roles reversed. In the movies, the woman is on the runaway horse and the man does the saving."

"Well, this isn't the movies, is it? I have to go now and give my children's grandfather a piece of my mind," she said as she gracefully swung herself into the saddle.

"Don't be too hard on him," Julian said, feeling brave enough to pat the horse's neck. Carefully. "Jim will just resent me more if you do. You are coming back this evening?"

"Yes," she said, looking down at him. "After dinner."

He watched her ride away. *Horses.* He always knew he didn't like them.

"Except you, Phyllis," he said, as he stopped to scratch the ancient mare's nose. "I'll bet you never went over a fast walk in your life, did you, old girl?"

THE MORE SHE THOUGHT about Julian on Barry's horse, the angrier Sara got. By the time she had unsaddled Hank and tended to him, she was well past the boiling point.

An apron tied around her church dress, Bea was in the kitchen preparing Sunday dinner. Rolls were rising on the kitchen table, giving off their warm, yeasty aroma. Jim had the Sunday paper spread out on the dining room table.

"I can't believe you encouraged my son to pull a stunt like that," Sara blurted out as she stormed into the dining room.

"Calm down, girl," Jim said, looking at her over the top of his reading glasses. "It was just a little joke."

"Julian could have fallen off. People die falling off of horses. I don't think it's the least bit funny and I'm telling you the same thing I told Barry. You go over there and apologize."

Bea was standing in the kitchen door, hands on her hips. "I don't like the sound of what I'm hearing, Sara Cate."

"I don't like it, either," Sara said back. "I count on my children's grandparents to set a good example for them. And then you encourage them to be rude to someone. Both of you. And I want it to stop. Julian Campbell came here in friendship, and my family has treated him poorly. I am embarrassed and humiliated."

Sara turned heel and marched to her room. She sat at her quilting frame, staring down at the tiny, even stitches, taking several deep breaths, then picked up the needle and thimble.

Quilting had a way of soothing away anger and frustration, and soon Sara felt calmer. The double wedding ring pattern was one of her favorites. The rings were in plaids and calicoes, with a natural colored background. It looked like something a pioneer woman might have made from scraps of old clothes by candlelight. When Sara quilted, she felt a kinship with those hearty pioneer women who'd lived hard lives but still managed to leave something beautiful behind. Sara's most prized possession was a quilt her grandmother had made out of feed sacks with perfect tiny stitches.

After a time, Mary Sue came to say that dinner was on the table.

"I'm not hungry, dear. But tell your grandmother to leave the dishes. I'll do them."

"You always make Barry and me come to dinner when we're pouting. How come you don't have to?"

"Because I'm the mother."

Mary Sue left the door open. Sara could hear Barry and Mary Sue recounting the episode with Julian on the runaway horse. They were all laughing.

At that moment, Sara didn't like her family very well.

She waited until the house was quiet to emerge. Bea and Jim would be taking their Sunday afternoon nap. The children had gone with friends to carnival in Chickasha.

The dishes were stacked neatly. It didn't take Sara long to put them in the dishwasher and clean the counter tops.

She got a package of ground beef out of the freezer and left it to defrost, not sure what she planned to cook with it. Sunday supper was her responsibility, the only meal she cooked on a regular basis.

She waited in the living room for Bea to wake up. She never napped as long as Jim.

And shortly, Bea came padding down the hall, carrying her shoes.

"You calmed down some?" she asked, sinking onto the sofa.

"Yes and no. I am very displeased at the way you and Jim continued to make a joke out of Julian's experience on Spanky even though you knew how I felt about it. I don't like you and Jim undermining my authority with the children, and I don't like you teaching them it's all right to make fun of people who are different than they are."

"Lighten up, Sara. You're about as sour as lemon juice on a green persimmon."

"Please don't make jokes. I'm dead serious about this. Those are *my* children."

"And this is *my* house," Bea reminded her.

"Yes, that does make for problems. Maybe it's time to rethink our arrangement."

Bea shook her head. "No. I shouldn't have said that. It's your house, too. And Jim and I were in the wrong. It's just that I don't like that man. I don't like to see you throwing yourself at him."

"Do you not like Julian, or do you not like the possibility of the children and me moving away?"

Bea sagged a bit. "Both, I guess."

"Bea, you have become more than my mother-in-law. You are my children's only grandmother. You are the closest thing I have to a mother. And you are my friend. And right now, what I need is a friend. Can't you take off your other hats and just be my friend and see as a friend would that Julian Campbell is a very nice man and that I might very well be falling in love with him? Can't you be happy that I feel alive and excited and that I really want to be with him?"

Bea sighed. "I don't know, Sara. That's asking a lot."

"No, it's not. It's only asking you to accept what is very normal and beautiful. I'm not saying I'm in love, but I'm at the point in a relationship with a man that I need to find out how I feel. I need to find out if I even want to love again. Maybe the best thing would be for me to put my life on hold until my children are older. But I can't know that until I spend some time with Julian. If I stop seeing him now, I'll be very angry and resentful toward you and Jim and my own children. Now, that isn't what you want, is it?''

"No, I suppose not," Bea admitted. "So, what is it that you want of me?"

"I want to spend the night with Julian tonight. And I want you to help me make it seem normal and proper to my children."

Bea squared her shoulders and set her jaw. "You can't ask such a thing of me! I won't have you sleeping around—not while you're living under my roof."

"One man in three years hardly constitutes sleeping around," Sara said wearily.

"Well, it's not proper. You can't expect me to tell those children that it's all right for their widowed mother to sleep with a man. A *divorced* man."

"I slept with your son before we were married. That helped us know that we wanted to get married. If we hadn't enjoyed each other in bed, I doubt if the relationship would have continued."

"Well, maybe that's the modern way, but sex before marriage is wrong in my book." Bea leaned over and tugged her shoes onto her feet.

"Wrong for whom?" Sara asked. "The whole world? Wrong even when two people have both been married before and want to make *damned* certain they are not making a dreadful mistake? If you were widowed, would you marry a man you hadn't been with in bed?"

"Don't you go saying things like that. Jim's a healthy man."

"So was Ben!" Sara said, struggling not to raise her voice. "I'm not saying it will happen. I'm just asking a hypothetical question. What *if?* Would you tie the knot without being intimate first?"

"I don't know. Maybe so. Maybe not. The best I can do for you is not to say anything at all. If you must, spend the night over there. I won't pass judgment."

"Maybe not with words, Bea. But pressing your lips together like that is just as condemning. Can't you be my friend and know that I need your support and understanding?"

Sara went to sit next to Bea on the sofa. She put her arms around her mother-in-law. At first Bea was stiff, but then she wilted into Sara's embrace. "I don't know why Ben had to die," Bea said.

"I don't either. But he did. And I'm still alive. Don't be mad at me for that, Bea."

They cried together, the two women on the sofa. That's how Jim found them.

"I take it you two have made up," he said.

"Sit down, Jim," Bea said brusquely. "We need to talk."

SARA WAS BROWNING the ground beef for spaghetti sauce when the children came in. Mary Sue was carrying a huge teddy bear that she won at the ring-toss booth. The Ferris wheel made her sick to her stomach, she reported. Barry insisted one of the heads on the two-headed cow was fake, but Mary Sue claimed the eyes on both heads blinked.

"Why's the overnight bag out?" Mary Sue asked, glancing over her shoulder at the small suitcase sitting by the back door.

"I'm going to spend the night over at the Warren place," Sara said as matter-of-factly as she could.

"With *him?*" Barry demanded accusingly.

"Yes, with Major Campbell."

"But he's not your husband," Mary Sue protested.

"No, he's not. But I may want him to be someday."

"Does Grandma say it's okay?" Barry challenged.

"It's not Grandma's decision to make," Sara explained carefully. "It's my decision. Something I want to do. Normally it's something two people do very privately. But for a mother with half-grown children sometimes that's difficult. So, it's still private—that is, it's nobody's business but this family's. But I thought you two should know what's going on. I didn't want to lie to you."

Mary Sue buried her face against Sara's middle and began to cry. "I don't want a new daddy. I don't want to move away from Grandma and Grandpa."

"Me neither," Barry added, feet apart, arms folded across his chest—the way his father used to stand when he didn't plan to budge. "Geez, the guy is such a wimp. He doesn't know how to do anything—'cept *cook.*"

"You have only one daddy," Sara said, caressing her daughter's back. "And I don't know that we'll move away. I don't know a lot of things, kids. This isn't easy for me, either. But I'm an adult woman, and a woman sometimes likes to be with a man. I miss your daddy very much. I don't want to always be lonely."

"Why can't you just go for a drive?" Mary Sue persisted, looking up at her mother.

"Maybe that's all we'll do," Sara said, "but probably I'll sleep in the same bed as him—like Bea and Jim, like your daddy and I used to do."

BEA AND JIM CHATTERED too much at dinner. Bea told about Jim falling off a horse once, in the middle of a Statehood Day parade. "He'd been partying too much the night before and fell plumb asleep right up there on the horse. Next thing I knew, he was on the pavement. Had the biggest knot on his head you've ever seen."

"Is that true, Grandpa?" Barry demanded.

"'Fraid so, son," Jim confessed.

Sara nibbled at her food. And kept looking at the clock. Finally, heart pounding, she rose from her chair. "You kids do your homework, hear."

No one said a word as she picked up her bag and walked out the door.

Oh dear, she thought as the screen door banged behind her. *Have I done the right thing?*

Half expecting lightning to strike her dead, she climbed into Jim's truck. She started the ignition and put her hands on the steering wheel.

She could go back. She could take her bag and go back in the house, and no one would ever say a word to her. Yes, maybe that would be better. After all, she didn't even have a decent nightgown. Her underwear was plain cotton. Her only cologne came from the drugstore.

Women who went off to spend the night with a man had *lingerie,* not underwear.

Sara clung to the steering wheel as though anchoring herself to the truck. And thought of Bea's words. *Why did Ben have to die?* Sara felt the same way. If Ben was still alive, she wouldn't be put in this hideously awkward position.

But she was still alive—never more so than last night with Julian's arms around her, his mouth pressed on hers. Alive. Very, very alive.

She put the truck in gear and drove away.

Julian was cleaning paint brushes on the back porch. He and the dogs ran up to the truck.

"You came," he called out. "I was so worried that you'd change your mind."

Then he looked at her face.

"Are you okay?"

"No. I feel..." She paused. How did she feel? "Wicked," she said. "I feel very wicked. I am going to get out of this truck, and I don't want you to tell me I'm not wicked. I don't want you to touch me. And I don't want you to carry this little overnight bag into the house. I'm not sure I'll be needing it.''

She waited on the back step while he got two beers from the refrigerator, and they took a walk around the farm. The beer tasted good. A soft breeze cooled Sara's hot brow. Such a pretty time of evening, with the night sounds starting, the stars beginning to put in an appearance in the eastern sky, the warmth of the day still rising from the ground.

Julian showed her what projects he'd started—fence mending and patching the barn roof. She asked him about a stack of lumber by the barn.

"For porches."

"More than one?" she asked.

"Yes, I agree with you that the house needs one across the front with a porch swing for sitting out in the evening. But everyone goes in and out the back door, so there should be more than just steps back there. I've never built anything more complicated than a fence in my life, but I'm going to give it a try. Actually, I'm kind of excited. Come on in the house, and I'll show you the plans I've made."

She looked over the detailed plans he had drawn and re-alized a porch was more complicated than she had thought. Books on home improvements were scattered about the ta-ble. A roll of linoleum stood in the corner of the kitchen. A brick pattern. It would look nice.

"You can hold me now," she said in a small voice. "For the second time in one day, I think I'm about to cry."

JULIAN HELD HER, rubbing her back, letting her cry softly against his shoulder.

What now? he wondered. All day, he had thought about making love. The instant she walked in the door, he wanted to swoop her up and carry her off to the bed. Rachel's bed. Strange thought, to make love in that bed.

Now, he wasn't so sure they would even make love and, oddly enough, that was okay. He would be content to hold Sara and soothe her and have her sleep beside him in the bed.

All he wanted was to be with her.

Finally, she calmed herself, had a drink of water. And admitted her stomach was growling. "I haven't really eaten since breakfast. Do you have any popcorn?"

She watched quietly as he popped enough corn to fill a huge bowl. At first she only nibbled, but then she helped herself to handfuls, washing it down with another beer.

"Feeling better?" he asked.

"Much," she said with an appreciative smile.

"Pretty rough over at Bea and Jim's house?" he asked, nodding his head in the direction of their house.

"Yes. *Their* house. Isn't it strange how I say that, too. 'Bea and Jim's house.' But the children and I also live there. Anyway, yes, we had quite a discussion about you and the horse you almost rode. I hope we got some things straightened out, but I'm not so sure."

"I don't know if it's indelicate to bring it up, but what about the overnight bag? Does that mean that you might stay over?"

"Yes. And they know I *might*. At least I've established that I am a grown-up woman with the right to visit a man if I choose. But it didn't make anyone very happy. There's no joy at the Cate household tonight."

"So, what now, Sara? I confess I'm not very good at this. Last night, it would have been the easiest thing in the world to bring you here and fall into bed with you. We were in quite a state, as I recall."

"And now it seems so calculated, doesn't it?"

"Too strong a word. Try 'awkward.' "

"Whatever. I'm not sure how we get from here to there," she said, tilting her head toward the bedroom. "In the movies, there's music playing and clothes miraculously fall away. But as we've already discussed, this isn't the movies."

Suddenly Julian felt his face breaking into a broad grin. "I have the solution," he said. "We can recreate last night. Right here in Rachel's kitchen."

First, he went racing down to the dirt-floored cellar—what Rachel used to call the 'fraidy hole,' where they went when tornadoes threatened—and found her stash of candles. He grabbed a handful and climbed back up the rickety steps. He rummaged through cupboards and found two mismatched wine glasses—actually they were sherbet dishes, but they had stems.

He dusted off a stack of Rachel's records and put them on the record player in the living room.

Then he lit the candles, turned off the light, poured beer into the sherbet glasses and started the music. "Star Dust," was first.

Then with a formal bow, he asked for the next dance.

Around and around the old kitchen table on the worn linoleum floor they danced, and kissed, and laughed and drank more beer from sherbet glasses. It was silly and carefree, and Sara was very beautiful.

Chapter Seven

As though by mutual consent, they avoided kissing and concentrated only on the dancing, on their bodies touching and responding.

She didn't need the accoutrements of an Eagle's Nest, Sara realized. The view, the wine, the food and the service last night had been fantastic, but this shabby, candlelit kitchen was just as romantic. All she needed for romance was this very special man.

She felt him grow hard and aroused against her belly and rubbed her body against him, thrilling to the maleness of him. She had done that to him. He wanted her *that* much.

His hands roved up and down her body, stroking her buttocks, the sides of her breasts, her neck, her shoulders, her hips, her hair.

When he slid a hand between their bodies to feel her breasts, she reached down to explore the bulge in the front of his jeans. "Oh, my," she said quite breathlessly. "How lovely you feel."

They kept dancing while the records changed, listening for a few beats of their own internal rhythms as their hips worked in unison. Then they would adjust their steps to the music of the new song, sometimes twirling 'round and 'round until they were dizzy and breathless, other times simply swaying.

"I'm going to die if I don't kiss you," he said finally.

"Yes, kiss me now."

And with his mouth he devoured her lips, her neck, her face, always returning to her mouth, to plunge his tongue deep, to make her moan.

His mouth was so hungry, so insistent, the kissing itself became a sexual act—a beautiful, honest sexual act. Sara wanted to kiss him forever. Endless kisses. Soul kisses.

He began to undress her, and she him, never allowing themselves to disconnect, continuing to kiss and touch as though their very lives depended on it.

Sara kicked off her shoes. He rolled her jeans far enough down her legs for her to step out of them, and she returned the favor for him. Then shirts fell away. She buried her face against the hair on his chest, inhaled the musky male aroma of him, tasted the salt on his skin.

Then she took a step backward, unclasped her bra and allowed it to fall away, wanting him to look at her, knowing that her breasts were swollen and full of her desire, tingling with her need of his touch, his mouth. She closed her eyes, thinking of that—his mouth on her breasts—and felt weak with longing.

"Oh my God, Sara, you are so beautiful," he said hoarsely. He reached out to feel her naked breasts reverently, caressing them gently as though they were overripe fruit that would bruise to his touch.

Slowly, she stepped out of her panties and was nude before him, illuminated only by the flickering candlelight. Then she reached out to peel his briefs down his body, to relish the sight of him and his arousal.

With only fingertips touching, they stood away from each other to feast their eyes. He was lean and sinewy, not an

ounce of fat, his belly tight and flat, the moist sheen of his
flesh reflecting the candlelight—a beautiful male body that
was boldly exhibiting its desire for her.

"I don't think I've ever wanted anything more than I
want you this minute," he said.

"And I want so desperately to give myself to you," she
said as she slid her arms around his neck. The feel of naked
flesh on flesh took her breath away. "Oh, my," she gasped
before their mouths began devouring one another once
again.

His torso moved back and forth, rubbing against her
breasts with his bare chest as he slid his hand between her
legs. *Oh, yes,* Sara's mind called out as he explored her, en-
ticing her to even greater desire.

Still kissing, they stumbled across the short distance to the
bedroom. Julian sat on the side of the bed and with his
hands on her waist, her hands guiding his face to first one
breast and then the other, her nipples growing hard and alive
with sensation. How glorious to be a woman, to have breasts
so that Julian could do this to her!

He fell back on the bed, pulling her on top of him. She
kissed his mouth endlessly, then his neck, his chest, his belly.
He groaned loudly when he realized what she was about to
do. But she teased, making him crazy as her tongue flick-
ered up and down his torso. She could tell how badly he
wanted to take her head in his hands and guide her mouth
to where he wanted it the most, but he resisted, letting her
carry out her sweet torture. And finally, she plunged him in
her mouth, feeling him arch his back to meet her. Was this
really her—this bold, wanton creature? Ah, the mystery of
his manhood. So erotic. So perfect. *And all hers.*

Quite deliberately, she ministered to him, bringing him
closer and closer to the edge until, with hurried roughness,
he pulled her away and threw her onto her back so that he

could mount her. She grasped at his shoulders and wrapped her legs around his thighs, pulling him toward her. But for a moment, he held back, hovering above her.

"Open your eyes and look at me, Sara. I want you to know that it's me making love to you."

"I know it's you, Julian," she said, looking into his eyes. "You and no other."

Then he plunged deep inside of her and the passion took them, owned them, made them one.

As AWARENESS RETURNED, Julian lay very still, savoring the honey-sweet feeling of contentment that permeated his every pore.

She was awake—he could tell by her breathing. But calm. Satiated, like himself. She had cried out again and again in ecstasy. No need for a polite "Was it all right for you?" with Sara. He *knew* she had reached that high glorious place of blinding white light and waves of warm sensation, each wave more intense than the one before until the mind explodes and satisfaction comes floating down like a blessing. And he felt smugly pleased with himself as he thought about it. He had been able to do that for her. In fact, he realized he was grinning at the ceiling.

"I had planned to be gentle," he said.

Beside him, her head on his outstretched arm, Sara offered a soft, throaty laugh. "That'll teach you to plan."

"May I ask you to marry me?"

"No."

"May I say that I love you?"

"Can't you find some less scary words? How about you like me a lot?"

It was his turn to laugh. "I *like* you, Sara. A lot."

"So mellow," she said taking a deep, contented breath. "I feel so mellow. Isn't it just the loveliest feeling in the world?"

"The very loveliest."

Their speech was slurred as though they'd been drugged. He knew they would both doze now, but he hung on a minute longer, clinging to this feeling of utter contentment.

She curled her body in closer to him, and he reached down to pull the spread over their nude bodies.

Yes, they would sleep, and in the night they would wake, reach for each other and it would start again. And then in the morning when they woke...

"You're a miracle," he whispered into her ear.

But already her breathing was deep and even. And he felt himself slipping away with her.

IN THE NIGHT, the lovemaking was different, more deliberate, more prolonged as they explored each other and took as much joy in giving pleasure as receiving it. Sara wanted to tell him how very special he was, how much she hoped that this was the beginning, but she had no right to make promises or to ask them of him.

Instead, as the afterglow waned, they talked into the darkness about other things.

Again, he explained how he wanted her and the children to come to North Carolina. Maybe if he could be with Barry and Mary Sue away from their home environment, they would stop judging him by Murray's standards.

They talked about his Aunt Rachel and her inability to love a small lonely boy. And Sara told him about her own mother, who had been almost fifty when she was born. "She called me her miracle baby and worried all the time that she was too old to be a good mother."

Finally though, they talked themselves out, and Sara sank into a deep sleep. But Sara slept only fitfully until dawn when she slipped out of bed and crept into the bathroom to shower and dress.

Julian was awake and sitting on the side of the bed when she came out of the bathroom.

"I need to go," she said.

"I want to fix you breakfast. I've got ham and eggs and honey for biscuits."

"Some other time," she said, gently planting a kiss on his forehead, sidestepping as he reached out for her.

"Why are you leaving so early?"

"I need to be at home when they wake up," she explained.

"Why?"

"I just do."

"Will you come back tonight?"

"No. Not two nights in a row. I thought maybe we could go on a little trip in a day or two. Just the two of us."

He didn't understand her need to leave, Sara thought as she drove away. But she wasn't strong enough to walk in the back door, with the four of them sitting at the breakfast table, turning to stare at her. *The Scarlet Woman.*

No, it would be easier to just be there—good ol' Mom baking muffins in the kitchen as they came stumbling in for breakfast.

Bea was already up though, and dressed. Instead of muffins, she was making biscuits. Without a word, Sara began to set the table.

"You okay?" Bea asked.

Sara nodded, feeling herself blush.

"I take it you are now completely infatuated with Julian."

"Something like that. Were the kids okay?"

"I suppose. They were both pretty quiet and went to bed without being told. I can't believe..." But she stopped midsentence, apparently deciding not to chastise.

But Sara got the message. *Good mothers didn't go off with men.* And maybe there was some truth in that. She wouldn't feel so strange now if it were perfectly okay.

"Are you going back over there?" Bea asked.

"Not tonight."

"Are you going to marry him?"

"I haven't the faintest idea."

"You know that Barry is planning to wear his dad's old number when he plays football for Murray High School this fall? And you know how much he wants to ride junior rodeo?"

"Yes. I know."

"And you know how much Mary Sue is looking forward to being in pep club with all her friends, maybe even trying out for cheerleader? And how much she wants to be a rodeo barrel racer?"

"Stop it, Bea!"

"No, I won't stop it. Someone has to speak up for those children. And Jim and I have some rights in this matter, too. We've got a lot invested in you and those kids. A lot of time and money and love. Just don't do anything lightly, Sara. Please, that's all I ask."

SARA WENT RIDING with the children after breakfast. They followed the creek bed across the Cate property down to the river bluff. Only Sara had bothered with a saddle. Both shorts-clad children were riding bareback—bare, strong, brown legs gripping the sides of their horses as they made their way along the narrow path. Except for their light hair, they could have been Indian children from a hundred years ago, born to this land, to ride and fish and live as one with nature.

She thought of the lines from the state song—about belonging to the land, and the land they belonged to was grand. Her children had a true home and a proud heritage.

Mary Sue and Barry knew the names of the birds in the sky and could recognize their calls. They knew the names of the prairie creatures and could identify their tracks. They knew the fish in the rivers and lakes and how to catch them. They knew where the wild blackberries grew and how to find sassafras roots.

Barry knew how to hunt and knew not to waste. Just as they killed chickens to eat, if he wanted to shoot a rabbit, he must skin it and bring it home for rabbit stew.

Like their grandfather, the children liked to watch the seasons come and go, and from him they learned about farming and caring for the land. They learned gardening from their grandmother, and their father had put them on a horse even before they could walk.

But even more than their love of nature, her children had seen evidence of its awesome power after tornadoes had ripped across the prairie and rivers had flooded, destroying homes and crops and lives. They understood about the food chain and survival of the fittest and that nature was about dying as well as living.

Her children respected the intricacies of nature, loved its beauty and feared its caprice—and because of this, Sara believed, were better equipped for life.

She had always known this was where she wanted to raise her children. For years, she had begged Ben to give up his job on the road and take them back to Murray.

This morning, Sara had wanted to scream at Bea and tell her how selfish she was for wanting to keep them all here.

But wouldn't she herself be just as guilty of selfishness if she took her children away from a life that suited them so well?

She thought of the trip that Julian wanted them to make to North Carolina. He wanted to show the children a good time, to make friends with them on his own turf.

Did she dare hope that his plan would work? Did she even want it to? He insisted she needed to show the children the world outside of Murray, that even when they were on the road with their father, most of what they saw was the sameness of rodeo arenas and trailer parks—which wasn't altogether true, but what they had seen and experienced was fading as the years went by.

Julian wanted to take them to Williamsburg. To Mount Vernon. And to the seacoast. They had only seen the ocean once when they were very little.

A lovely trip for Julian to court her children, to win them over—the more she thought about it, the better Sara liked the idea. They could see a military base and watch the soldiers march and the flag being lowered. They could see the vast hospital where Julian worked. They could see other children living there with their military families and leading interesting lives.

"Look, Mom, a red-tailed hawk!" Barry called out.

Sara shaded her eyes and looked heavenward at the magnificent bird coasting on the air currents in the vividly blue sky. Such a beautiful bird. So free.

Or was it? Maybe it had a nest of babies waiting for their next meal. Was anyone or anything ever really free?

But with responsibility came love. And that was the gift that made life worthwhile.

BEA AND JIM TOOK the children on a three-day fishing trip to Lake Texhoma down on the Texas line. Sara helped prepare the food and pack the camping trailer, and she helped

Mary Sue pack her clothes. But when they insisted she come, too, she firmly informed the children and Bea and Jim that she had other plans.

No one asked what her other plans were. They carefully avoided ever mentioning Julian's name.

Sara felt giddy with relief when Jim finally drove away, the camping trailer in tow. She offered one last wave, then turned to go in the house. As soon as she closed the door, she let out a war whoop. Three whole days! What a glorious gift!

Her own suitcase was already packed and waiting under her bed. After everyone was in bed last night, she had made a celebration out of packing, carefully choosing garments from her meager wardrobe, pressing them to perfection, shining shoes, shaving her legs, giving herself a pedicure. Yesterday, she and the kids had made a trip to Chickasha. She bought them bathing suits. And bought herself a summer gown and robe. Nothing fancy—just white lawn trimmed with a little lace. But they were pretty, and it gave her pleasure to fold them and lay them carefully in her small suitcase, to imagine herself wearing them with Julian while they had a glass of wine in their hotel room before they went to bed.

She even had a new toothbrush. A new hairbrush. A new tube of lash-lengthening mascara. Even those were fun to pack. She felt like a new woman. *Three days with Julian!* Everything was going to be perfect. It had been years since she had felt such anticipation.

And when a small voice inside of her asked if it was wise to get this involved, she didn't answer. She didn't want to be wise. Maybe the situation between her and Julian was an impossible one, but for three days she wanted to do what was best for Sara and not worry about being a good mother.

Whatever happened in the future, she wanted these three days.

Sara changed into a pair of black walking shorts, a pink cotton shirt and white sandals—quite a departure from her usual jeans or cutoffs. She added gold-hoop earrings and bangle bracelets. And decided she looked pretty good even if the whole ensemble—including earrings and nail polish—came from a discount store.

She turned the horses out in the paddock and called Casey Little Shield, the teenager who looked after the animals when the family was out of town. She reminded him one more time about the animals over at the Warren place and latching the gate. "And give Bea's garden a good soaking tomorrow if it doesn't rain."

Julian arrived on schedule, wearing a knit polo shirt, khaki slacks and a grin. He leaped out of the car and twirled her around and around in the driveway.

Then he grabbed her suitcase, and they were off!

"I feel like singing," he said as he pulled out onto State Highway 9.

"Well, why don't you?" Sara said, laughing.

He broke into a rousing rendition of "Bicycle Built for Two." Sara joined him with a little close harmony. They hit a few sour notes and were flat in places, but they tried it a second time and decided they were ready for the talent scouts.

She directed him first to the town of Anadarko, where they visited the Indian museum there and toured Indian City, which had authentic replicas of the various dwellings used by North American Indian tribes. Each lodge, hogan and tepee was outfitted with the possessions a family would have used in their daily life.

In front of a surprisingly large tepee used by the Plains Indians as they migrated back and forth across Oklahoma, following the buffalo herds, Sara said, "This is Oklahoma past. Tomorrow, I'll give you a sample of Oklahoma future."

They had lunch at a mom-and-pop cafe that reminded Sara of the B & J. Julian ordered chicken-fried steak with mashed potatoes and gravy. Sara settled for a chef's salad.

"I must admit that no one does chicken-fried steak like they do in Oklahoma," Julian said. "And would you look at this okra fried in cornmeal! I don't think I've had anything this good since I lived with Rachel. Oh, how I remember all that down-home cookin'. Black-eyed peas cooked with ham hocks! Hash-brown potatoes. Corn bread with black strap molasses. Hominy grits with eggs in the morning. Pickled watermelon rind. God, I loved her food even if I didn't love the woman."

"Are you sure you didn't love her?"

"Yeah. No love. The only time she ever touched me was to see if I had a fever. I used to like to be sick just so she'd put her hand on my head. Now, that's pretty starved for affection, if you ask me."

"Are you bitter?"

"No. Just sad. What about your mother? Did you love her?"

"Oh my, yes! After my dad died, we lived with my older sister, who was married and had kids older than me. Mom had arthritis, so my sister really took care of me. But my mother would play cards with me by the hour. And read to me. That's what I remember best—curling up beside her and listening to her read stories. I guess that's why I still read to Mary Sue if she'll let me. It makes me think of my mother."

"Where is your sister?"

"She lives in Alaska. We write some. But we're not as close as we should be. After I married Ben, Bea and Jim seemed like my parents. They still do."

From Anadarko, they drove to Norman and checked into a Holiday Inn.

"I've always thought this was such a pretty town," Sara said. "Don't you love all the trees?"

Sara insisted he drive by the sprawling regional hospital where Barry had had his tonsils removed. The hospital was only an hour's drive from Murray, she pointed out. "Do you want to go inside?" she asked.

"Not really," he said. "Touring hospitals is business. This trip is for pleasure."

"Well, it's a real nice-looking hospital, isn't it? Did you notice all the landscaping?"

Yes, he agreed. The hospital had nice landscaping.

Just at dusk, they took a walk around the university campus with its traditional collegiate Gothic buildings, spacious lawns, spectacular flower beds, stately trees and the carillon in the student union tower playing "The Battle Hymn of the Republic." Julian didn't need any prompting to say that it was a lovely place.

Some of the summer-term students were playing catch on the dormitory lawns. Others were taking an evening stroll, walking hand in hand. "I'll bet they think we're students, too," Sara said.

"I feel young enough to be one. It must be something in the air," he teased, slipping his arm around her waist.

"I used to dream about coming to school here," Sara confessed. "I knew I would have to wait tables and not be one of the sorority girls, but I wanted to make something of myself—maybe be a teacher or an accountant. I love history and was always good at math."

"Why didn't you?"

"I fell in love. I couldn't live without him."

"Any regrets?"

"No. Not a one. Ben and I had two wonderful children. And we had a great life for a while. I just realized it was time to make changes before he did, and then he got hurt and things went sour. But I'll never want to forget those good years. What about you? You have regrets?"

"No. In a way, I needed to marry Brenda to figure out a lot of things. She came from a different world—a world I thought I wanted to be a part of. She had grown up spoiled and rich. I thought that marrying a woman like her would change me—make me sophisticated and charming. And she thought that we would have a couple of years traveling about seeing the world, living the novel life of a military couple, then I would dutifully resign my commission and join the ranks of the idle rich. But one day I realized that I was no longer impressed by her family and friends, that I preferred people who were more genuine and sincere. Being with Brenda and her people helped me figure that out. I know myself a lot better now. Maybe my years with her had more of an impact than I realized, but I absolutely can't pretend to be something I'm not. So, I gained something from our marriage. Brenda didn't. It's really quite unfair."

They went to a quaint little Italian restaurant near the campus for dinner. Pasquale, the owner, tried to seat them in a booth, but Julian requested a table instead.

"Don't you like booths?" Sara asked.

"No. I couldn't touch you in a booth," he said, seating himself catercorner from her, their knees touching, their elbows, their shoulders.

"I see what you mean," Sara said. "This is much better."

When Pasquale discovered that Julian had traveled in Italy and even spent time in his hometown near Bari, he fixed them a special order of black mussels—on the house.

Sara regarded the platter suspiciously. She had never eaten anything you had to pull open and dig out of a shell and wasn't sure that she wanted to. But Julian encouraged her to try just one and showed how to dip the bread in the cooking juices. And soon Sara was ready for a second order of both the mussels and bread.

"You'd better watch out for those things," Julian warned as Sara tackled the second platterful.

"Why? They taste wonderful."

"The Italians say that shellfish are aphrodisiacs," Julian said in a conspiratorial whisper.

"Poor Julian. I hope you have been taking your vitamins."

Julian offered a playful groan and ordered another carafe of wine. "For strength," he explained. "Italians say that a man with a woman eating shellfish must always drink red wine."

"And what else do Italians always say?" she asked playfully.

"That falling in love can make two adult people act like kids."

There was that word again. *Love.* Sara changed the subject. She wanted to go to Italy someday. Was the Isle of Capri really as beautiful as the pictures?

The mussels were followed by heaping plates of spaghetti and garlic bread.

"Do you know that food tastes better when I'm eating it with you," Sara said. "And suddenly I love wine. The music is lovelier. Isn't that interesting? Do you suppose that means I'm attracted to you?"

They managed to drink the entire second carafe of wine. As they left, Sara had to concentrate on how to walk to the door without bumping into a table, which made her giggle.

"I loved the mussels," she told Pasquale with a wave.

In the car, Julian began kissing her. "For the past two days, I've thought about nothing but making love to you. While I painted the barn, I thought about it. While I pulled weeds, I thought about it. While I mended fences... You've put a spell on me, and I love it."

"I know. It's been the same for me. Every minute. I get dizzy remembering," Sara said. She felt dizzy now, thinking of the lovemaking that awaited them.

"How long do you think it will take us to get back to the motel?" she asked.

"About five minutes."

Sara groaned. "That long?"

In their room, she started stripping off her clothes the minute they walked into the door. "Would you like to take a shower with me?" she asked over her shoulder, trailing her shirt behind her.

Julian was already unbuckling his belt.

Showering was incredibly erotic as they soaped every inch of each other's bodies then rubbed against each other, the hot water pouring over them.

"I love your body," Sara said, spreading the soap suds over his smooth, firm chest.

Being with him like this made her feel young and giddy. Before he came into her life, she was beginning to wonder if she would just slip quietly into an uneventful middle age, love and romance something she only remembered. She would probably get a third recliner to place alongside the pair that Bea and Jim dozed off in every night in front of the television.

But now, here she was showering with a lovely, sexy man. Her life had possibilities—if only she could figure out a way to love Julian and be a good mother, too.

They kissed under the shower spray like two natives in a rain forest. The water poured over them like a benediction.

They dried each other with big fluffy towels and fell naked across the king-size bed.

"Can I say those scary words tonight?" Julian asked.

"No, not yet. But it helps to know you really want the kids and me to come visit you. To know that you don't hate them."

"Of course I don't hate them. If I were them, I probably wouldn't want my mom getting involved with someone who could change their life. But no talk about children. I want to please you, Sara. I want to fulfill your every fantasy. Will you help me do that?"

"You already are."

"Tell me what you want."

"For you to kiss me. I want endless kisses. All over my body. And then, I want to return the favor."

Chapter Eight

Sara chattered away during the short drive from Norman to Oklahoma City, telling Julian how much the state had changed since he left. Industrial diversification. New jobs. People from the East and West coasts moved to the state in search of a better quality of life, to get away from pollution and crime, to buy an acreage so they could keep a horse for their kids.

Julian understood perfectly well what Sara was trying to do. Like a tour guide for the state chamber of commerce, she was trying to sell him on Oklahoma. Sara wanted it both ways. She wanted to continue raising her children in rural Oklahoma and form a committed relationship with him.

And the only way she could figure out to do that was to convince him to give up his military career and settle down in Murray or someplace close by. He wondered if she was really that sold on the value of country living or just so beholden to her in-laws she couldn't bring herself to leave them.

Probably both motivations were playing a role in her determination to stay where she was. If Sara had a fault, it was that she consistently put other people first. Julian could already see that just in the short time he had known her. And, of course, unselfishness was an admirable trait, but if practiced all the time it became selflessness. Self got erased and all that remained was a good little robot running around doing what other people wanted. Sara sincerely believed that good mothers had to put their own lives on hold, that what was good for them personally could not be factored into any decisions they made about their family's future.

His wife and Sara couldn't have been more different, but even so, Julian felt a sense of déjà vu as he listened to Sara. Brenda had wanted him to resign his commission and go live in posh beach-front property in Florida among wealthy socialites. Whereas, Sara wanted him to resign his commission and come live on the prairie in landlocked Oklahoma among country folks. But the end result was still the same. He would be giving up a way of life that he valued—one that had given him a chance to finally rise above his difficult childhood and become the man he wanted to be—a life that combined an orderly military existence with his chosen career field of health-care administration. Being an Army officer brought him security and respect. It had given him the opportunity to live abroad and learn a great deal in the process.

What Brenda had wanted and Sara now wanted was for him to give up a life to which he was eminently well suited. Oddly enough, he felt Brenda had been more justified in her position than Sara. Brenda had tried his way and found out it wasn't for her. For their marriage to survive, one of them would have to make a huge sacrifice. He wasn't willing to live her rich and spoiled life-style. Brenda wasn't willing to be an Army wife. So they parted.

But he and Sara had reached an impasse almost before their relationship had even begun. She wasn't willing to try his life, wasn't willing to consider the benefits for herself and her children of living another way.

Julian had even wondered about asking Sara to come away with him and leave the children with their grandparents in Murray. She could go back to Murray for long visits. The children could come visit them—even if he and Sara were living abroad. Somehow, he would find the money for all the necessary plane tickets, telephone calls, presents, whatever to keep Sara in close touch with her children.

But Julian kept his mouth shut on that account. Sara would never agree to such an arrangement, and his suggesting it would probably make her angry. No matter how inconvenient it might be, Sara was a package deal. She came with two kids or not at all. And while, at least in theory, he wasn't opposed to the idea of marrying a woman with children, he and the children in question at least needed to like each other.

He was going to work on that. Really hard. He would take up fishing. Maybe even practice his marksmanship and go hunting on occasion. But horseback riding was out.

Absolutely.

But Oklahomans were really horsey people, he was discovering. He had observed an amazing number of pickup trucks and other vehicles traveling up and down the highways with horse trailers in tow. Sara explained that people transported their horses around so they could ride them in rodeos, horse shows, parades, polo matches, trail rides, and on fishing and hunting trips. And when the residents of the Sooner state weren't riding horses, they apparently went to the races, Julian decided, and watched someone else ride horses. That's where he and Sara were heading now. To the races. At Remmington Park, Oklahoma City's new track. Her idea.

He was expecting a county-fair type racetrack—a tumble-down grandstand with a poorly maintained dirt track. He'd seen races on such tracks several times when he and

Rachel would take her canned goods and produce for the annual judging to determine the best homemakers and farmers in the county.

But he and Sara were sitting in a several mile-long, double row of cars waiting to enter the sprawling parking lot of a facility that had nothing to do with country fairs. The huge enclosed grandstand looked like something out of that old television show "The Jetsons," with a space-age look that didn't jibe with Julian's image of Oklahoma.

"It's the best racetrack in the world," Sara told him proudly. "State-of-the-art everything. The track has become a real tourist attraction."

Next to fishing, coming to the races in Oklahoma City was Bea and Jim's favorite weekend pastime, Sara explained. Bea had won so many daily doubles, they put an article about her in the track newsletter.

Once again, Sara launched into her tour-guide routine, pointing out how Murray was a rural community but was close enough to a large metropolitan area so that its citizens could enjoy the races, zoo, amusement parks, symphony, big-city shopping....

"Sara, I'm happy that Murray is such a nice place to live," he said finally, "but could you please curtail the chamber-of-commerce stuff. I get the picture. If I weren't in the Army, I might want to live around here someplace. But I am in the Army. And I suspect that by this time next year, I'll be living in Europe, not in Murray, Oklahoma."

"But would it be so bad? Murray is a wonderful little town with lots of fine people. You already own a home there."

"I have a master's degree in health care administration," he pointed out. "What am I supposed to do in Murray? Pump gas? I don't really like the town, Sara. My memories of Murray are not happy ones. And I hate what that town is doing to you. Do you want to wait tables for the rest of your life? You're a prisoner of your own good intentions."

Sara grew very silent as Julian occupied himself with paying the gate attendant and being directed by parking attendants to the far side of an enormous parking lot. She didn't say a word as they joined the stream of people hurrying toward the entrance. When he took her hand, it was limp.

"Look, Sara," he said, "I'm sorry if I hurt your feelings. I enjoy hearing you talk about Oklahoma. Really I do. I think it's wonderful you're proud of the state. And I'm flattered you would want me to live here."

"I am not a prisoner," she said, her lower lip quivering. "I have chosen of my own free will to live in an environment I think is best for my children."

"Are you sure? If you hadn't already been living there and hadn't turned up destitute after Ben died, would you really have chosen to stay on in Murray?"

"Yes," she said, her tone growing angry. "I'd been trying to get my family back there for years."

"Look, I'm just as frustrated about our situation as you are. And I suspect the solution isn't going to be an easy one. But I refuse to believe that when two people are as right for each other as we are, that there isn't a way for them to work things out."

"You really think so?" she asked.

Julian was surprised to see that she had tears in her eyes. "Yes, I think so, dear lady. And I know I'm not supposed to say that 'L' word out loud. But I'm thinking it, Sara. I'm thinking it a lot."

She sniffled a bit and said with a small smile, "Well, maybe tonight we can say it out loud."

The river of people heading for the entrance had to detour around them as Julian gathered Sara into his arms.

"Dearest Sara," he said, kissing her eyes, her hair. He thought his heart would break from sheer joy. Tonight they would speak of love.

The inside of the racetrack was even more spectacular than the outside. Built on the rim of a large natural amphitheater, the huge grandstand was surrounded by a soaring glass wall that offered a perfect view of the track and the surrounding countryside, which included the city's sprawling zoo and public golf course. One had the feeling of being out in the country, even though downtown Oklahoma City was minutes away to the south of the track.

They had to hurry to place their bets on the first race. Julian bet two dollars to win on a horse named Sweet Thing—based on its name only—and lost. Sara checked the tip sheets and took into consideration each horse's breeding, trainer, jockey, record of past performances, and bet on a horse named What Luck's Prince—and lost.

The next race, Julian closed his eyes and stabbed at the program, his random choice being number six—Alma's Boy. Once again, Sara carefully studied all the statistics and also chose Alma's Boy.

"In that case, the horse is a sure thing," Julian said. "I think that calls for a twenty-dollar bet."

"Heavens, no!" Sara said, eyes wide in mock horror. "I don't believe in more than a two-dollar bet."

"But we might win," Julian insisted.

"We also might lose. If there's one thing I've learned from horse racing, it's 'there's no such thing as a sure thing.' But if you have to gamble the whole twenty, bet the horse to show."

Alma's Boy came out of the gate last and stayed in last place almost until the final turn when the horse shot forward like a bullet. Sara and Julian were on their feet yelling.

When the horse crossed the finish line third, Sara jumped up and down. "We did it!" she said.

Julian went to collect their winnings and returned with $29.45. The horse was one of the favorites, so their profit for a show bet was modest. "Not even enough to pay for our tickets," Julian said. "But that was fun. Now, let's have some pizza and beer and do it again."

The rest of the races, they won a few and lost a few, finishing in the hole, of course, but having a wonderful time doing it. Julian loved it when the horses were coming around the final turn and the crowd was on its feet, everyone yelling for his or her selection, Julian and Sara with them, even if they only had two dollars riding on the outcome. It was lighthearted and fun.

From the track they checked into the Marriott on Northwest Highway. He insisted they return to Eagle's Nest that night for the view and the food and the dancing. "But I'll have to wear the same outfit I wore last time," Sara warned him.

"So what? I'm wearing the same uniform. It will be exactly like before—except this time, I get to keep you with me all night."

Once again, they danced until the music stopped. Julian had to stop himself repeatedly from whispering in her ear that he loved her. *Later,* he told himself. *Make the first time you say the words special. Wait until you can show her just how much you mean it.* He felt like a champagne bottle about to explode, so great was his need to tell Sara exactly how he felt about her.

And finally, primed with wine and music, they were in the hotel room, their bodies nude, holding each other in the middle of another king-size bed. Julian left a lamp on so he could see her body and her face as he made love to her.

They kissed and caressed endlessly. Her body was like silk, her breasts a miracle. And she responded so appreciatively to his every touch.

He loved learning about her—what things made her murmur with contentment and what made her groan with desire.

And how incredible that she seemed to enjoy doing all those delicious things back to him, indeed she *insisted* upon it, at times wanting him to be completely passive while she ministered to his body.

He had not entered her yet, forcing himself to wait and wait and wait, until their coupling would be the glorious union they both wanted.

Finally, when he knew that he hadn't the strength to resist much longer, Julian hovered over her, looking down at her lovely face. "I love you, Sara. I love you with all my heart and soul, and I want to be with you forever."

And then he plunged himself deep into her sweet, burning flesh.

"I love you, too," she cried out. "I love you, Julian. I really do. I love you. I love you. I love you."

IN THE MORNING, they slept late and when they awoke made lazy, morning love—silly, teasing, nibbling love that made them laugh.

After a wonderful, decadent breakfast in bed, with the morning newspapers and two pots of coffee, they packed up and hit the road once again. Sara had planned to stay in Oklahoma City another night, wanting Julian to see the Cowboy Hall of Fame Museum and the zoo, but Julian decided that two could play the tour-guide game and headed toward Fort Sill in the southwest corner of the state.

He had never visited the Army's sprawling artillery center before, but he knew it was one of the fine old bases and would serve his purposes well.

Sara admitted she had never been on a military base before but assumed they were stark places with no-nonsense buildings and weapons everywhere.

Driving into Fort Sill was like entering another world. Every curb was painted white. The lawns and parkways were all carefully manicured, the shrubbery trimmed, groves of trees everywhere. No place was there a building in disrepair. And men and women were smartly uniformed, their shoes and boots polished, their shirts tucked in, their brass insignias gleaming, their hats on straight.

"Are all military bases so beautiful?" Sara asked.

"All are well maintained, but old ones are the most beautiful," Julian said. "Fort Sill has been here since the 1830s when they built it to control the warring tribes."

"How do you know?" she asked.

"Oh, I'm a bit of a military history buff. And Fort Sill is a famous place for all us Army folks. Geronimo was incarcerated here for years—as were a lot of the last of the renegade Apaches after they finally surrendered. And a lot of famous generals were commandants here at some point in their career."

They had lunch at the officers' club. Julian pointed out the ballroom, the huge swimming pool and the outdoor pavilion for summertime dances. "Every post has an excellent officers' club," he said. "Army people love to dance and party. They're really a very friendly lot. And the wives have their own clubs and service projects. There are always lots of organized activities for the kids. Army kids play baseball, too," he added.

They drove through the residential areas where officers and their families lived. Julian could tell that Sara was im-

pressed with the gracious old houses. He didn't tell her that
all Army posts didn't have such wonderful quarters. And he
didn't tell her that every single set of Army quarters had
cream-colored walls throughout. Brenda used to hate that.
No painting or wallpapering allowed. She couldn't put car-
pet on the hardwood floors. She couldn't replace drab
kitchen flooring. And what would be the point? They'd
probably get orders the day she finished redecorating. She
hated living in a house just like the one next door. Some of
the wives accepted the challenge and enjoyed personalizing
their quarters in spite of the restrictions. But Brenda balked
at the restrictions. She said that the walls were symbolic.
Army life was too damned colorless for her.

Their next stop was the guardhouse-turned-museum that
once had housed Geronimo. From the museum exhibits,
Sara discovered that the famous Indian chief had actually
spent very little time incarcerated there. Mostly, he lived in
a white frame house with his family and was allowed to tour
with Wild West shows.

They toured the several post museums, which offered exhibits not only on the Indian wars but also on the role of
Army Artillery in other wars. Julian was a bit surprised at
how knowledgeable Sara was about the historical events
portrayed.

"You must read a lot," he said.

"Not as much as I used to. Mostly now, I listen to the radio and quilt. But I still read some at night to put myself to
sleep. I like biographies and historical novels best. I guess
I've picked up a little information here and there. If I ever
went back to school, I'd probably major in history—and be
a history teacher. I loved my history classes in high school.
It was like having a story hour every day."

"Most larger military bases have arrangements with uni-
versities for extension courses right on the post," Julian

said. "Military personnel and their dependents can get college credit by attending class in the evenings."

"Now, who's doing the chamber-of-commerce bit?" Sara teased. "First we have a tour of your basic, attractive military post followed by an explanation of the education opportunities offered by the Army."

"Turnabout is fair play, I've always heard," he said.

Julian wore a uniform for their evening meal at the officers' club. Sara was surprised when he ran into two officers that he knew from previous postings—one a pediatrician and the other from the post quartermaster's office.

"That's not unusual at all," Julian explained. "Army folks move a lot but seldom do you move to a new posting without finding people there you knew from someplace else. And the semi-mandatory socializing that goes on at military bases is really a good idea. People do get to know one another—spouses and children included."

"Do you really think you'll go to Germany?" she asked.

"I've requested it. And I'm due for an overseas assignment. You would love Germany, Sara," Julian said, taking her hand. "You can't imagine how beautiful it is, and it's like living in a history book. And it would be good for your children, too. They'd learn so much, see so much. They could even learn another language. And just think what living there would do for them. They could grow up to be citizens of the world instead of narrow-minded provincials."

"I wish you'd stop talking about folks from Murray like that," Sara said angrily. "We may not be well traveled and sophisticated, but we're honest people who believe in being good to our neighbors and our families."

After dinner, they went outside to the dance pavilion. Strings of Japanese lanterns were lit, and a dance band was playing. The setting couldn't have been more romantic, but Sara was stiff in his arms.

"I'm sorry," he said finally, taking her back to a small table on the edge of the dance floor where a waiter had placed their after-dinner brandy. "I was out of line. You have very good reasons to like living where you do, and I shouldn't put you down for it."

"I suppose we're both right," she said with a sigh. "I'd love to live abroad. I'd love for my children to travel. But they are so happy where they are. I don't see how I can disrupt their lives and those of Bea and Jim. And I can't have it both ways."

"You have the right to some happiness, too," he reminded her.

"If I stay in Murray, will you come to see me often? Maybe let me visit you when I can? We can write and call each other."

"For a while, that might be okay. But I want a wife, Sara. I'd like to have a child or two before I get too old to be a good father. I can't promise that I'll dangle out there on a string forever."

"I want to say that if you loved me enough, you would wait forever," Sara said. "Or at least until my children are grown. But that's not fair. Love by itself isn't enough. If I were you, I'd want a wife, too."

Their lovemaking that night was poignant, with both of them wondering what was going to happen to them. Sara cried. Julian wondered if he was wrong. Could he give up his military career and the prospect of a good pension someday? Could he move into Rachel's house?

Could he live in Murray and become the man who married Ben Cate's widow?

Aunt Rachel had just barely eked out an existence on her wheat farm. Bea and Jim obviously didn't make enough money with their farming and had to run a cafe on the side. Ben Cate had gone bankrupt trying to raise wheat and cattle. Try as he might, Julian could not imagine himself earning a living in that town—or even living in that town.

But love was supposed to conquer all. Wasn't that what the songs and stories said?

Trouble was, he could see Sara's side. Her kids would have a hard adjustment if they moved away. And Bea and Jim would be devastated. They had wrapped their whole life around their two grandchildren.

They started back to Murray after breakfast, neither one having the heart for any more sight-seeing.

It was mid-morning when they arrived home. Sara was surprised to see Jim's truck and the camper already parked in the driveway.

"They never come home this early," she said, alarm in her voice. And in a flash, she was out of the car and running toward the house, Julian following.

Barry met them at the door. "Mary Sue's in the hospital over at Norman. Grandma and Grandpa said we're to come right over."

"In the hospital?" Sara said, grabbing her son's shoulders, color draining from her face. "What happened?"

"She got sick yesterday, and we came on home. This morning, she was worse and started throwing up all over. She said her belly hurt real bad. So Grandma and Grandpa took her to Norman and told me to wait here for you."

Julian drove as fast as he dared. Sara was trying very hard to stay calm, but he could sense the panic just below the surface. Barry was quiet in the back seat.

At the hospital, the attendant at the front desk directed them to the pediatrics ward. The nurse at the desk in pediatrics directed them to surgery.

A worried Bea and Jim were in the waiting room.

Bea jumped up when she saw Sara. "We had the high-way patrol out looking for you. The doctors wouldn't operate without your permission. But finally, they got a court order, and the surgeon went ahead."

"What's wrong with her?" Sara asked.

"Appendicitis," Jim said. "Poor little thing, she was hurting real bad."

"And she wanted her mother," Bea said, collapsing into the closest chair. "Lord, I was scared to death. She got so pale. That drive to Norman was the longest ride I ever had in my life."

Julian tried to hold Sara, but she would have nothing to do with him. Instead, she clung to her son.

Julian felt very much the outsider as they waited through the next half hour in the chilly room with its vinyl-covered furniture. Magazines were neatly displayed in racks, but it didn't look as though anyone had been reading them. This was a room for apprehension and prayers. Magazines seemed out of place.

When the surgeon, still in her green scrub suit appeared, they all rose to their feet. Julian thought Sara was going to faint as she hugged her son to her, waiting for the verdict.

"The appendix had ruptured and released a lot of infection into her abdominal cavity," the doctor explained. "She's going to be pretty sick for a few days, but I think she'll get over it just fine. Would you like to see her?"

"Oh yes," Sara said. "Please."

The two women went off together, leaving Julian alone with his silent accusers. The unsaid messages were clear. *Sara shouldn't have gone off with you.*

He went to the rest room, then hung out by the vending machines, drinking horrible coffee, waiting until Sara reappeared.

Sara was calmer now, but still Julian felt like a fifth wheel in this grim family gathering.

Finally, he asked Sara if she wanted him to stay.

"No. Just bring in my suitcase from the car. I'm staying here with Mary Sue tonight."

"I'll come back this evening. Okay?"

Sara nodded.

IMMEDIATELY, SARA felt regret. She should have reassured Julian, told him that nothing was his fault—that what was wrong here lay between her and her family.

She wanted to run after him, to tell him not to go. She felt helpless and alone as she watched him depart. But she needed him out of the way while she faced the scene that lay ahead.

But first things first. She went to the admitting office and signed the necessary papers. She ate a sandwich and took some aspirin to ward off a threatening headache.

Then she needed to see her daughter once again.

All those tubes! Again, Sara had to brace herself at the sight of her pale daughter, with tubes in her arm and nose.

But Mary Sue was less groggy now. Her eyes opened, and she smiled at her mother.

Sara's heart turned over in her chest. She kissed Mary Sue's forehead, her cheeks, her sweet mouth. She caressed her daughter's shoulders, her arms, her sturdy brown legs. She smoothed Mary Sue's silky hair back from her brow. "I love you so much, honey. God, how I love you."

"I got real sick," Mary Sue said, her words still slurred from the anesthesia. "I had 'pendicitis."

"I know, honey. I'm sorry I wasn't with you."

"I was scared without you," Mary Sue said.

"Yes. I need to be more careful about letting Grandma and Grandpa know where I am. I'll do better in the future."

"Will you go off with Major Campbell again?"

"I don't know, honey."

"I don't want you to, Mom. I like it better when we're all together. It's more fun that way."

Sara sat with her daughter until she had drifted off to sleep, then kissing her once again, she squared her shoulders and went to face her son and in-laws.

They were waiting for her. Jim was slumped in a chair. Bea's back was straight, her lips a narrow line. Barry looked anxiously from one adult face to the other.

"I know you think Mary Sue's illness somehow proves something," Sara began.

"Why don't Barry and I go down and have a Coke?" Jim offered hopefully.

"No," Sara said. "I want you here."

"Well, her getting sick does prove a mother's place is with her children," Bea chided. "It proves you shouldn't have been off with that man."

Jim put a hand on his wife's arm. "Watch it, Bea. Don't go saying things now that you'll regret later."

"No, it doesn't prove that at all, Bea," Sara said. "It proves that I should have been more careful about staying in touch. That's where I erred. I thought as long as they were with you, I didn't need to worry. Now I know I should have given you an itinerary with phone numbers where I could be reached. Or made arrangements for you to leave messages with one of the neighbors and for me to call in periodically. Next time, I'll plan better."

"So, there will be a next time?" Bea demanded. "Maybe Jim and I don't want to take care of the kids so that you can go off like that."

"*Bea,*" Jim cautioned.

"If you are uncomfortable doing that, I'll make other arrangements next time," Sara said. "They can stay with friends, or come along with us. Yes, I expect if there is a next time, we'll just take the kids along."

"I wish Rachel had disinherited Julian," Bea said, her shoulders shaking. "I rue the day he ever came back to our town."

Chapter Nine

Sara finally convinced Bea and Jim to take Barry home. "I'll call you if there's any change. Go home and get a good night's sleep and come back in the morning. I'll probably be ready to go home for a while then to take a shower and change clothes."

Mary Sue had been moved from recovery to a room in the pediatrics wing. The second bed in the room was empty. Sara was glad. She didn't want to meet anyone and feel as if she had to socialize. All she wanted was to be with her daughter—and Julian.

She kept looking at her watch. No time had been set for his return, but it was already after seven. Once again, she went to the mirror. She had already washed her face and put on fresh makeup. But she touched up her lipstick and patted her hair.

The television was on, but Mary Sue didn't seem to be watching it. And she had hardly touched her dinner. Sara blamed her daughter's listlessness on the painkillers she was being given.

But Mary Sue's forehead seemed warm. Yes, definitely warmer than before.

Sara rang for the nurse, who felt Mary Sue's forehead, then took her temperature and made a notation on the chart. "I'll give Dr. Carter a call about this," the nurse said. "She has developed some fever."

The nurse returned and explained the doctor had altered Mary Sue's medication and wanted her temperature taken every hour.

An hour later, Mary Sue's temperature had risen still higher. "I'll check back with the doctor," the nurse said, hurrying from the room.

Sara paced back and forth, stopping every few turns to feel her daughter's forehead. Mary Sue was more than just listless now. She could barely mumble in response to Sara's questions.

In less than thirty minutes, Dr. Carter arrived. At first, Sara didn't recognize her. The physician's hair was swept up on her head, with tendrils gracefully fringing her face and neck. She was wearing a green shantung evening suit and high-heeled pumps to match. Obviously, she had been called away from an elegant social occasion.

Sara watched as the doctor checked Mary Sue's chart, then deftly examined the barely responsive child.

"We'll increase her doses of IV antibiotics and give her alcohol baths to get this fever down," the doctor told Sara.

"Is it serious?" Sara asked, her voice trembling.

"It's not good," the doctor admitted. "But Mary Sue is an otherwise healthy child, and her body should be able to throw this off. We'll just have to watch her closely. I'm going to have one of the other pediatricians look at her. And I've ordered her moved to intensive care, which means you can only be with her ten minutes on the hour, but she'll be monitored more closely there."

"You're worried, aren't you?" Sara asked, her heart sinking.

"Just precautions," Dr. Carter assured her. "I have a little girl, too. I know how precious they are. And we don't want to take any chances."

Sara nodded. Somehow it made her feel better to know the surgeon was a mother, too.

She called home but downplayed Mary Sue's condition and made Bea promise they would not come back. "Everything is under control," she said with more confidence than she felt. But she really didn't want them rushing back over here. That would make everything seem too dramatic, too serious. Sara didn't want to look at their worried faces all night and feel even more concerned than she already was. And she didn't want any more of Bea's snide remarks.

The only person she wanted with her was Julian.

Sara promised Bea she'd call back if there was any change. Yes, she knew they'd come in an instant.

She was relegated to another waiting room, this one adjoining the intensive care unit. The nurse on pediatrics assured her they would send Major Campbell up as soon as he arrived.

Sara kept watching the door. She needed for Julian to hurry up and get there! She needed his strength. Needed for him to tell her that it wasn't ominous that her daughter was in intensive care. Needed for him to talk to the doctors and nurses. He would know better what questions to ask. Hospitals were his domain.

Other people in the waiting room. An anxious wife and her grown son. Two elderly women who looked exhausted.

Sara kept to herself. As did the others.

It was almost nine o'clock before Julian arrived. In uniform. So handsome. So much concern in his eyes. And love. A beautiful man. A caring man.

He held her, soothed her. She told him she was sorry about today. She had been upset. Of course, she didn't blame him for anything. Only herself.

"Why are you in uniform?" she asked.

He guided her out into the hall to tell her. "I have an eleven o'clock flight out of Oklahoma City," he said.

"You're leaving?" she asked incredulously, stepping back from his touch.

"The rest of my leave has been canceled. There's been a fire at the hospital. No one was hurt, but things are in a terrible mess. A telegram was waiting for me when I got back to the house."

"But can't you tell them you have an emergency here? That you need to stay longer?" Sara asked. "I want you here with me."

He shook his head. "You're not my wife. Mary Sue isn't my child. I have no basis to request any sort of emergency consideration."

"Isn't love a basis? I thought we loved each other."

"We do," he said, pushing his hand through his hair, his agony written on his face. "Look, Sara, emergency procedures at the hospital are my responsibility. I've already spent hours on the phone, getting repairs under way and arranging for some of the less seriously ill patients to be housed in the nurses' quarters. But that aside, I'm an Army officer under orders. I really have no choice. I'd be considered AWOL if I didn't report at Fort Bragg by tomorrow."

"Then I hate your Army! And maybe it's just as well I figured that out now instead of later."

"Look, I can stay for another hour," he said, checking his watch. "Can we go someplace more private? I don't want to leave you upset like this."

"No, you go on. I'd hate for you to miss your plane. I'm sure it's the last one out of Oklahoma City, and your wonderful Army might throw you in the brig if you didn't get on back."

"Sara, don't be this way."

"How would you have me be?" she said crossing her arms, hugging her middle as though she was afraid she would fall apart. "You think I should be thrilled to death that you're leaving?"

"Just understanding would suffice."

"If I said I understood, it would be a lie," she said, and started to cry.

She let him take her in his arms. She tried to tell herself that she was being unreasonable. But, unreasonable or not, she felt betrayed. He was leaving her when she needed him the most.

She went in for her ten minutes with Mary Sue, who seemed not one iota better, but at least she wasn't any worse.

Julian had a steaming cup of coffee waiting for her when she came back. They carried their cups down the hall and sat on the low wall of an indoor planter.

"Promise me you'll come to Fort Bragg when Mary Sue gets better," he said. "Before the kids' school starts."

"What if you have another emergency and can't be with us?" she asked contritely.

"I think you know without asking that that's not likely. But I can't promise to be with you every minute any more than I can promise a tornado won't carry us away or the world won't come to an end. All we can do is proceed as best we can and hope for the best."

She clung to him after he kissed her goodbye. He was really leaving her. She wanted to scream and curse and kick down doors. But all she could do was kiss him one last time.

Mary Sue seemed better the next hour.

By three a.m., her temperature was almost normal. "Children get well just as quickly as they get sick," the nurse told her. "Why don't you stretch out on the sofa in the waiting room. I'll get you a pillow and a blanket."

Sara started to protest, but the nurse promised she'd wake her for the next ten-minute visit.

The room was so cold. She wondered if there was a reason why hospitals were cold. Maybe it kept the germ count down.

Even with the blanket, she shivered. She tried to dream of the comfort and warmth of Julian's arms but couldn't. She felt as if she was in a refrigerator.

She didn't realize she had slept until the nurse woke her.

Mary Sue was definitely better. And hungry. "Could I have a chocolate milk shake?"

Sara felt weak with relief. Any child who wanted a milk shake couldn't be too sick.

By the time Bea, Jim and Barry arrived, Mary Sue was already back in the pediatrics wing, the crisis past.

Sara couldn't look at Bea as she told them Julian had left. She didn't want to see the look of relief on her mother-in-law's face.

JULIAN CALLED every few days. When was she coming was always his first question.

First, Mary Sue needed to get better, she explained.

Then Mary Sue's softball team was headed for the state play-offs. Still recuperating from her operation, she wouldn't be able to play, but she wanted to be there.

Martha, the B & J's only hired help, got sick, and Bea and Jim needed Sara at the cafe.

Barry's Explorer Scout troop was going on a week-long trail ride and camping expedition in the Wichita mountains. When they returned, two-a-day football drills would begin.

Finally, she told Julian, "I think it's best if I come alone—just for a few days. The children can come with me during their Thanksgiving break. Bea is big on Thanksgiving, but I convinced her that she and Jim really needed to visit her niece in Dallas this year. Nelda had been wanting them to come for Thanksgiving several years now—although I'm not sure why. Bea won't let her do a thing in her own kitchen."

"When can you come?" he asked. "Is tomorrow too soon?"

Sara laughed. "No, but how about next Thursday. I'll stay until Monday."

"I'll send money for a ticket," he said.

"No, I'll get this one. You'll have to get the tickets when we come at Thanksgiving."

The ticket was a lot more than Sara thought it would be. The agent at Carefree Travel in Norman explained to her about 21-day-advance purchases and told her next time she wouldn't have to pay so much if she planned ahead. As she made out the check, Sara tried not to think of how many hours of late-night quilting the trip was costing her. But her pride dictated that she pay for this ticket or not go. And she desperately wanted to go.

She fretted over her wardrobe. After spending all that money on her ticket, she dared not buy any new clothes—not with the children needing school shoes and winter coats. She'd take the navy blue evening outfit, of course. And the two summer dresses she alternated for church. But as she got them out and looked at them—really looked at them—she realized how tired and faded they were.

Bea surprised her by bringing in a really nice white linen suit. "It hasn't fit me for years," she explained. "Maybe you can take it in and shorten the skirt."

"That's very nice of you, Bea."

"Jim says I'm being too hard on you. He says you have a right to fall in love. And I guess he's right. But people like Julian who grow up unhappy don't make good marriage partners. They always think someone is going to hurt them, and life becomes a self-fulfilling prophecy. Just be careful, Sara. If you want to be romantically involved with him, that's one thing. But marrying him involves those children. And it involves Jim and me. But whatever happens, I do love you, Sara. You know that, don't you, honey?"

"Of course I do," Sara said.

"Then can I have a hug?"

Sara obliged, then tried on the suit. Bea marked the hem and fitted the jacket. A few tucks here and there and it would be perfect.

This time, Sara left a list of phone numbers. Julian's apartment. His office at the hospital. The home phone number of Julian's commanding officer. And the Fort Bragg military police.

She wore one of the two cotton dresses for her flight. A muted pastel plaid. A white leather belt dressed it up a bit.

Jim drove her to the airport.

"Do you really love Julian?" he asked.

"Yes. But I'm a big girl. I know that love doesn't automatically make everything work out just fine."

"You have to decide what's best for you and the kids," he said. "I know Bea thinks she'll just die if those children go away—and you, too, honey—but she won't. She survived Ben's death, and if she survived that she can survive anything."

"I've often thought that we all survived Ben's death because we had each other," Sara said.

Jim nodded and wiped his eyes with the back of his hand. "The smartest thing that boy of mine ever did was marry you," he said.

Sara had been in a plane only once in her life—when she had to fly back to Oklahoma City from a West Coast rodeo for her mother's funeral. She and Ben had been in thirty-eight states, by actual count, but they always went in their truck with their trailer in tow.

As she boarded the plane, Sara tried to act blasé, but she didn't feel that way. She was not only flying on a big, wonderful airplane, but she was going all the way to North Carolina to visit her handsome Army major. She felt like a child on Christmas Eve.

From her window seat, she watched the ground recede below her and saw Oklahoma City under her like a map—but a wonderful map with moving cars and emerald green baseball diamonds and blue sapphire swimming pools in the backyards of little toy houses.

She had to change planes in St. Louis and felt like a real country girl as she made her way through what must be the biggest building in the whole world. And this was only the Delta terminal. There were other buildings for other airlines. Amazing.

It was dark when the plane banked over the Raleigh-Durham airport. The earth below her was sparkling with a million lights. And Julian was down there. In just minutes, she would see him!

Nervously, she looked at her reflection in her compact mirror once again and couldn't decide if she looked wonderful or ugly.

She added some blush and looked again. And still couldn't decide.

Would she look the same to Julian? Would he look the same to her?

God, she was nervous.

But suddenly the plane was on the ground, taxiing toward the terminal. *Soon,* Sara thought. *Soon.*

It took forever for the door to be opened, forever for people to gather up their possessions and file out. Sara was in the back of the plane. *Forever.* Her stomach was in knots. Her palms sweating.

Then, finally, she was hurrying down the connecting hallway, through the door.

And into Julian's waiting arms.

He had both flowers and balloons. He was hugging her along with her purse and her cosmetics case.

And saying her name. How sweet was the sound of her own name when it came from his lips.

All around them people were watching and smiling at the sight of two happy people so obviously in love.

"I can't believe I'm here," Sara said as they managed to walk with arms entwined and carry balloons, flowers and the cosmetics case as they made their way to the baggage claim area. Everyone they met along the corridor smiled. The balloons were silver and had hearts all over them. The flowers were red roses. The man beside her was beautiful. And apparently she didn't look so bad in her old dress, judging from the admiration in Julian's eyes.

He was wearing a navy blazer and tan slacks. His hair was freshly trimmed. Even out of uniform, he looked so perfectly groomed, his carriage so elegant, his whole demeanor so handsomely military. But at this moment, he was wearing a decidedly unmilitary grin.

Her suitcase didn't make the flight. The attendant promised it would be delivered to Julian's apartment in the morning.

"Oh dear," Sara said in mock horror. "I don't have anything to sleep in," and they dissolved in laughter. *Nothing to sleep in.* It was the funniest thing they'd ever heard.

More smiles came from those around them. She and Julian were leaving a trail of smiles as they went.

In the car, they kissed. And kissed. And kissed some more. He felt her breasts, roughly, deliciously. He was dying for her and she for him, the heat of passion consuming them, demanding satisfaction. Such sweet agony.

"Do you want dinner?" he asked.

"Do you mean before or after? I want it after."

The drive to Fort Bragg took far too long. Over an hour. She was having a terrible time keeping her hands off him, but she didn't want to distract him from driving. She had to satisfy herself with stroking his strong, firm thighs, touching his neck above his collar, playing with his hair.

But finally they were there. Sara had glimpses of a pleasant apartment with light-colored walls and lamps lit in welcome. But she would look around later.

They began undressing each other the minute they were in the door. As they made their way to the bedroom, they left a trail of clothing in their wake.

The covers were turned back. A small lamp on the bureau gave off just the right amount of light.

Naked they fell on the bed.

"I've missed you more than I can ever say," Julian said. "Every night, I imagine you here in this bed with me. I fall asleep thinking of you in my arms."

"And I have dreamed of being here. I love you, Julian. And I desperately need for you to make love to me."

With a low animal moan, he covered his mouth with hers, and it began. *Oh yes,* Sara thought. *This is what I want. So beautiful. So very beautiful.*

She loved the feeling of warmth that infused her veins, loved the rapture that ignited her soul as they journeyed together to the pinnacle, calling out to each other in their passion, saying each other's names over and over.

THE AFTERGLOW had its own kind of sweetness as they lay entwined in each other's arms, Julian's fingers softly caressing her flesh, his lips pressed against her forehead.

Forever, Sara thought. *I want this man forever.*

She was floating in a sea of pure pleasure. Drifting. A lovely feeling.

She might have dozed. She wasn't sure. But suddenly she realized she was starving.

"Do you have anything to eat?" she whispered in his ear.

His eyes popped open. "Are you kidding? I've been cooking for days."

The table was already set, the candles ready to light, the wine in a cooler chilling.

Sara wore Julian's terry robe and sipped wine as she watched him putter about the kitchen, putting a quiche in the oven, tossing a salad, slicing a loaf of French bread that he'd made himself. A chocolate mint cake—his own recipe—waited on the sideboard.

"I made the quiche, too," he said proudly. "And I can assure you that this real man not only eats quiche but makes a mean one—with bacon, baby Swiss cheese, real butter, cream and calories. But the salad dressing is low fat."

"Thank goodness for that!" Sara said, laughing. She didn't care about calories. She didn't care about anything except being here with the man she loved.

He looked over at her and grinned. "Sara in my kitchen, wearing my bathrobe! God, what a beautiful sight."

THEY SLEPT VERY LATE the next morning. The doorbell awakened them—the delivery man from Delta with Sara's suitcase.

Julian made pecan waffles, and they lingered over coffee. Then he gave her the grand tour of Fort Bragg and vicinity. The post reminded Sara of Fort Sill with many of the buildings having identical tan stucco walls and red tile roofs. Its museums weren't as impressive, but nice.

The nearby town of Southern Pines was pretty with wonderful old hotels surrounded by lush green golf courses. The town was aptly named with pine trees everywhere. And beautiful magnolia trees with their huge fragrant white blossoms lined the streets.

That evening they were invited to dinner at the quarters of Brent and Margaret Gordon. Sara was grateful for the white linen suit Bea had given her.

Brent was Julian's commanding officer, and the two were obviously very good friends.

The Gordons had a thirteen-year-old daughter named Susan and a sixteen-year-old son named Chris. Sara was impressed with the teenagers' wonderful manners as they stepped forward to shake hands and inquire about Sara's trip and how long she was staying.

"I'm looking forward to meeting your children," Susan told Sara. "Major Campbell said they both have their own horses. I've always wanted a horse. Daddy says I have to wait until he retires to have one, but that's three more years!"

Sara didn't look at Julian, but he would know what she was thinking. Murray did offer advantages for her children. Having their own horses out back was one of them.

The children joined the adults for dinner, and once again, Sara was very impressed with their manners and their ease in conversing with the adults. She knew her own children wouldn't seem as polished. Julian had explained that a lot is expected of military families. Officially, an officer's advancement is not based in any way on his wife and children, but officers who got promotions always seemed not only to be competent but to have gracious wives and well-behaved children.

And as Sara looked around her in the handsomely furnished set of quarters, she could see many mementos of the family's travels. The Gordons had lived in both Hawaii and Germany as well as numerous Stateside assignments.

"Don't you children mind moving all the time?" Sara asked.

Chris shrugged. "Sometimes. But you get used to making new friends. I'd really like to stay here to finish high school, but we're moving to Alaska in March. That will be cool, too, though. Dad and I can hunt and fish."

"I like to see new places," Susan said. "Dad said we can take a cruise up the coast of Alaska next summer, all the way into the Arctic Circle. And we can see Eskimo villages and maybe even a polar bear."

Both children thought they would like to attend college at West Point and become regular Army officers. They loved Army life and could imagine no other.

Margaret Gordon, however, shared the old adage that "Army life is great for the men and kids, but hell on wives and pets."

"There is some truth in that," she admitted as she started the serving dishes around the table for second helpings. "We've moved nine times in seventeen-and-a-half years. But Alaska will be the last assignment. Brent is going to retire at twenty years."

"I didn't know you could do that," Sara said.

"Sure. You don't get as much of a pension, but Brent will be young enough to try something else," Margaret said. "And now that the children are older, I'd like to start some sort of mid-life career. Mostly, though, I want to go home to Vermont. I've loved our Army years, but I'm tired of all the moving around. I want to plant tulip bulbs in the fall and know I'll be there in the spring to see them come up. And I want to wallpaper everything. I think I'll even wallpaper the ceilings. God, I'm tired of all this cream-colored paint.''

"You mean the walls have to be this color?" Sara asked.

"Every one. In every set of quarters," Margaret said with a laugh. "My dream house is in Technicolor."

Later, in the kitchen, as Sara helped her serve the coffee and dessert, Margaret admitted that her husband didn't really want to retire. "But he promised me when we got married that we'd have a permanent home before we were too old to enjoy it. I think he's hoping I'll change my mind and let him off the hook."

"Will you?" Sara asked, putting scoops of whipped cream on the wedges of strawberry pie.

"I don't know. It's almost a case of who gets to be happy—him or me. I've been a good Army wife for twenty years, now I want for him to be a good civilian husband. But I know he'll miss the Army. And maybe he'll resent me for having to give it up. It's a no-win situation."

IT WAS TWO HOURS EARLIER in Oklahoma, still early enough for Sara to call home when they got back to Julian's apartment.

Mary Sue answered. "Are you with Julian Campbell?" she asked.

"Yes, I am with Julian. How are things at home?"

"Grandpa has indigestion and went to bed early. Barry's over at Kirk's. It's just me and Grandma, playing cards and watching television. Do you want to talk to Grandma?"

"No. Just tell her I called."

"You're still coming back on Monday, aren't you?" Mary Sue asked, her voice anxious.

"Yes, honey. I'll be there for dinner."

JULIAN AND SARA SPENT an idyllic three days, sight-seeing at their leisure. Sara enjoyed the picturesque countryside with fields of tobacco and the tumbledown drying sheds left over from another era. It was so green and lush here, quite different from the rolling prairies of western Oklahoma.

They took a day-long drive to the seaside, where they picnicked, swam, walked on the beach and fed the gulls by throwing pieces of bread high in the air to be caught mid-flight.

Sara loved the ocean. Its power and majesty filled her with awe. And it was so deserted here. Not mobbed with people like other beaches she had visited.

The next day, they went to see the impressive state capitol at Raleigh. And on the way back, they stopped at the Bentonville Battlefield near Smithfield. Julian explained that it was the scene of one of the last great battles of the Civil War, where General Sherman's Union forces defeated the Confederate troops of General Johnson.

"It looks so peaceful now," Sara said. "It's hard to believe men fought to the death here."

They got back to Julian's apartment in time to change and go to the officers' club for dinner. Julian introduced her to several couples.

"Ah, Julian's secret lady," the wife of one of the officers said. "No wonder he's been resisting all our efforts at matchmaking."

Then, too soon, it was time for the last night of lovemaking and talk of the future.

"I have my orders, Sara," he told her, holding her close to his bare chest. "I'm leaving in two months for Germany. I want you to marry me. I want you and the children to go with me as my dependents."

Sara was stunned.

She got out of bed and put on her robe. She couldn't have such a serious discussion in bed.

"It's too soon for anything that drastic," she insisted. "I can't go home and tell my children we're going to pack up and not only leave their home and grandparents, but move to a foreign land. What about their school? What about their animals? What about what they want?"

"You're their mother, Sara. You don't have to ask them. Just explain to them that you want to make the four of us a family. And some things will be difficult, and they will probably be homesick some. But at the same time, they will be living an exciting life, seeing things that most American youngsters never get to see. They can ski the Alps. Sail the Rhine. We'll go to Paris, Rome, Geneva and Vienna. And to Venice and Florence. Can you even imagine those cities, Sara? Florence is the most beautiful city in the world, Venice the most incredible. Going to Venice is like going through a time machine. You almost expect to see Michelangelo or Leonardo da Vinci come walking across the piazza. We are still young, Sara. I want to take you places, to share the beauty and the excitement with you. Don't you want that, too?"

"Of course, I do. I can't even imagine anything that wonderful. But you don't understand," she said, sitting on the side of the bed, her back to him.

"I understand that you're not even going to try."

Chapter Ten

"Promise me you'll come back to Oklahoma," Sara said in the airport coffee shop. All morning she had been talking about when he came back to Murray, unable to face the prospect of an open-ended separation—or perhaps never seeing him again.

Julian had listened politely, been noncommittal. Now, she desperately needed a promise from him. They *would* see each other again. "Please say yes," she begged. "Please say this isn't goodbye."

"I'll come only if there's some point to it, Sara," he said, "only if it will make a difference."

He looked tired. The furrows in his forehead seemed deeper. His eyes were bloodshot. Neither one of them had slept much. Hours of agony, knowing the other was awake and not knowing how to reach across the gulf that separated them.

"What about just being together?" she asked, her cup of coffee untouched. "Isn't that enough?"

"At first it was," he said, pushing his fingers through his hair. His gesture. What he did when he was frustrated. How well she had come to know this man. And love him.

"At first, I lived for the next moment," he continued. "But I fell in love with you, Sara. And now the next moment isn't enough. In fact, it's torture unless I know it isn't just that minute, that others will follow. I either need to marry you or figure out how to survive without you. Life is a gift, and it's immoral to waste it. I don't want to be one of those people who sit around feeling sorry for themselves or always waiting for something good to happen without doing anything to *make* it happen."

"But getting married is too much of a gamble," Sara insisted. "We'd be skipping over too many steps. You and the children need to get to know one another. They need to gradually get used to you and the idea their mother might get married. Then, when they are older..."

"I will be leaving the country in two months and don't have the luxury of time. And even if I did, I'm not sure I would want to take advantage of it. Sometimes it's better to go ahead and take the plunge. But obviously you're one of those people who goes into the water an inch at a time. I won't be back in the States for at least two years. Maybe longer. And when I come back, I will not be taking up residence in Murray. It's now or never, Sara."

"What if we get married, and it doesn't work? What if you and the kids don't get along? How can I deliberately disregard my children's happiness?" she asked miserably. She was losing. She didn't know if she wanted to reach across the table and shake Julian as she would an errant child or fall on her knees and beg him to change his mind.

"How will we know if we don't try?" he said, exasperation in his voice. "I know it will be rough. But surely at some level those selfish kids of yours want to see their mother happy."

"My kids aren't selfish!" Sara said indignantly. "But I have always put their needs before my own because that's what mothers do, Julian. I guess you just can't understand that since you've never had children and obviously don't know the first thing about what it means to be a parent. To me, you're the one who sounds selfish.''

''Then if mothers always put their children first, are the men in their life always second?'' he demanded.

''No! Of course not. You're twisting my words.'' She was angry now. Maybe that was better. She wouldn't cry if she was angry.

An announcement came over the public address system. Sara's flight was now boarding.

''Then explain it to me,'' he said, shoving away his cup of coffee and leaning toward her, his forearms on the table.

Sara took a deep breath. ''*Parents* put children first. Ideally, the man in a woman's life is the father of her children. They both want what is best for the children. It gets a little difficult when that man isn't the father.''

''The question was, Sara, 'Do the men come second?' ''

''Damn you, Julian! It's not a question of first or second! It's whether or not two adult people can manage their lives given the circumstances they find themselves in. My children are not going to go away. Whatever we do, they have to be considered.''

''And I have considered them. Basically, they seem like bright, likable kids I could enjoy getting to know. I could probably have a positive impact on their lives if they'd let me. For starters, I'd like to get them out of an unnatural environment with two doting grandparents and a passive mother turning them into spoiled brats!''

Sara grabbed her purse and carry-on and almost pushed over her chair as she stood. *Damn him.* Anger brought tears, too. She could feel them starting.

She marched out of the coffee shop ahead of him, heading toward the security gate.

Julian caught up with her. ''Sara, damn it, slow down. We can't let it end like this.''

"You are the one who is ending it," she reminded him. "Not me. You are the one putting down the ultimatums. Do it your way or else!"

He grabbed her arm, but she jerked it away. "Okay, Sara, what is your way? I'm thirty-eight years old. Am I supposed to wait around until your kids are grown? What about *our* kids? Don't you want that, too?"

They were at the security gate. People were circling around them. Sara's flight was being announced a second time.

"What now?" he asked.

"I don't know. Will you call me?"

"No. I don't want to have this conversation again. Call me if you have anything new to say."

"Will you kiss me?"

He was crying, too. Sara could taste the salt of his tears. They kissed each other as if it was the last time.

Such pain. Sara felt as though she could die of the pain.

"Maybe it's for the best, Sara," he was saying. "Your kids scare me. I dream of being with you, not of being with them. Maybe it was just a fool's dream on my part to think that it would work. But I'll always be sorry it didn't."

She put her purse and cosmetics case on the conveyer belt. One more embrace. One more kiss. Then she hurried through the gate.

He was still standing there for one last wave. Sara had to wipe the tears from her eyes to read the sign overhead. Her gate was to the right. The last call for her flight was being made. She hurried away without looking back.

The flight attendant asked if she was ill.

"No. Not really," Sara said, struggling for control. "Thank you."

"The flight isn't full," the young man said, his expression concerned. "Would you like to move to the back and have a row to yourself?"

Sara nodded and followed him to the back of the aircraft, where there was an empty row. The flight attendant supplied her with a pillow, blanket and glass of water.

Miserably, Sara curled herself into the corner. *My Julian,* she thought. *My darling, Julian. What have we done!*

He was right in everything he said. And she was right, too. Sara was overcome with a sense of hopelessness.

But deep inside of her a comforting thought was struggling to the surface of her consciousness. And finally Sara calmed enough to heed it. Even if that was goodbye, even if her heart was breaking, she wouldn't have missed Major Julian Campbell for the world.

She knew something about herself she hadn't known before. She could and would love again. Julian had given her that knowledge.

EVERYONE WAS WAITING for her at the airport, Bea and Jim wearing their Sunday best even though it was Monday, Barry in a pair of new cowboy boots.

And Mary Sue with gold studs in newly pierced ears.

"Bea, how could you?" Sara demanded.

"All the girls in her class were getting them pierced," Bea said, bristling. "You wouldn't want her to be different."

"I am the girl's mother," Sara said, furious. "You should have asked me first. And Barry didn't need those eelskin boots. I already told him he couldn't have them."

Engulfed in stony silence, the five Cates walked down the corridor toward the baggage claim area.

This is not how it should be, Sara thought miserably. She needed her homecoming to be happy. She should have waited until later to tell Bea of her displeasure.

"You guys got your Wal-Mart lists made out?" she asked her children. School was starting next week, and Sara had promised to take them to Chickasha for school supplies and new shoes. Barry didn't need shoes now, but he still needed notebooks and pencils.

Everyone relaxed. Sara was going to be nice now. They picked up her suitcase and headed for home.

"I've been practicing my cheerleading," Mary Sue said once they were on their way.

"She sure is noisy, but she's pretty dang good," Bea said affectionately from the front seat.

"Tryouts for seventh-grade cheerleaders are next week," Mary Sue said. "Oh, Mom, I'll just die if I don't make it!"

"No, you won't die, honey. You'll go on and do other things and be perfectly happy."

"But I want it so much," Mary Sue protested.

"And I want you to get it too," Sara explained, holding her daughter's hand. "But you have to understand that you can't have everything you want. And sometimes the things you want the most are the things you don't get."

Bea turned around from the front seat and patted Mary Sue's leg. "I'll tell you what, honey. If those judges are stupid enough not to pick you, your grandpa and I will buy you that buckskin jacket with all the fringe that you've been wanting so bad."

"*Bea!*" Sara said, horrified. "Those jackets cost a fortune."

"No more than a plane ticket to North Carolina," Bea said.

"Meaning what?" Sara demanded. "That I should have bought her the jacket myself instead of taking this trip?"

"Well, you could have. But you didn't. You deserve to spend money on yourself, Sara. I know that. But don't get all upset if Jim and I spoil these children. It gives us pleasure.''

Barry's big news concerned the football team. He was doing well in two-a-day practices and had been named second-string quarterback. By the time he was a junior, Coach Johnson said he'd be first string for sure.

"I got Dad's number on my jersey, Mom. Wait until you see it. It's really cool.''

And they babbled on, this happy family of hers. The vet had checked Mary Sue's mare, and she was definitely in foal. A new girl had moved to town from Kansas, and Barry was a little sweet on her. Barry even blushed when Mary Sue teased him about her.

Bea was planning her entries in the state fair. A crocheted tablecloth and a pie, of course. Rhubarb this year.

"Why don't you hurry and finish that double-wedding ring quilt, Sara, and enter it? I'll bet it would be a sweepstakes winner. You just get better and better.''

Only Jim looked at her with concern.

Murray looked the same—and different. Her home. She would always think of it that way. The place on earth closest to her heart, the place she would always want to come back to no matter how far away she roamed.

"You okay, honey?" Jim said, his words just for her, as they walked into the house.

His concern brought those damned tears back to her eyes. "Just a little sad," she said. "And scared maybe.''

That night at dinner, when Jim said grace, he offered a special tribute to Ben on the third anniversary of his death.

Sara was startled. Three years!

She stared at her plate and listened while her dead husband's father invoked God's help in "keeping them true to Ben's memory.'' She could hear Bea sniffling.

"We took the children to the cemetery this morning," Bea said. "They put a wreath on their father's grave. Did you not remember what today was, Sara, when you made your plans to go off?"

So, she had missed the visit to the cemetery. That's why they were dressed up—not to pick her up at the airport but to make the pilgrimage to Ben's grave. It was required not only for the anniversary of Ben's death, but also on his birthday, Easter, Father's Day, Memorial Day, Thanksgiving, Christmas and most other holidays. Lots of wreaths. Lots of remembering. Lots of long prayers before dinner.

They were trying to make a saint out of Ben.

Sara couldn't eat. Bea kept passing food her way. "For the fourth time, I'm not hungry!" she snapped.

Sara passed on dessert and drank coffee while the others ate peach cobbler with ice cream. When they were finished, she asked them to stay at the table for a few minutes. She had something to discuss with them.

"Julian will be leaving for Germany in two months. He wants to get married and for me and Mary Sue and Barry to go with him. There are good American schools there, and we can travel all over Europe in the next two years. You kids can see things that most people just read about—the Leaning Tower of Pisa, the Eiffel Tower, Buckingham Palace, the Matterhorn, the canals of Venice, the windmills in Holland. Just think, kids, what an incredible opportunity that will be. And it would make your mother very happy. I love Julian, and I would like very much to be his wife."

They all stared at her, stunned expressions on their faces, their bodies motionless.

Bea moved first, burying her face in her apron and bursting into tears.

"I want to stay here and be a cheerleader," Mary Sue said, her eyes also filling with tears. "I don't want to leave Grandma and Grandpa."

"Me neither," Barry said. "Why can't Julian come here to live?"

Only Jim said nothing.

Sara stood up from the table. "You kids do the dishes," she said.

"I'm going to Jenny's after dinner," Mary Sue protested.

"You will go to Jenny's *after* you and your brother do the dishes."

Sara went to her room. She sat in the chair in front of her quilting rack, not even bothering to turn on the light. She heard Bea telling Mary Sue to run on—that she and Barry would clean up.

I will not be unhappy, Sara told herself. Julian was right. Life was a gift, and it was wrong to waste it with unhappiness. Somehow, she would get through this. *Somehow.*

And to do that, she was going to have to make changes.

Julian had also said she was passive. She hated him for saying it. But he was right.

She went to the kitchen just as Mary Sue was heading out the door. Bea was at the kitchen sink. Barry was bringing dishes from the table.

"Mary Sue, *I* said for you to help with the dishes, and I meant it," Sara said.

"But Grandma said—"

"I heard what your grandmother said," Sara interrupted. "Your grandmother is just trying to be nice. But there will be plenty of time for you to go visit Jenny *after* you do as I asked."

"I don't mind," Bea said. "I don't have anything else to do."

"Bea, whether or not you have anything else to do is not the issue here."

Sara turned back to her daughter. "Mary Sue?"

"You sure got mean after that man showed up," Mary Sue said, returning to the sink. "I don't like you as much anymore. If you go to Germany, I want to stay here. Grandma said I could. Didn't you, Grandma?"

Bea looked at Sara miserably. "I didn't exactly say that," she told Mary Sue. "I just said that would be a possibility if your mother was so hell-bent to leave."

Bea followed Sara down the hall. "I'm sorry," she said. "I shouldn't have told the child that. I'm really sorry, Sara. It's just that this whole business has gotten so out of hand. One minute, we're this nice happy family, and the next you're trying to tear us all apart."

"Did you think the children and I would stay forever?" Sara asked, sinking down on the edge of her bed. "Someday they'll grow up and move away. Children are not a permanent condition, Bea. Someday you and Jim were going to have to find something else to live for."

"I knew you might get married again. I hoped you'd find a nice widower in a town nearby. But you're talking about me and Jim not seeing those children for *years*. You're talking about taking them away from everything they know."

Jim appeared in the door of Sara's bedroom. "Leave the girl alone, Bea. You've said enough."

Bea started to protest, but closed her mouth and left Sara sitting there. She closed the door quietly behind her.

My Dearest Julian,
I sincerely hope that you will reconsider and come to Murray before you depart for Germany. I still can't believe my visit with you ended on such a terrible note.

I've spoken with my children about Germany. And as I suspected, they do not want to leave Murray. And yes, I suppose they are spoiled. And I know you've compared them in your mind with the Gordon children. But Susan and Chris have grown up with the Army. They've always known that each place they live is temporary. They have never allowed themselves to develop long-term expectations. But Mary Sue and Barry have structured their priorities based on the expectation that they would graduate from high school here in Murray, that they can ride junior rodeo and play on Murray athletic teams and have the same friends for a lifetime. They have not been raised Army, and for that reason it hardly seems fair to expect them to change horses midstream.

I know you are thinking that you and I have both faced a lot of changes in our own lives and managed to survive. But we are adults. And children cannot and should not be expected to respond like adults. You had to grow up too fast, and I'm sure you wouldn't wish that fate on someone else.

And there is another very important factor that makes my children's situation more difficult. They lost their father and still suffer from that loss. As you know, they are very close to their grandparents, and I simply don't have the heart to pull them away from all that love and concern.

Yes, Bea and Jim spoil them. And perhaps I have been too passive. I have learned a lot from you, Julian. And I feel myself growing and changing because of it. For that, I thank you.

And I thank you for your love. Being loved by you is perhaps the most special thing that has ever happened to me. You came along at a time in my life when

I had all but trained myself not to expect too much. I'm not like that anymore. I expect a lot out of myself and my children and life. I can feel myself changing, taking charge. And I will find a way to go to college even if it's only one or two classes a semester.

I can't begin to tell you how much I want to see you again. You have become so dear, so important to me. I wish you were over at Rachel's farm now, so I could go over and we could cook dinner, sit at the kitchen table and talk about everything under the sun, drink a little too much beer. And then we would go to bed. God, how glorious it is to make love with you. I long for you so. I think of you constantly. I am lost without the comfort of your arms, the joy of your presence.

Take care, my beautiful Julian, and come to me if you will. If not, I do understand. But I will always miss you, always wish it could have worked between us.

With such love,
Sara

"THANK YOU FOR COMING BY, Sara," the portly attorney said, indicating that she was to take a seat in one of the armchairs on the opposite side of his desk.

"I admit, I'm very curious," Sara said. "What is it you need to see me about?"

"Rachel Warren's farm."

"What about it?"

"Major Campbell was considering turning it back to the bank rather than assume the mortgage, but I had a better idea. The farm is really worth more than the mortgage, even at today's low prices. But most people are looking for acreages these days, not big tracts of land. You know how city folks like to move to the country so they can run a few cattle and their children can keep horses. So, we're going to subdivide the Warren place into ten-acre tracts. We already have a couple of interested buyers. Julian should be able to pay off the bank and make a modest profit.''

"That sounds like a good plan, but what does that have to do with me?"

"Major Campbell wants you to have the house and ten adjoining acres. Rent free. When you move out, he'll sell it. But in the meantime, he wants you to have full use of it and treat it like it was your own."

"I don't know what to say," Sara said, overwhelmed. "Will he be coming back here to dispose of her things?"

"Oh, didn't you know? He's already left the country. His orders were changed. He says for you to store his grandfather's rifle and anything else you think constitutes a family heirloom. And to give away his aunt's personal things to whatever charity you think appropriate. And then consider the rest of Rachel's possessions yours.

"He's already left for Germany?"

"Yes, just yesterday, in fact. I talked to him day before yesterday. He had some sort of temporary assignment in Washington and left directly from there for Europe. I have power of attorney to make all the arrangements for the property. So, if you will just sign this agreement I've drawn up, the house is yours for as long as you want it."

"Is he ever coming back?" Sara had to ask.

"Well, obviously no time soon. I don't think he likes our little town very much, do you?"

Sara shook her head. She read the papers the attorney put in front of her and signed them. Mr. Mason handed her the keys and the title to Rachel's old truck. And just like that she had a house of her own.

Julian's gift. Such sweet sadness she felt. A place of her own was a dream she had had long before Julian arrived.

But then that dream had been set aside for one that had him in it. Sharing a kitchen with Julian would have been a delight.

But now she was back to the original dream. And she supposed that having one dream come true was better than none at all.

She drove Bea's Buick to Rachel's farm. Not Rachel's anymore. *Hers.*

"Thank you, Julian," she whispered as she fitted the key in the lock.

She stood inside the back door, seeing herself and Julian at the kitchen table. Seeing them dance around the room with candles glowing everywhere—on the table, on the stove, on top of the refrigerator. Remembering the reflections in Julian's eyes as he looked at her with love.

Slowly, she walked into the bedroom and remembered how it was to be naked on the brass bedstead with Julian making love to her.

She sat on the bed and touched the pillow where his head had lain. Then buried her face in it and cried.

Her letter to Julian was waiting in the mailbox when she got home. The words "not at this address" were written across the envelope.

SHE KEPT THE SECRET to herself for a few days, sneaking over to *her* house several times, planning how she would fit her little family within its walls.

The second floor was finished space that had apparently never been used for anything but storage. But it had two dormer windows and was wired for electricity. She would put a heater of some sort up there and use it as Barry's bedroom.

The bedroom that had been Julian's would be Mary Sue's. It was much smaller than the one she had now, and she would probably complain that it was not fair for Barry to have a bigger room. But Barry was older and needed more privacy, Sara decided as she planned her case. She would put up shelves for Mary Sue's books and collections and paint the walls any color she wanted.

The big old-fashioned kitchen had plenty of room for a sofa and television set. And Sara loved the big round table that was already in place. She would put rugs on the floor and hang pictures on the walls to make it look more like a combination kitchen-family room. And then she could turn the front parlor into a workroom for her quilting.

Sara really couldn't get over it. *Her* house. And maybe it was the booby prize, but it would help her get over Julian.

And she had to get over Julian.

She had to find things to laugh about. She had to stop being short with her children. And the customers at the B & J. She had to stop being so hard on Bea.

But her heart ached. Sometimes, it went beyond ache, all the way to pain, and she had to stop what she was doing and put her hand to her breast in an attempt to block it. *Julian was gone from her life.*

She had known him such a short time. But it was going to take a long time getting over him. So quickly, she had pinned her hopes and dreams on him. So completely, she had fallen in love with him.

She couldn't concentrate on television programs. She'd start to read a page in a book or magazine and lose her place. She could quilt only in short segments before her shoulders would sag and tears clouded her vision. She not only lost interest in food, she didn't even like to be around food.

God, if there was one thing in the world she hated, it was self-pity. Yet, here she was being pitiful. Feeling sorry for herself. But she missed Julian so. Missed having the anticipation of him in her life. If she just knew for sure she'd see him again *sometime,* she wouldn't hurt so much. But the prospect of never seeing him again was more than she could bear.

She found herself imagining grand reunions with him, even down to what she would be wearing, where she would be sitting, what she would say or do when she saw him.

Then she would realize what she was doing. *Grow up,* she would chastise. *It's over.*

She was making herself sick. No doubt about it. She had to shape up. Get herself out of the dumps. She wasn't doing herself or her children any good like this.

She'd tell them about the house tomorrow, she decided as she lay in bed. She'd kept it to herself for three days, almost unwilling to open Julian's gift up to scrutiny. She couldn't bear for them not to be glad about it. She didn't want to get angry when Bea protested even that much of a move. But surely she wouldn't. Surely Bea would be able to see it was for the best.

And Sara feared she would explode if one whiny word came out of either of her children. They had talked her out of marrying the man she loved and taking them to Germany, but by golly, she was moving her family across the pasture and that was the end of it. No discussion. No whining. Just pack up and move.

Yes, at breakfast she would tell them. Maybe tomorrow after school, they could start taking some things over.

But in the morning, she could hardly get herself out of bed. And it wasn't just loneliness that was making her feel this way.

She stared at herself in the mirror. Same face. Was she pale? It was hard to tell.

She ran her hands down her body. And wondered.

As soon as she pushed open the door of the kitchen, the smell of bacon cooking overwhelmed her. She put her hand over her mouth and raced back down the hall to her bathroom.

She didn't have much in her stomach to throw up. Sara bathed her face with a damp washcloth and tried to get control of her stomach.

Bea's lips were drawn into a very straight line when Sara returned.

"So, you're pregnant," she said.

"I don't know. Maybe," Sara said, pouring herself a glass of water. But even a sip of water didn't set right. And that bacon! She took several deep breaths and went to the cupboard for a cracker.

"That's a fine kettle of fish, Sara Cate," Bea said, shaking the spatula at her daughter-in-law. "The widow of my son, living under my roof, getting herself *pregnant.*"

"I won't be living under your roof much longer, Bea," Sara said wearily as she lowered her aching body into a chair.

"And just what do you mean by that?" Bea turned to face her, putting her hands on her ample hips.

"Julian is letting me have Rachel's house and ten acres of land for as long as I need it. The kids and I are moving out. Maybe that will help ease your humiliation of having Ben's widow pregnant."

"Are you going to... to stay pregnant?"

"I thought you didn't believe in abortion."

"I don't. But this is just awful, Sara. Just awful. Everyone will talk. Julian Campbell has to come back here and marry you. For Mary Sue and Barry's sake. Imagine having their mother pregnant and unmarried! The poor babies."

"I'm not going to make any man marry me," Sara explained. "I turned Julian away because my family didn't want me to marry him. And now I'm not going to use an unwanted pregnancy to force him back here."

"We'll have to lie," Bea said, waving the spatula around while she conjured up a plan. "Yes, we'll have to say that you're married, and your husband is overseas someplace where you can't go. Or maybe that he was killed in an automobile accident right after you married him."

"Bea, no! If I really am pregnant, you and Jim and the kids and citizens of Murray will just have to get used to the idea."

"Then you're not really sure. Maybe you've just got a stomach virus."

"Maybe. But I doubt it. I'll make a doctor's appointment tomorrow to find out."

"Oh, Sara," Bea said, sinking down into a chair next to her. "How could you? My goodness, if you were going to have sex with him, couldn't you have used something? It's not like you were new at it."

Sara sighed. "I haven't taken birth control pills since Ben died. I thought it was a safe time of the month. It appears I was probably wrong."

"You mustn't tell the children!" Bea said. "We've got to protect them."

"I won't. Not until I'm sure. But then they've got to know, Bea. I'll need their help and support. Yours, too. And Jim's. God, Bea, I'll need you all so much," she said as the tears began.

"Lordy, girl," Bea said, opening her arms. "You've really made a mess of things. But somehow, we'll muddle through. That's what families are for."

Jim pushed open the kitchen door, regarded the two women then went over to the stove to turn the bacon.

"I don't know what this is all about," he said. "But I gather the war is over. Thank God, for that!"

"Hush up, Jim, and bring us some tissues," Bea said. "And get this girl a cracker."

"A cracker?" Jim shrugged and did as he was told.

Chapter Eleven

"Let's see," the receptionist said, looking over the new patient form Sara had just filled out. "'Mrs. Sara Cate.' You live in Murray. And your husband's name is James Cate."

"No, James Cate is my father-in-law," Sara said, pointing to the upside-down form. "See, he's on the line for 'close relative or friend to notify in case of emergency.'"

"So, what is your husband's name?"

"I'm a widow," Sara explained.

"Oh, how sad," the plump young woman said. "Your husband won't get to see his own baby. But we do need to write his name on this line right here."

"That line's for the child's father," Sara pointed out. "My husband has been dead for three years. He's not the father."

"I see. Well, what shall we put on the line for the child's father?"

"Why don't *we* just leave it blank?"

"As you wish," the woman said and wrote "unknown" in the blank.

"No, that's not correct. I know who he is, but I choose not to name him."

The receptionist put a line through her last entry and wrote "unmarried" in large letters across the top of the form.

The nurse was more understanding.

"I heard that little exchange," she said as she weighed Sara. "The girl is new. The doctor needs to speak with her. Please don't think you're the only unwed mother to walk through the door."

"I bet you don't get many my age, though."

"Not too many. Do you plan to keep the baby?" she asked, wrapping the blood pressure cuff around Sara's upper arm.

"Yes," Sara said, lifting her chin. "It's my baby. I'll raise it."

"Good for you. My sister's trying to raise one like that— without a daddy. It's rough, but that little guy is the light of her life. She says she doesn't know what she would do without him. This is a university town, though, and it's not uncommon for unmarried women to raise children. But a little town like Murray isn't as liberal as a college town. You sure you can handle it?"

"I guess I'll have to," Sara said.

The obstetrician took about two minutes to confirm Sara's pregnancy. "Of course, we'll run some lab work to make sure, but you appear to be about a month along. That means we're looking at a May delivery," the petite woman said as she completed her examination and helped Sara to a sitting position on the end of the table.

"How have you been feeling?" the doctor asked.

"Pregnant," Sara said.

"Have you lost weight?"

"Some."

"Are you depressed?"

"I guess a little. I would prefer to be happily married and expecting. But I'm not. It's hard on me—and my family."

"What about the father?"

"He doesn't know," Sara explained.

"Is that fair?"

"I've thought about that and decided that no, it's not fair. But few things in life are. If I'm going to be the one to raise the child, I'd rather do it without his involvement to confuse the situation."

"What about child support?" the kindly woman asked. "Can you manage without it."

"Other women have managed on less."

"Are you sure you're not just being proud?"

"No," Sara acknowledged. "I'm sure he'd come back here and marry me if I'd asked him to. But I have two older children, and it just wouldn't have worked."

The doctor gave her a prescription for prenatal vitamins, a pamphlet with a recommended diet and health tips for the pregnant woman and a brochure on childbirth classes held at the Norman hospital.

Sara stared at the brochure and had an image of husbands with their pregnant wives attending class together, preparing to share the adventure. And a feeling of loneliness dropped down on her like a heavy mantle, making her shoulders sag and her knees feel weak. With effort, she walked down the long corridor to the exit and crossed the parking lot.

She put her head against the steering wheel and closed her eyes. *Julian, where are you? Do you ever think of me?*

THE CHILDREN were out in the barn with a new litter of kittens. Sara sat with them on a bale of hay and admired the tiny little animals born just yesterday with Mary Sue and Barry in attendance.

The mama cat hovered nearby, not sure she wanted her babies held.

Sara nuzzled a white kitten. She loved the softness and the sweet, innocent smell of new life whether it was animals or people.

And she loved this barn. It smelled of hay and animals and was full of space—almost like a church—with a high peaked ceiling soaring above them, crisscrossed by sturdy beams. Slanting downward from the high hay door was a single shaft of sunlight, illuminating millions of dancing dust motes.

Rachel's barn was just a long metal shed—not wonderful like this one. But Sara was going to put a weather vane on its roof and paint its door barn red. And the rail fences in front of it white.

"They're so helpless," Mary Sue said, holding a tiny, spotted kitten against her cheek.

"Yes, but in a few days, they'll open their eyes and in a few weeks they'll be all over the place—not like people babies at all," Sara said, taking a deep breath. *Now,* she told herself. Get it over with. "And that's what we're going to be having pretty soon, next May as a matter of fact. A people baby. Our baby."

Both youngsters stared at her, puzzled frowns on their faces as they tried to figure out her meaning.

"But Grandma's too old, and you don't have a husband," Mary Sue said.

Barry said nothing, but a wary, knowing expression crept over his handsome face. He looked more like his father every day. Sometimes Sara would see Bea or Jim staring at his young face with a sad, poignant expression on their aging ones as they remembered Ben.

He was shaving now. His voice was as deep as a man's. Would Barry be indifferent to this baby growing inside of her, or would he become a surrogate father for the baby's missing one?

"You're right on both counts," Sara told Mary Sue as she put the white kitten back in the wooden box hidden between bales of hay. "Grandma's too old. And I'm not married. But sometimes women get pregnant without a husband. They may want to marry the man, but by the time they figure out they can't, they're already pregnant. That's what happened to me. I loved Julian very much and thought we might get married. But you children and your grandparents made it very clear that you didn't want me to marry him. And by then, it was too late. I know I should have been more careful, and I'm embarrassed about what has happened. And I'm worried about how I will pay for everything. I'm concerned about the problems it will cause for my family. But I can't be sad about having another baby."

"Shouldn't Julian come back here and marry you and take care of you?" Barry asked.

"I don't want to make him marry me," Sara explained, choosing her words carefully. "Julian shouldn't have to marry a woman whose children don't want him. That wouldn't be any fun for him, now would it? And I don't want to be married to a man if it will drive a wedge between me and my children."

"But won't people think you are terrible?" Mary Sue asked. "Like when Betsy Mae Hart had to marry Buddy Henderson."

"Some people will. But if our family is happy about this baby, and we show everyone that we want it, I hope they'll get accustomed to the idea."

"The baby will be one of those 'halves,' won't it?" Mary Sue asked.

"You mean a half-brother or a half-sister? Yes, it will. But that's just a technicality. We will think of the baby just as your and Barry's brother or sister. No halves."

Barry looked away, no longer able to meet his mother's gaze. Mary Sue concentrated on the kitten in her lap.

As Sara looked at the puzzlement and fear written on her children's faces, she felt very, very sorry. They had a pretty good sense of the gossip their family would be facing. It had happened in Murray before.

But only to teenagers. Sara couldn't remember ever hearing of an adult woman in this situation. Would that make her all the more scandalous—or less so?

If she had it all to do over again, she would have taken every precaution to prevent a pregnancy. She had been stupid and irresponsible—for surely at some level, she knew she was tempting fate. But she also had still believed love would find a way for her to be with Julian forever. She had been living in a romantic fog.

Well, the fog was clearing, and reality was emerging all too clearly.

She wanted to take both children in her arms and smother them with kisses, but held back, fearing their response. Her poor children—their father got himself killed. And their mother got herself pregnant. What a bum draw!

"And now I've got some more news," she told them in as cheerful a voice as she could muster. "We're moving to Rachel's farm! The house, the outbuildings and ten acres are ours for as long as we want them. Julian sent word through Percy Mason that he wanted us to live there. And we don't have to pay a dime."

"Why would he be nice to us when we weren't nice to him?" Barry asked, his brow creasing in a frown.

"I'm not sure, son. Except that he's a very kind person, and I think he felt we needed to have a place of our own. He thought Grandma and Grandpa spoiled you and Mary Sue too much, and that I was letting them get away with it. He was afraid you two were growing up expecting other people to do your work and not willing to carry your fair share. Sometimes people like that never really grow up. They spend their whole life whining. And Julian knew that every woman wants a place of her own. I feel like a visitor in Bea's house—especially in her kitchen. I want to decide how to arrange the furniture and what to have for dinner. Women are like that."

"I like it here with Grandma and Grandpa," Mary Sue said, looking toward the brick house that had been her home for three years. "Rachel's house is ugly. And she died there. The kids at school say that makes it haunted. They say that Rachel was a witch."

"Do you think she was a witch?" Sara asked.

"No," Mary Sue admitted. "But she did die there. I don't want to live where someone died. I want to stay with Grandma and Grandpa."

"I know, honey. But we'll just be across the pasture. You can see Grandma and Grandpa every day—after you finish your chores. We can even cook dinner for them sometimes. Won't that be fun?"

"Can we take our horses?" Barry asked.

"Yes. But you two will have to take care of them. You can't count on Grandpa to make sure their water buckets are full and they get brushed and fed and their hooves cleaned out. And Barry, you're going to have to be the man of the family. Our ten acres needs to be cultivated, and that will be your responsibility. When shingles blow off the roof, you're going to have to fix it. And tend to all the things that require a man's muscles. Mary Sue and I will keep house and plant a very large garden. We can save a lot of money by growing our own vegetables and melons. And we'll raise our own chickens."

"Will we be poor?" Mary Sue asked.

"We're already poor. Grandma and Grandpa have been taking care of us."

"But I don't understand," Barry admitted. "Why should we have to work hard over there and not have very much when Grandma and Grandpa give us everything we need?"

"Because it's time, Barry."

"I don't want you to have a baby," Mary Sue said, tears welling. "And I don't want to move."

"Well, sweetie, you better start getting used to both ideas. Because both this baby and that house are now our responsibility."

"JUST WHAT DO YOU THINK you're doing?" Bea demanded as Sara walked through the kitchen carrying her rocking chair.

Without waiting for an answer, Bea took the chair from Sara and called, "Barry, come here and carry this chair out to the truck for your mother."

"There's no call for you to be lifting heavy things like that," Bea chastised.

"Well, I hate for Barry to do everything when he's not too sure he even wants to move in the first place."

Bea handed Sara a glass of lemonade and pointed to a chair. "Sit down. You look hot and tired. And skinny. Lord, girl, it'd take two of you to cast a decent shadow. Are you sure you want to do this, Sara? Jim and I have talked it over, and maybe we're not too happy about the idea of your having a baby like this, but we can learn to live with the idea, if it means keeping our family together. This big old house is going to seem awfully empty with just Jim and me. Jim's always said I'm too dang bossy. Well, I can tone it down.

What if we take turns with the cooking? And Jim and I won't interfere with the children. Not one bit. You assign them chores, and we'll back you up. You decide how much allowance they deserve, and we won't slip them one thin dime on the side. And we won't buy them anything without clearing it with you first."

"Bea, I'm not moving because I'm pregnant. At least, not altogether. I would have wanted to, baby or not. In fact, I've been saving money to buy a house trailer to put out back. At the rate I was going, however, I'd be an old lady by the time I had enough money. I need to be on my own with the kids. I need for you and Jim to come have dinner at my house once in a while. Can you understand that?"

"I suppose," Bea admitted. "I loved Jim's mother, but I wouldn't have wanted to live with her. I thought our family was different, though. I thought we'd really made it work."

"We did. God, I love you and Jim so much. And I could have lived here with you forever, but it's better this way. Especially now with this baby on the way. I can't ask you to take in another man's child."

Bea nodded. That would not be easy.

"Well, if that's the way it's going to be," she said, slapping her plump thighs for emphasis, "then we'd better get organized. Jim and Barry can do the carrying over. Mary Sue and I can give the place a good cleaning. All those cupboards will need to be emptied out and scrubbed, all the dishes washed."

"Bea, I'm not helpless."

"You can decide where things go," Bea said, ignoring her comment. "I always thought Rachel should have put that big old buffet on the west wall, and..." But she stopped herself. "Just listen to me. Trying to run the show. Sara, would you like Jim and me to help?"

"I'd be honored. But let's leave the buffet where it is."

"BUT GRANDMA AND Grandpa have a big screen and a satellite dish that gets forty channels. I don't see why we have to sit here and watch that crummy little television that only gets four," Barry challenged.

"Because this is our home, and I prefer for you not to go over there every evening," Sara said.

"But that's our home, too. Or at least it was," Barry said. "I don't like it here, Mom. My room up there in the attic is as hot as an oven. The whole house is hot. Why can't we have air-conditioning?"

"We can trade bedrooms," Sara offered. "I'll take the upstairs room. I don't mind the heat as long as the windows are opened."

"Naw, that's okay. I just got all my posters hung," he said.

"I mean it, Barry. We'll move everything around tomorrow. I'd like it up there. When I was a little girl, we didn't have air-conditioning, and I'd push my bed over to the window of my upstairs room and put my pillow in the window sill. I could hear the traffic over on May Avenue. All night long. I used to wonder where people went all night."

"Mom," Barry said uncomfortably. "I don't want to sleep in there where Miss Rachel died. That's spooky. I don't see how you do it."

"It's not spooky. Rachel's old heart just stopped beating. I can't think of a better place to die than in one's own bed."

"I keep thinking about what everyone says—about the house being haunted. Sometimes I hear things."

"It's an old house, son. It creaks a lot. And if there were such a thing as a ghost, which I don't for one minute believe there is, Rachel's ghost wouldn't ever hurt you, now would she? She might bawl you out, but she wouldn't hurt you."

"Can't we buy a window air conditioner to put upstairs?" he asked.

"The hot weather is almost over. Just tough it out and I'll find a second-hand window unit for next summer. I promise. Okay?"

Barry nodded and returned his gaze to the television screen. Football. Mary Sue had gone to pout in her room because she didn't want to watch football.

Barry didn't like his room. Mary Sue predictably didn't like her little cell-like space even though Sara made her a new bedspread and dust ruffle for her bed and frilly curtains for the window.

Sara went into the front room and sat at her quilting frame. Maybe the move hadn't been a good idea. The house was hot. The children were accustomed to all those television channels and a VCR for rented movies. The three of them sharing a bathroom had already caused problems. Barry complained because there was no shower.

And having her own kitchen wasn't without its own set of problems. The old refrigerator wouldn't keep ice cream and took forever to make ice. The thermostat didn't work on the oven. Sara didn't mind not having a dishwasher but missed a garbage disposal. She had forgotten how much of a problem disposing of garbage could be.

The washing machine down in the cellar was an old wringer model that was out-of-date forty years ago and should be given to a museum. And there was no clothes dryer. Only clotheslines out back. Sara took most of the laundry over to Bea and Jim's. The kids went over there to watch television.

Sometimes Sara had a hard time remembering why they moved. *Oh yes, she needed to unspoil her kids and regain control of her little family.*

Except she herself had been spoiled, too. She hadn't really thought about that.

Evening meals alone with her two children were not the warm, cozy occasions Sara wanted them to be. Meals used to be noisy affairs with Bea's one-liners and Jim's stories. The children enjoyed an audience of three adoring adults to report on the happenings of their day. Now with just the three of them, dinner seemed subdued—strained. Sara did most of the talking, asking lots of questions and getting sullen, one-word answers.

The best part about the house was keeping it. And fixing it up. Sara had loved moving in and arranging everything. Hanging her few pictures. Incorporating her few possessions in with Rachel's. Jim had laid the linoleum that Julian had bought, and Sara used a hooked rug to define the corner of the kitchen where she put the television on the 1930s-vintage buffet and moved the 1950s-vintage divan and easy chair from the parlor along with a lovely glass-topped coffee table and graceful lamp table. Actually, the kitchen/family room looked very cozy, and Sara found immense pleasure just standing in the doorway and looking at it. Her home. Her very own home. And it wasn't on wheels.

Sara had lots of plans. In addition to making curtains for all the windows, she was going to recover the lamp shades, make slipcovers for the sofa and easy chair, make rag rugs for the bedrooms. She loved polishing the furniture, oiling the hardwood floors and thinking of inexpensive decorative touches to make the little house more homey—more her own. Plants had helped tremendously. Eventually, she would put up wallpaper and paint the woodwork.

And she wanted to stock the shelves of the small cellar with canned fruit and vegetables from the garden she planned to put in next summer.

Already, they had returned some of Rachel's laying hens to the place. Sara had bought some hatchlings so they could raise chickens for eating.

Julian had begun cleaning out the barn and shed, but the task needed completing. And Sara had never gone through Rachel's personal possessions. In her rush to get settled, she and Mary Sue had shoved everything from her closet and bureau drawers into boxes and stored them in the upstairs closet.

BEA ANSWERED the phone. It was eight o'clock in the morning, Oklahoma time. Julian could imagine her standing by the phone in her kitchen, apron on, frying bacon.

"It's Julian Campbell," he told her.

"Hello, Julian," she said, sounding wary. "Where are you?"

"In Heidelberg, Germany. I just called to see how Sara is." Julian carried the phone to the sofa of his new apartment. Unpacked boxes were stacked in the corner. It didn't yet feel like home. But he was determined. Pictures on the walls. Rugs on the floors. Lamps on the tables. *A home.*

"To see how Sara is?" Bea parroted, her wariness in her voice increasing. "Are you asking for any particular reason?"

"Well, yes. Because I care about her. And I wasn't sure she'd want to hear from me directly. In fact, I'm not even sure I want you to tell her that I called. I don't want her to think I've changed my mind. I'm not getting out of the Army and moving to Murray. Although, I might have done that if it weren't for the kids. But then, if she didn't have the kids, she would have come with me. I think about her all the time and would just like to know that she's okay."

"She's fine."

"Did she move over to my aunt's house?"

"Yes, she did. Jim and I live here alone now in this big old house, and she and those two children are all cramped up in Rachel's little old house that's hotter than Hades in the summer and drafty as a sieve in the winter. And that lawyer of yours is going to sell off tracts of her land to poor people who live in house trailers. That's what Jim and I can look forward to—looking out our windows at a bunch of house trailers."

"Did Sara ever talk to the children about coming over here?"

"She did."

"And?"

"They didn't want to. In fact, the whole notion got everyone pretty upset. Mary Sue wants to be a cheerleader. Barry is playing football with his dad's old number. Both children ride rodeo. Barry has a girlfriend. They belong here in Murray, and they know it. Of course, they aren't as happy as they used to be—before you came. You've got your nerve, telling her those children are spoiled! All the time you were growing up, you would have given anything to have had the love and concern those youngsters have. But now, Sara's worried that she's raising them all wrong. She's after them all the time to do chores. She's got them with a paint brush or a hoe in their hands all the time. And she won't let us buy them the things they want and need. Lordy, what are grandparents for if not to spoil their grandkids! I told Sara the other day she's not only living in Rachel Warren's house, but she's turning into a crotchety old woman, just like Rachel was. Jim and I, we miss our sweet Sara. And we eat down at the cafe every night 'cause we can't bear sitting at a table with only the two of us. I wish that Rachel had left her place to the Methodists, like she threatened. Then you never would have come back here and messed everything up like you did."

"Yes, that would have been better," Julian agreed. "Does Sara ever talk about me?"

"No."

"Are you going to tell her I called?"

"I'd rather not. But if you asked me to, I will."

"No. I guess it's best to make a clean break. I do love her, you know."

"I know, Julian. And she loves you. And in a way, it breaks my heart to know you're both unhappy. But it just wouldn't work. You hated our little world and left it behind years ago. Such a sad boy you were. And that sadness is still there inside of you, isn't it? But Sara and her kids aren't the ones to make it go away. Even if you married Sara and took them all away from here, you'd have more problems than Carter has little pills. You'd end up wishing you hadn't. Those children are too old to let another man be their father. They remember their daddy and would resent you. And Sara can't take sides against her children. It's better to end it with love."

"I suppose you're right," Julian said.

"You take care of yourself, hear. And, Julie Boy, keep your windows clean."

"BUT I GAVE YOU permission to enter the roping events *only,*" Sara told her son, feeling her anger rise. So that was why Jim had come over. Barry wanted his grandfather's support when he told her.

"I won't have you riding bulls and broncs," she said, getting up out of her chair to pace, to look down at the two conspirators as they sat side by side at the round kitchen table. "God, Barry, surely you remember all those cowboys getting trampled and injured for life. And remember what one of those bulls did to your father? He had to walk with a cane because of a bull."

"Come on, Sara," Jim said, hat in hand. "People get struck by lightning and hurt in automobile accidents. Barry's a natural-born rider. The boy could be a high school rodeo champion like his father."

"He also could be a cripple like his father," Sara said flatly. "If Ben hadn't been crippled by that bull, he probably could have jumped free when that tractor started tipping over. Stop trying to turn my son into a carbon copy of his father, Jim. I won't have it!"

"The roping events are sissy," Barry said. "If you won't let me ride the broncs and bulls, then I want to go live with Grandma and Grandpa. They'll let me do what I want. I don't like living in this house anyway."

"I am your mother, Barry Cate, and that means you live with me and do as I say," Sara said, then took a deep breath to calm herself. "I'm sorry, son. I know you don't like some of the changes I'm making. And I know you think that nothing is ever going to hurt you. But mothers know that bad things happen. They worry. And it's their job to protect their kids."

"What about if we compromise?" Jim suggested. "Barry can rope and ride the broncs. But since you're so worried about the bulls, Sara, he'll stay away from them."

"No, Jim. Roping only."

"If Dad was alive, he'd let me," Barry said, standing to face his mother.

They were the same height now. Soon he would be taller. But that didn't make him a man.

"Maybe he would. But your dad is dead. I am your only parent, and I feel very strongly about this. I know too well what can happen. I saw it too many times. And I vowed a long time ago that no son of mine is ever going to get carried out of a rodeo arena on a stretcher."

She held up her hand before Barry could say another word. "The discussion is over, son."

THE NEXT MORNING, when Sara called up the stairs to Barry, there was no answer. She climbed the stairs to see a neatly made bed and no sign of her son.

She raced to the phone, but Bea and Jim hadn't seen him. By the time Bea and Jim arrived, Sara had determined that he had taken a large duffel bag and several changes of clothes. Sara's small stash of cash was missing from her dresser drawer.

The sheriff came and explained that Barry would be classified as missing after twenty-four hours. But no great law enforcement effort would be used to find a runaway teenage boy. "He could be out of state by now, Sara. We'll send out his picture, and you call every place you can think of that he might go to—like any of Ben's old buddies who still hang around the rodeos."

For the next four days, Sara lived in a nightmare. She made dozens of phone calls. Afraid to leave the phone in case there was news, she sent Jim and Bea out to drive up and down the county roads and the streets of every nearby town.

Neighbors brought over food—as though someone had died. Funeral food, she thought, unable to eat more than toast and some fruit and that only because she got sick if she didn't eat. Every time the phone rang, she jumped. And offered a hurried prayer as she answered it.

Finally, the phone call she had lived for came. An Oklahoma City police officer called to say they had found her son. He had hopped a freight train and been accidentally locked in a boxcar.

"He's a lucky boy," the policeman said. "A yardman just happened to hear him calling out. That boxcar could have set on that siding for weeks before anyone looked inside."

Sara called Bea and Jim to give them the news. "I'm on my way," Jim said.

"No, Jim," Sara said. "*I'll* go get him. Mary Sue and I will go."

"Going to a jail house is a man's job, Sara," Jim said sternly.

"In this case, it's a mother's job."

Sara cried with relief when she finally saw her son. He was skinny and filthy, but she hugged him gratefully.

And he hugged her back. Crying. "I'm sorry, Mom. Really sorry. It was a dumb-kid thing to do."

Barry sat in the middle on the way home. When she wasn't shifting the gears of her old truck, Sara couldn't stop touching her son. He was alive. He was all right. Her little family was going to make it.

She fixed Barry's favorite meal of fried catfish, slaw and corn bread. After dinner, she explained to her children that there were going to be some more changes in their lives. "I love Grandma and Grandpa, and I'll always be grateful to them for looking after us after your father died. And Murray has been a good home for us, but now I need to think about the future. I don't want to wait tables any more. And I don't want to accept any more charity from your grandparents. When the baby is old enough, I plan to find a job in Oklahoma City. And when I do, we'll move there—probably after the next school year. I can get student loans to go to school in the evenings and help with expenses, but I'm going to need a lot of help from you kids. You'll have to cook and do laundry. You'll have to help me with the baby and do your homework without being told. We will still see Grandma and Grandpa often, and you can spend school vacations in Murray. But I have to take charge of our family again. And I have to think about the rest of my life."

"You're sorry you didn't marry Julian, aren't you?" Mary Sue asked.

"Yes, as a matter of fact, I am."

"Is it too late?"

"I'm afraid so. And quite frankly, I'd have serious doubts about any man who would be willing to marry a woman with two children who had gone out of their way to make him feel inadequate and unwanted."

"But he wasn't special like Dad," Barry protested. "He can't ride or rope or shoot. He can't do any of the things Dad could do."

"Julian is special in other ways, son. He grew up with no advantages whatsoever. He was raised by a hard old woman who didn't know how to love. As a young man, he made up his mind he was going to make something of himself. He put himself through college. He became an Army officer in the service of our country. The woman he married decided she didn't want to share his life. But he didn't let any of these things ruin his life. And in spite of all the pain he's lived through, he was brave enough to try love again, brave enough to offer to take on two children who were pretty hateful to him. He is kind, hardworking and unselfish. In my eyes, Julian Campbell is just as much of a hero as your father ever was. And I miss him. If he ever comes back, I will beg him with all my heart to give me another chance. But that may never happen. So, in the meantime, I've got to do what is best for the three of us."

"Do you miss Julian more than Daddy?" Mary Sue's tone was accusing.

"I am still sad that your father died young. And he will always be my first love, my first husband, the father of my children. I am proud to have been his wife. No one can change that. But the man I miss is a living man."

"And you want to hug and kiss him?" Mary Sue challenged.

"Yes. Very much."

"I'VE BEEN HEARING a most disturbing rumor," Brother Carmichael told Bea. He had asked her to stay after the deacons' meeting, and they were seated in the church office, the clergyman behind his tidy desk, a familiar religious picture in an impressive gilded frame hanging on the wall behind him, his hands folded prayerlike under his chin.

"About Sara?" Bea asked, knowing full well what rumor the minister was talking about. "And why does this 'rumor' disturb you, George? Sara has chosen to bear a baby. That takes a lot of courage in a little town like Murray, don't you think?"

"Yes, I suppose it does," he admitted with a nod of his handsome gray head. "But what happens when she starts to...ah...to show?"

"What do you mean, 'what happens'?"

"Well, surely she doesn't plan to continue as if nothing was amiss."

"What are you trying to say—that you don't want her sitting in your congregation with a pregnant belly?" Bea demanded.

Brother Carmichael winced at Bea's bluntness. "Well, it would be a bit unseemly. Surely you can see that. I mean, for me to be in the pulpit preaching about morality, and her sitting there like that—unmarried. Yes, definitely unseemly," he said, his head bobbing as he agreed with himself. "I'm sure some of the church members would have a problem with it."

"I always did say you preached too much, George Carmichael. Your daddy *talked* to us. There's a world of difference, you know."

"Yes, you've explained that to me many times. But that's off the subject. What about it, Bea? What are Sara's plans?"

Bea shrugged. "To continue working at the cafe. To continue taking care of her children. To continue coming to church."

Then Bea leaned forward in her chair and narrowed her eyes. "And if you say one more word, George Carmichael, I'm going to remind you what a hell-raiser you were back in our high school days. I'm going to remind you that your firstborn son was the heftiest *premature* baby I've ever seen. And I'm also going to remind you that when I took over your ladies' circle, it had half-a-dozen ladies—all over the age of seventy—and church membership was at an all-time low. But the circle started putting on potluck suppers, picnics, talent shows, benefit auctions, square dances, quilting bees. We fed folks after funerals and decorated the sanctuary for the holidays. We made cushions for the pews so people could be more comfortable during all that preaching. And now, not only does every woman in the church participate in circle activities, but the church has more members than the Methodists. As you once so wisely pointed out, the strength of a church comes from its women—that where women go, families follow. And I seem to be the ramrod around here, don't I, George?"

"Bea Cate, are you blackmailing me?" Brother Carmichael asked indignantly, leaning forward in his high-backed chair, his hands planted on the desktop.

"Maybe so, but I'd rather be a blackmailing granny than a sanctimonious preacher man any day of the week. I think this church should set an example for the community by supporting my Sara and welcoming her innocent little baby when it arrives."

Brother Carmichael stared at Bea for a minute, his mouth slightly ajar, then broke out laughing. "Bea Cate, the good Lord knew what he was doing when he sent me to this pulpit. He knew you'd be here to keep me in line."

"The Lord be praised," Bea said, picking up her purse. "Now, if we're finished with this little discussion, I need to get on over to the cafe and get the pies made. Stop by for a piece, George. It'll be on the house."

Chapter Twelve

Julian enjoyed watching Frieda eat. There was something terribly sexy about a beautiful woman who loved to eat and didn't pretend otherwise. She never picked at her food, never nibbled like a little bird. When she found a food especially tasty, she would moan with pleasure, sometimes even closing her eyes to better savor a particularly tasty morsel.

Frieda ate with the same gusto that she danced, shopped, cooked and argued politics. Julian had no doubt that she would make love with the same energy and enthusiasm.

At this moment, she was attacking a plate of sauerbraten, pausing every now and then to bite off a chunk of chewy rye bread, take a swallow from a large stein of strong, dark beer or to make another point about the European Common Market, the topic of their dinnertime conversation.

"You do not like the food?" she asked, pointing at his half-eaten plate of food.

"Yeah, it's great," he said. "But it's more fun to watch you eat."

She rewarded him with a smile. "Eat," she commanded. "It is better hot."

Did she have any idea how gorgeous she was? Julian wondered. Frieda had flawless fair skin, deep blue eyes, sleek pale blond hair and full pouting lips. She spoke fluent English with just enough of a sultry German accent to make her seem sexy and exotic—reminiscent of Marlene Dietrich in all those old World War II-era movies. Frieda even wore a belted trench coat and jauntily slanted beret. Except that, unlike Dietrich, Frieda made no attempt at sultriness. Joviality was more her style.

She had lived in both New York and San Francisco, loved American movies and music and had obviously enjoyed Julian's American presence in her life.

Julian was fascinated by her self-assurance, by her intelligence, her sense of style, the easy way she moved her lanky body and the way she frequently erupted in wonderful spontaneous laughter that said life was meant to be enjoyed and to hell with anyone who didn't agree.

She loved to travel, had never been married, had no children and had celebrated her thirtieth birthday.

In short, Julian couldn't find a single thing the matter with Fräulein Frieda Berger. And no one could accuse him of trying to duplicate his former love. Frieda and Sara were quite different. Frieda took risks. Sara was cautious. Frieda didn't worry. Sara worried a lot. Frieda was responsible only for herself. Sara had two children and a set of parents-in-law who dictated her life.

Julian was "living on the economy"—as it was called when military personnel lived off-base—in downtown Heidelberg, where he had found lodging in an apartment building managed by the intriguing blond Frieda, who was finishing a graduate degree in European history at the Johanne Wolfgang Goethe University.

Julian assumed it was only a matter of time until he and Frieda went to bed together, before they fell in love, before they made a serious commitment to one another. Frieda obviously thought the same thing.

So, why was he holding back?

He had met Frieda almost four months ago, the first week he arrived from a temporary-duty assignment at the Pentagon in Washington, DC, where he had been a member of a think-tank session held by the Support Preparedness Group in the office of the Joint Chiefs of Staff. The think-tank participants had been brought together to assess current military procedures concerning the establishment of wartime field hospitals and make recommendations for speeding up and improving the process, with special emphasis on desert locations.

Julian had been a last-minute replacement at the month-long session, taking the place of an officer who had suffered a heart attack the week before the meetings were scheduled to begin. Julian had been only too willing to hasten his departure from Fort Bragg and leave behind his lonely apartment with its constant reminders of Sara.

She had only been with him for four days and not every hour had been wonderful, yet everywhere he looked in his apartment, he saw Sara, felt her presence, heard her voice. That first night without her had been torture. The pillows on the bed bore her fragrance.

He made arrangements to leave for Germany directly from Washington rather than return to Fort Bragg. The busyness of moving had been just what he needed. No time to think. So much to do. In less than a week, he tied up loose ends at the hospital and left things in order for his successor, who was scheduled to arrive at the end of the month. At his apartment, he cleaned out drawers, closets and cupboards, deciding what went to Germany, what got put in storage and what got tossed.

The day before he left, a packet of papers arrived from Brenda's lawyers. Her lawyer and his lawyer had finally worked out the final terms of the divorce settlement. All Julian had to do was sign it.

There should be a ceremony, he had thought as he stood alone in his empty kitchen, signing papers. There was a ceremony to get married. There should be one at marriage-end to call it all off. Like a funeral. Something with dirges and tears and the floral wreaths.

The think-tank environment was intense and stimulating. Julian had written his master's degree thesis on field hospitals and was able to make a valuable contribution to the project, which could mean the difference between life and death to wounded American servicemen in the event of another war.

Members of the group who were not stationed in the Washington area often continued their discussions in the evening over cocktails and dinner—pleasant evenings during which Julian even tried a little halfhearted flirting with an attractive fortyish major representing the nurses' corps at the meetings. But he was relieved when she held up her left hand and pointed to a narrow gold wedding band. He was out of practice. He should have noticed.

"But thanks for the compliment," the nurse major said. "It's nice to know I still get noticed."

In his hotel room at night, exhausted from a day of intensive thought and sluggish from an evening of cocktails and wine, Julian would fall gratefully into a deep, mindless sleep. If he dreamed, he didn't remember. But he never felt particularly rested in the morning and drank coffee to the point of gastric rebellion, spending the rest of the morning popping antacid mints into his mouth.

"Are you getting over someone?" Helen, the nurse major, asked at lunch one day.

"Does it show?" Julian responded.

"Like a tattoo. What happened?" Helen asked.

"Kids."

"Yours or hers?"

"Hers."

"I live in one of those households with his kids, my kids and our kids," Helen said. "It's a zoo. We have both sibling and interfamily rivalry. Sometimes I take it out on him because of stuff his kids have said or done. And he gives me a hard time because my children have been little monsters. And both sets of children claim we like the baby better than them. It'd make a cute television sitcom, but have you ever tried living in a sitcom?"

"Is it worth it?" Julian asked.

"Some days I wonder," Helen admitted. "But I've been away almost a month now, and I'm crazy to get home and see them all. I miss them—even *his* kids—so much I'm getting tears in my eyes just talking about it. Of course, after I've been home fifteen minutes, I'll probably be ready to get back on a plane and go anywhere at all. But yes, it's worth it because through all the trauma and arguments and skinned knees and kids whining 'that's not fair,' there is love. And my husband is the best kisser on the face of the earth. He can eat crackers in my bed anytime. Now, what's the matter with your lady love's kids?"

"They don't like me personally, and they don't want the military life-style I offer, and they are old enough to make their voices heard."

Helen nodded. "So you gave up?"

"It was pretty mutual."

"But you and the lady in question let the children decide?" she asked, with one eyebrow raised quizzically.

"Not exactly. I found that I wasn't too crazy about them either. I love their mother—a lot. But the kids and I—we were pulling her apart. The best thing for me to do was bow out."

"Well, better luck next time," Helen said.

"Next time, I'll find out if a woman has children *before* I fall in love with her."

"Then, my dear boy, you are eliminating most women over the age of thirty, and you don't seem like the kind of guy who needs to court young babes."

After the group compiled their final report, they disbanded. Julian said goodbye to the major. And headed off to Germany and the next chapter. After a failed marriage and a disastrous love affair, he was determined to make it a better one.

On the seemingly endless transatlantic flight, he took a long, hard look at his life. The professional part was satisfying. But his personal life was a flop. He wanted a family. He'd never had one, at least not the sort he envisioned—with a man and woman who loved one another and shared a home and children. For Julian, children meant family. And without having ever had that sort of family, he wasn't sure how he knew that was what he wanted, but he felt a need for it from deep inside.

Julian's father had never been a part of his life. His memories of his mother were of a tired, sick woman struggling to take care of him. Finally, she had sent him away to Oklahoma. He remembered the last time he saw her, her skin gray, her breathing labored. He was curled up in bed, snuggling against her side. She was crying as she stroked his hair and told him to be a good boy and to always remember that she had loved him.

"Try not to remember me the way I am now," she had told him. "But think of the time we spent a whole month in that cabin by the lake and swam everyday and roasted wieners and marshmallows over a fire at the water's edge. We had ourselves a real good time, didn't we?"

Julian no longer had any recollection of the time his mother had spoken about. But it was nice to know that she hadn't always been sick. That they had gone swimming in a lake and cooked over a fire. He had always thought that someday, when he had children, he would take them to a lake and do those things with them to honor his mother.

In a few months, he would be thirty-nine. He didn't want to be one of those over-the-hill fathers who sit in an easy chair reading a newspaper instead of playing with their young children.

He had thought of the nurse major—Helen—and her family. He wouldn't mind living in a zoo if his wife could honestly say—as Helen had—that in the midst of all the chaos there was love.

The first thing Julian found out about Frieda—after her name and marital status—was if she had kids. "Not yet," she said, "but someday I want babies with a nice man."

He was relieved. No more women with children, he vowed. He'd learned that lesson well!

After four days in his new apartment, he invited Frieda out to dinner. And in the evenings and weekends that followed, she had shown him Heidelberg, a jewel of a city on the Neckar River, with wonderful medieval ruins and an ancient university. They took a cable car to visit the city's most famous landmark, the ruins of the Heidelberg Castle, which stood high on a steep bank of the river.

Frieda introduced him to the city's nightlife with visits to the many rathskellers and cabarets. He learned to love onion tarts—or *zwiebelkuchen*—with good vintage wines and sausage with his beer. His favorite restaurant was Roter Oschsen, made famous by the operetta, *The Student Prince*.

They talked a lot, laughed a lot. That first night over dinner, he had explained to her that he was getting over someone and wasn't ready to get involved on more than just a friendship level.

Frieda had nodded sympathetically and left it at that. She never asked him about Sara, never asked if he still thought about her, never pushed him to make promises or even make love.

But she wanted to make love. When they danced together, she made that obvious. And when they kissed good night.

And Julian would become aroused at such moments. He had no doubt he and Frieda were well suited for each other. No, more than just well suited—they seemed perfect for each other. But he could not bring himself to cross over an invisible line that he had drawn between them. To do so would signify he was ready for a commitment. And he wasn't. He was still numbered among the walking wounded. He still thought of Sara constantly. It was still her face he saw when he closed his eyes at night, still her kisses and sighs he missed, still her body he dreamed of making love to.

"Why are you so patient with me?" he asked Frieda after the waiter had brought the black cherry torte she insisted he must try. The restaurant was famous for them.

"Because you are a man worth being patient for, darling," she said. "Taste the torte. It is *wunderbar!*"

"I feel like a louse," he said.

"A *louse?*"

"A person who behaves badly," he explained.

"And why do you feel this way? Because you fear that you will never forget the woman back in America?"

"Yeah. Something like that."

"But we should never forget those we have loved," Frieda insisted. "I remember every man I have loved. Some with fondness. Some with loathing. But I will never forget them."

"No, you're right. I wouldn't want to forget her," Julian admitted. "I guess what I'm saying is that I seem to be stuck in neutral."

Frieda put down her fork and wrinkled her brow as she considered his statement. "You Americans have such a strange way of explaining things. You mean to say that you cannot go to the front and you can not go to the back?"

"Right."

"So, perhaps it is time for you to tell me of this woman," Frieda said, leaning on her elbows, folding her hands under her chin. "What is her name?"

"Sara."

"And Sara is what sort of person?"

"Sara is sweet. Dear. Passionate." He shrugged helplessly, unable to find the right words for Sara. *A flower in the snow. A soft evening breeze. A haunting melody.*

"Ah, now I see," Frieda said, her blue eyes wise and sad. "So now you are with a woman whom you suspect is passionate, but not sweet and dear. You are right, my darling. I gave up sweet and dear a long time ago. And now, be a gentleman and beg a cigarette from the waiter."

"A cigarette? I've never seen you smoke."

"I only smoke when I am about to cry."

Julian did as he was bidden, then watched as Frieda lit up and inhaled deeply. God, she had style. And a patina of toughness that he suspected was just a facade.

"But I think you are sweet and dear, lovely Frieda. You just pick your moments to show it. I can honestly say that I wish I'd met you first. I wish I'd taken you with me to Murray, Oklahoma. I wish I'd never fallen in love with Sara. But I did, and it was stupid of me to think I could find another woman to cure me of my pain. I have to deal with the pain first. Then maybe I'll be ready to move on."

"And so, I can either wait and hope—or wish you well and find myself another pretty man to fall in love with."

Julian nodded, feeling miserable, like a cad, like a stupid oaf. Like a louse.

"Ah, you should see your poor face, my darling Julian. You look like someone who just shot their best friend in the back."

"I guess that's how I feel."

"JULIAN, IS THAT YOU?" the early morning caller asked.

Julian struggled to wakefulness. And looked at the clock. Almost three o'clock in the morning.

Then he realized who was speaking. *Brenda!*

"Is something wrong?" he asked, struggling to a sitting position and turning on the lamp.

"Wrong? In what sense? Like an emergency or just life in general?"

"Both I guess," he said. Nothing was ever simple with Brenda. She would never just say up front why she was calling.

"No emergencies. But we need to talk."

"What about?" Julian asked, shivering as he reached for his robe. The wind howling outside the windows even *sounded* cold.

"What do you think we need to talk about?"

"If I knew, I wouldn't be asking."

"Is it cold there?"

"Very."

"It's lovely here. I'm calling from poolside. The ocean is as blue as sapphires."

"You wanted to talk about something," he reminded her.

"Well, next Wednesday is the first of February. The waiting period will be over."

"Yes. And the divorce will be final."

"But we have one more week to call it off before it becomes engraved in stone," she pointed out.

"Are you suggesting something?" he asked.

"Would you like me to suggest something?"

"Are you happy?"

"Yes and no. I like being here with my friends and family. My golf game is fabulous. I'm taking lessons from the most wonderful pro, who's taken six strokes off my score. And I'm putting in a cabana by the pool. My tan is great. I'm a perfect size six. And I've had my teeth bonded. Wonderful process. Everyone should do it."

"Everyone doesn't have ten thousand dollars to spend on white teeth," Julian said. "Do you realize it's three in the morning here?" he asked.

"No. I knew it was either later or earlier. So you are in bed?"

"Yes."

"Alone?"

"Yes."

"Come home, Julian. We didn't have a perfect marriage, but it was better than no marriage. I'll do better. If you still want to adopt a child, I would agree to it. I wouldn't be a very good parent, but you'd do a good enough job for both of us."

"Where is this home you want me to come to?" he asked.

"Why here, of course. With me."

"And what would I do in Palm Beach?"

"Whatever you want. I'm sure you could find some sort of work. Or you could become a very good golfer. Work on your tennis game. Or there's always charity. Some of the more serious-minded of my friends are into volunteerism—

like teaching English to the Cubans, looking after the homeless, that sort of thing. A lot of the social functions are benefits. They're very nice, actually. I've gone to several of them. Come on, Julian. You expected me to give the military life a try and I did. I gave better parties than the generals' wives. But even you could tell I wasn't suited for government quarters. And designer dresses didn't go over very well when the other officers' wives had to shop at department stores. Of course, a few of them actually managed a modicum of style on their budgets, but they wore poverty like it was some sort of honor. It was so boring. Anyway, I tried your life, but you've never tried mine. Don't you think that turnabout is fair play?"

"I'd have to get out of the Army to give it a try," he reminded her.

"Would that really be so awful? You wouldn't need your precious pension if you were married to me, Julian. Don't make me beg. I'd really like it if we could try again—my way this time."

Brenda was exactly right. She had tried. And it seemed unfair that he was unwilling to try it her way.

"I'm no jet-setter, Brenda. Without my uniform on, my lack of polish would show. Your friends would see that I'm just a poor farm boy who pulled himself up by the straps of his muddy work boots."

"That's not so, and you know it. I trained you well, Julian, and you polished up nicely. I invested a number of years in you, and now I want the payoff. I don't like the men here. They are shallow and spoiled. Just like me. Can you imagine me marrying one of them?"

Julian laughed. Same old Brenda. Honesty had always been her long suit.

"You were a good balance for me," she continued. "I realize that now."

"It wouldn't work, but I love you for wanting it," he said.

"You sound sad, Julian. You can just as easily be sad with me as sad by yourself. At least we can distract each other. Remember Paris? God, Julian, we were good in Paris. We could go back, you know. Stay in the best hotels. But I'd want to find that same sleazy little restaurant where we sang with the piano player half the night."

"I can't, Brenda."

"You're in love, aren't you?"

"Yes."

"And she's pure and good and wouldn't wear diamonds if she had them."

"I suppose."

"Then why are you sad? God, Julian, you were always kind of sad. Sometimes I wondered if it was a chronic condition with you."

"I'm sad because it didn't work out with her and me. Her kids hate me," he said. "I'm in no shape to enter into a relationship, but that aside, it wouldn't work for us, Brenda. We managed to get out of our marriage with good feelings and nice memories intact. I'd hate to change that. If I came to Florida, I think we'd end up hating each other."

"My therapist told me not to call you. She said I had to learn to live alone and make real friends—as opposed to superficial friends, I suppose. Then if the right man came along, I could marry him because I wanted to be with him and not because I was afraid to be alone."

For a long time after they said goodbye, after meaningless promises to stay in touch, Julian lay with his hands behind his head, staring at the shadows on the ceiling. *Sadness.* He had dragged it around since childhood. Was he one of those people who was destined to watch others enjoy life but never really get plugged into it himself?

But he liked his work. He was a good administrator. He had broad knowledge of health-care delivery. He found satisfaction in a job well done. But he had had few close friends in his life. Maybe none at all. At personal relationships he was a failure.

Brenda had always managed their social life. Julian never had to invite anyone to do anything. Brenda kept conversations going. She programmed him at the beginning of the evening, telling him who was going to be at a function and what the political currents of the group happened to be.

Basically, he was a very shy person. When he was in his administrator's role, he managed just fine. When he was in a group of acquaintances, he was comfortable. He wasn't afraid of flirting and dating. But there was a script of sorts already written for such occasions.

However, when it came to simple friendship outside of the realm of business, marriage or romance, he was at a loss.

Palms sweating with nervousness, the morning after Brenda called, Julian forced himself to invite a bachelor colleague out to dinner. The following week, he enrolled in a duplicate bridge class. And then he joined an investors' club that met weekly at the officers' club.

He stopped refusing hostesses who invited him to their parties. He even took Frieda with him sometimes. Frieda was good for him. With romance no longer an issue, she became his friend and helped him replot his life.

He didn't try to date, but he did try to explore relationships with both men and women at a meaningful level.

And for the first time in his life, he had a best friend of his own sex. Col. Jerry Ferrier was a tall, lean surgeon from Arkansas. A widower with grown children, he was as alone in Heidelberg as Julian.

They started having dinner a couple of evenings a week. They went to movies, played chess and shared their mutual love of good jazz as they cabaret-hopped around the city.

But mostly they talked. Julian discovered it was possible to talk to another man about something other than sports. Jerry said they talked like two women—heart-to-heart. No secrets. Hopes and fears. Sharing.

Julian played matchmaker with Jerry and Frieda, and suddenly they were three. Jerry moved in with Frieda and asked her to marry him daily.

And one cold morning in March, while Julian was shaving in his chilly bathroom, he had a revelation. He was enjoying life. He looked forward to being with people. On this particular morning, he was looking forward to a busy day at work, an evening with his friends and a skiing trip next weekend.

"How about that?" Julian said to the face in the mirror. "You're a whole person. So there, Aunt Rachel! I think I just got over you."

And would he ever get over Sara? Probably not, but in a sense, he didn't want to. He would sort through his memories of her, selecting the best ones and storing them away like precious jewels.

Chapter Thirteen

Bea and Jim closed the cafe for a week to paint and make repairs. Without her usual nine-to-two shift waiting tables, Sara was spending the morning cleaning house, baking cookies and chopping the ingredients for the beef stew that was now simmering on the stove.

She had planned to spend the afternoon at her quilting frame, but leaning over made her back ache. And she had been promising Barry for months she would clean out the upstairs closet, which was still stacked with boxes of Rachel's possessions. And she needed to empty out the cedar chest in the hall.

Now was as good a time as never, Sara told herself as she climbed the stairs to Barry's room.

She designated three categories. Trash. Items to be given to the Salvation Army. And Rachel's personal and family mementos to be stored in the shed in case Julian ever came back to reclaim them.

Julian coming back. What a lovely thought that was!

Of course, Percy Mason said Julian had been quite firm about never wanting to return to Murray and had given the lawyer power of attorney to dispense with Rachel's property.

But having things stored for him made Julian's return seem like more of a possibility.

Rachel's clothing went into the Salvation Army pile. She obviously hadn't bought a new garment in years. Every article of clothing had been meticulously mended—including inexpensive cotton underwear and heavy cotton stockings.

Rachel's jewelry box contained only a few pieces—a couple of old-fashioned rings with modest settings, a nice cameo broach and a pocket watch with the engraved design on the case worn almost smooth. And there was a tiny gold key tied on a red ribbon in the corner of the box.

The jewelry box and its contents went into the "save" pile along with a box of old photographs of stiff, serious-looking people who were surely relatives. One snapshot, Sara decided after close scrutiny, showed Rachel as a young woman. She was standing on the front steps of the old Murray high school building, books tucked under her arm, smiling shyly for the camera—a slim, pretty girl wearing a middy blouse and a bow in her hair.

Sara found a shoe box with all of Julian's report cards and school pictures, arranged in order by year. Such a solemn little boy he was, Sara thought, as she looked at the unsmiling boy growing older in each picture.

There were no other pictures of Julian. Apparently no one ever pointed a camera at little Julian Campbell to record the landmarks of his life. Did he ever have birthday cakes and Christmas presents? Sara wondered. Did Rachel take his picture in his band uniform? If so, it wasn't in the box.

But still, Sara never could match the old woman who lived quietly next door to the Cate farm to the mean-spirited person Julian had described. Rachel certainly wasn't the friendliest person in the world and could be blunt to the point of rudeness. But Barry and Mary Sue got along well enough with her. And surely, the woman had cared for Julian. Why else would she have saved the contents of this shoe box?

The most incredible find of the afternoon came when Sara emptied out the cedar chest. Hiding under the quilts and blankets were a wedding dress and trousseau. The creamy silk wedding dress was of simple design but lovingly decorated with exquisite embroidery.

The collars of a white lawn nightgown and peignoir were edged with delicate crocheted lace.

Hand-hemmed towels and table linens were carefully monogrammed with the initial *R*.

And there were embroidered pillowcases and tea towels. Sara could imagine the young girl in the snapshot making careful stitches while her mind weaved romantic thoughts of a wedding and a home of her own with the man she loved.

Obviously Rachel had prepared for a wedding that never took place.

The last item Sara removed from the cedar chest was an old-fashioned locked diary. But Sara knew exactly where to find the key.

After retrieving the tiny gold key from Rachel's jewelry box, she inserted it in the lock and the book fell open. And there was a passage dated over thirty years ago:

My sister, Clare, writes that she is dying. She wants me to take her son to raise.

But what do I know of seven-year-old boys? And why should I make this sacrifice for a sister who ran off with the first man who came along and left me alone with our widowed father; whereas, I turned my back on love and fulfilled my duty as a daughter. I cooked and cleaned for Papa and worked like a man in the field. I nursed him when he was sick and listened to him rage every time Clare's name was spoken. And never once did he even say thank you. He said more words to the Lord in the blessing before meals than he ever said to me.

Clare had escaped, and I was a prisoner. Why should I do that again?

I don't want to take care of anyone. I can't love this boy. I have invested all my love in nature and this square of red Oklahoma earth. I thrill to hummingbirds at the feeder outside my kitchen window and find joy in sunsets. I love to watch the evening breezes ripple through my fields of ripe wheat and to hear my rooster greeting the sun.

No, I haven't any love in my heart for a child. And I will not take him in. I can't. I hate Clare for asking this of me. She always got her own way. She alone brought a smile to our papa's face.

I will write to her tomorrow. I am sorry for her problem, but she will have to make other arrangements for the boy. Julian is his name. She will have to find another home for Julian.

Clare dying. It's hard to believe. She was the youngest. I wonder if her boy looks like her. Such a sweet face she had—like our mother before the hard work made her old and tired.

Sara was compelled to read on, but a glance at her watch told her it was almost time for the children to come home from school.

She combed her hair and went to the kitchen to put out after-school treats.

This was her favorite time of the day. She sat with the children while they had a glass of milk and cookies or fruit. They showed her their schoolwork, and she questioned them about their day, listening while they shared school gossip, the day's achievements and disappointments. Sometimes, the little after-school ritual only lasted ten or fifteen minutes before ball practices and friends claimed them. But the minutes were special ones for Sara.

Barry was pleased to have the closet to himself and carried the repacked boxes of Rachel's possessions to their respective destinations, putting the Salvation Army items in back of the pickup. Sara would drop them off at the Salvation Army store in Chickasha tomorrow when she and Bea went to buy a car seat for the baby.

That evening, while the children did their homework, Sara sat at the table with them, reading Rachel's diary, occasionally sharing passages with her children. One entry was about an overnight train ride Rachel and her sister and brother took to Wichita with their parents for their grandfather's funeral. They had berths in a sleeping car, but Rachel was too excited to sleep and watched out the window all night as the prairie rolled past.

"Rachel saw Woodrow Wilson in person when he was campaigning in Kansas," Sara said.

The children didn't seem too impressed. They hadn't seen a president in person, but they saw the current one almost every day on television.

Several entries in the diary graphically spelled out the hardships of country women's lives before rural electrification, with laundry, ironing, housework and cooking all requiring inordinate amounts of preparation and back-breaking labor.

Rachel described how her mother's hands were always raw and bleeding from lye soap and wringing out clothes with her bare hands. And her back was stooped from a lifetime of carrying water buckets from the well and bending over washboards and ironing boards.

Rachel wrote:

My mother is only thirty-five years old and already she
looks like a tired old woman. I don't want her life. I
want to go away from here when I grow up and go
someplace where ladies have tea in the afternoon in
china cups.

Her mother died when Rachel was thirteen, and she quit
school to keep house for her father, older brother and
younger sister. Fortunately, in 1939, the long-awaited elec-
trical lines finally came. A pump was installed on the well
and for the first time the house had running water. And her
father bought a washer and an electric iron. Rachel took a
whole page to tell how much better her life was with electricity.

But even with electricity, I do not want to stay here. I
want to have people in my life, but I fear I have lived
apart for so long I could never learn how to carry on
polite conversations with gentle society. What if I was
tongue-tied or broke a teacup? But oh, I long so for
people and conversation. I like to look at ladies' magazines and see how other people live, but Papa said they
fill my head with silly notions. Probably he is right.

After the children went to bed, Sara continued reading the
diary, curled up in bed—Rachel's bed, where she had been
born and died, where her parents had died before her.

And finally, Sara read about a man named Samuel Rob-
bins entering Rachel's life. Samuel was a young pharmacist
who came to town to open a drugstore. For a year, he and
Rachel only saw each other in the store. But one day he put
on his good suit and came courting. By then it was just Ra-

chel and her father at home, Fred Warren's stern ways and harsh temper having driven away his other two children.

Rachel's father did not approve of Samuel or his family, who were of a different faith. She and Samuel continued to see each other in secret, but when it came to marriage, Rachel could not bring herself to go against her father's wishes.

More than anything, I want to go from this loveless house and live with my beloved. But who would keep house for Papa if I leave? Who would can the produce from the garden? Who will care for him when he is old and ill? Papa has never cooked a meal or ironed a shirt in his life.

Why did my mother have to die? Husbands should always die before wives so that daughters are not faced with this dilemma. Wives can live on by themselves. Husbands cannot.

Mama would have liked Samuel. She could have helped me prepare for my wedding day. She would have been so proud of the beautiful dress I made.

When her father had a stroke, Rachel felt as though her fate was sealed.

Samuel died in France during World War II, and Rachel vowed that someday she would go there and find his grave. Sara wondered if Rachel ever had. Probably not. But she must have loved him very much to want to make such a gesture. And been full of regret.

Rachel took care of her invalid father until he died. The year following his death, seven-year-old Julian was sent to her by her dying sister.

Free of her crotchety father, Rachel had looked forward to some peaceful years with only her animals. After much soul-searching, however, she honored her sister's dying wish and gave her permission to send the boy.

Rachel resented Julian's intrusion on her solitude and hadn't the faintest idea how to raise a child. She found herself resorting to her father's stern methods.

As time went by, Rachel developed some affection for the quiet little boy, but never could bring herself to express her feelings for him. Love brought pain. And Rachel would rather live a life devoid of emotion than suffer any more pain.

But the day Julian ran away, she made her last entry in the diary. "Twice, I refused to listen to my heart. Now my life is over," she wrote.

...*listen to my heart.* The words haunted Sara. Her heart had told her with every beat that she was in love with Julian. Yet, like Rachel, she let others convince her not to heed its message.

BEA HAD ALWAYS understood that the nature of gossip depended on the teller. Any interpretation one wanted could be put on the facts. So, when she had a vested interest in how gossip came down, she did the telling herself.

Sara's pregnancy had come as a shock to her. A terrible shock. She was angry and hurt. She felt that Sara had somehow betrayed Ben's memory—and put the whole Cate family in a very awkward position. And Bea certainly didn't want Julian Campbell's baby in her world.

But as the reality of the situation set in, Bea knew that, like it or not, the baby was going to put in an appearance in Murray, Oklahoma, and Sara and that baby and the whole Cate family would be the stuff of town gossip for years to come. The only question was—what sort of gossip? Sordid or romantic? Sordid was untenable. Therefore, it was necessary to present Sara's story in the best possible light—and to do so before people had a chance to form opinions of their own.

Bea announced the pregnancy to her church circle long before Sara had begun to show. And since it wouldn't take a genius to figure out who the father was, Bea announced that, too.

She reminded them that Julian Campbell came from nothing and was raised by a difficult old woman who hadn't had the foggiest notion about how to care for a boy. But that boy had pulled himself up by the bootstraps and was now a respected Army officer with a chestful of medals who would surely be a general someday. Bea explained that Julian and Sara had fallen instantly and deeply in love and planned to marry. But at the last minute, Sara realized she couldn't take her children away from the town and the grandparents they loved so much. Sara knew that, in Murray, Barry and Mary Sue would always be known as Ben Cate's children and would continue to feel that their dead father was a part of their lives.

Such a sacrifice Sara had made—giving up the man she loved for the sake of her children! And now she was faced with bearing this man's baby alone!

Bea paused at this point in her story for dramatic effect, waiting for the question she knew would come.

"You mean Julian doesn't know?" the ladies asked incredulously.

"No, Sara thinks it's better this way," Bea explained, her tone almost reverent. "She thinks it will be easier for Julian to put his life back together and find someone else to love if he's not tied to Murray and the past."

By the time Bea had finished the saga of Sara's love child, the circle ladies considered Sara a romantic heroine making a noble sacrifice in the name of love. And that was the story they carried throughout the community—just as Bea intended.

The results of Bea's campaign amazed Sara. When she waited tables at the cafe, people asked without innuendo how she was feeling and when her baby was due. Did she want a boy or a girl? One woman suggested she name the child Rachel if it was a girl. Customers even sympathized publicly with her decision not to tell Julian. It was better that way, they would say, sagely nodding their heads.

Thanks to Bea, Sara could hold her head up. She could ease her growing body into maternity clothes without fearing the consequences. Her children were saved untold embarrassment.

The whole town took a special interest in Sara and her pregnancy. Brother Carmichael—at Bea's suggestion—based a sermon on the Biblical admonition: "He that is without sin among you, let him cast the first stone." The Home Demonstration Club quilting section began a quilt for Sara's baby. Bob Barnhart, the best mechanic in town, offered to tune up Rachel's old truck—for free. And several men from the volunteer fire department spent one whole Saturday finishing the porches on Sara's house.

Percy Mason promised Sara that her pregnancy was the town's secret, and he would not reveal it in any correspondence to Julian.

"Where is he?" Sara asked, as she sliced a generous wedge of Bea's apple pie for the portly attorney. "Is he well?"

"His current address is an APO number out of New York," Mason explained. "And our dealings have been strictly of a legal nature. I don't know anything about his health or state of mind. Would you like the address?"

"No. And thank you for agreeing not to tell him about this," Sara said, patting her pregnant belly. "I don't want him thinking he has to come back here and marry me. And even though I tried to convince him to quit the Army and live in Murray, I realize now there wouldn't be anything for him here. Our little town is hardly the seat of prosperity these days. There's no opportunity here for administrators of any kind."

"Are you sure you made the right decision in staying here yourself?" Mason asked.

"Is one ever sure? Bea says all you can do is what seems right at the time and hope for the best."

SARA PULLED UP in front of the church community hall. "Why don't you run in with Grandma's glasses, honey," Sara told her daughter. "I'll just wait out here."

Mary Sue picked up the glasses case from the seat. "But Grandma wants you to come in. She needs to ask you something."

"Ask me something? She didn't say anything about that on the phone. She just wanted her reading glasses."

"She called back when you were in the bathroom," Mary Sue said. "She said it was real important that you come in."

With a sigh, Sara opened the door and extracted her heavy body from the cab of the elderly pickup. Thanks to Bob Barnhart, the truck was running well, but it was a rather disreputable-looking vehicle that a good cleaning and waxing didn't help much. But Sara liked having her own vehicle once again and not always having to depend on borrowing Jim's truck or Bea's car.

"You waddle when you walk," Mary Sue commented, following her mother up the drive.

"You haven't seen anything yet," Sara said. "Wait until next month."

"Did you look like that before I was born?" Mary Sue asked.

"Believe it or not, I was bigger. I've had a hard time gaining weight with this baby, and the doctor said he doesn't think it's going to be very big."

Sara pushed open the door of the community hall and was immediately greeted by calls of "surprise" from an assembled group of women.

Sara stopped in her tracks. And looked around the room, which was decorated with pink and blue crepe-paper streamers. A cardboard stork stood in the center of a table laden with gift-wrapped boxes. On a second table was a bowl of punch and a huge sheet cake decorated with pink and blue flowers.

Mary Sue was gleefully jumping up and down beside her. "She didn't want to come in, Grandma. I had to tell her you wanted to ask her something."

Sara was so shocked, she started to shake. And cry. *A baby shower.* For the town's Scarlet Woman. And so many women. Not just the ladies of church. Every woman in town and a couple from Chickasha were beaming at her.

She felt Bea's arms around her and put her head against her mother-in-law's plump shoulder. This was all Bea's doing—of that, Sara had no doubt. Of course, in typical Bea fashion, the other ladies would think it was their idea.

"I don't know how to thank you all," Sara said when her composure returned. "This is a mighty lucky baby, having the chance to grow up in a place like this. And I know you will all be as kind to him or her as you have been to me and my children."

Mary Payne, from the dry cleaners, made the cake, Bea told Sara. Martha from the cafe made the punch. Millie Renfrow, who had taught both Mary Sue and Barry in the fifth grade and also their father before them, was responsible for the table decorations.

Mrs. Carmichael, the minister's wife, presided at the tea table. Annabelle Mason, the attorney's wife, supervised the gift opening, recording each gift in the guest book.

Sara couldn't stop crying. Each gift set her off again. Her baby would have a real layette—not just hand-me-downs.

"You all are so kind," she kept saying over and over again, blowing her nose. Someone had found a box of tissues for her, and she was rapidly going through the whole box.

Bea's gift was a beautiful gown and robe for Sara to wear in the hospital. That made Sara cry, too.

On the way home, she continued crying. "I guess I'm just so happy," she explained to her daughter.

Mary Sue helped her fold the tiny garments and soft blankets and carefully put them in the drawer Sara had set aside as the "baby's drawer."

When everything was all arranged, Sara stared in the open drawer, and the tears began again. *Stop this,* she told herself. She was worrying her daughter. And the tears were for no reason. Everything was fine. She had nothing to cry about. True, those women had been nice to her. But she'd cried enough over that.

But a dam seemed to have been broken, and tears kept spilling over.

"Are you sick, Mom?" Mary Sue asked.

"A little, I guess. My allergies must be acting up. Go ask your brother if he'll put up that crib now. Now that we have a layette, I'd like the crib in here, too."

Barry obliged, putting together the crib that Nancy Payne had loaned to Sara some months ago, along with some very used maternity and baby clothes.

Mary Sue washed the assembled crib with soap and water, then rubbed the wood with furniture polish. She selected a yellow crib sheet and a yellow crocheted blanket from the shower gifts. And added a couple of her own stuffed animals for a finishing touch.

Bea called, seemingly for no reason, but really to mention that she was cooking at home for a change and had a bigger roast in the oven than she and Jim could ever eat.

"Do you want us to come over?" Sara asked.

"Only if you want to, honey. Only if you don't have plans and aren't too tired. But I thought if you hadn't cooked anything yet...well, you know me, I always cook too much."

"How about if the kids come without me? My back is killing me," she told Bea. "I think I'll eat a can of soup and go to bed early."

"How late can the children stay?" Bea asked, as she always did now. "Jim would like Barry to watch a basketball game on television with him. Mary Sue and I could put together a jigsaw puzzle."

"If they have their homework finished, they can stay until the basketball game is over."

Sara was relieved to see the children leave. She was trying to decide on tomato or chicken noodle soup when Jim appeared at the door with a plate of hot food.

"And here's a heating pad Bea sent over for your back," Jim said. "She said to stay off your feet tomorrow. She'll fill in for you at the cafe."

Sara opened a can of soup anyway and put the roast and potatoes in the refrigerator.

Sitting at the table with a bowl of tomato soup in front of her, the damned tears started again. She tried a few tentative spoonfuls of the soup. She was just tired and hungry, she told herself. The day had been an emotional one.

Billy, the three-legged dog, kept whining at the door. "Go away, Billy," Sara called. Sara had been fighting a losing battle to keep him and his fleas outside, but the children, like

Rachel before them, seemed to think his missing leg gave the animal special privileges.

Finally, Sara could ignore the whining no longer and let the dog in. He sat beside her and seemed content to watch her eat. "Do you miss Rachel?" she asked the homely animal. "You must have been her buddy if she let you in. I'll bet you slept by her bed at night and kept her from feeling lonely."

She managed half a bowl of soup and a couple of crackers, then—with Billy following—went into her bedroom to stare once again at the crib and the contents of the baby's drawer, which brought on more tears. Why all this crying now? Sara wondered. She'd hardly shed a single tear through the entire pregnancy. She had endured morning sickness, swollen feet, an aching back and chronic loneliness. But the shock of the baby shower shattered her carefully constructed composure, and all those unshed tears came pouring out in the course of one evening.

It shouldn't be like this, Sara thought. *I don't want to have a baby alone. I don't want to raise it alone. Pregnancy and babies are supposed to be shared.*

She took a hot bath and curled into bed with Bea's heating pad. The warmth was soothing against her aching back. She'd feel much better in the morning, she assured herself as she turned her attention to the book of suggested names for babies. Thousands of names. How could she possibly decide?

She dozed for a time, then awoke abruptly from a dream she couldn't quite remember. Something about Ben. Yes, Ben had been allowed to come back to life long enough to take her to the hospital and be with her when the baby was born.

Ben. He often came to life in her dreams. Sometimes he and her mother both were there, mixed in with the living people who made guest appearances in her dreams.

Ben had been the only man she'd ever loved until Julian came along. Now she had both men wandering through her dreams.

But Julian was alive. Julian was the one she ached for every waking moment.

Sara turned over and was startled by the unaccustomed baby bed standing in the shadowed corner of the room.

Soon. All was in readiness. Sara cradled her belly protectively until she felt some fluttering movement. *Her baby. Her and Julian's baby.* Then it was more than tears. She sobbed so hard her shoulders and neck hurt.

Suddenly her children were there at her side, awkwardly trying to comfort her. "It's okay," Sara kept telling them. "I'm really all right. Pregnant women just act weird sometimes."

"Do you want us to call Grandma?" Barry asked. "I told her you'd been acting funny, and she said we were to check on you when we got home and call her if you needed her."

"No. Really, kids. I'm fine."

"You miss Julian Campbell, don't you?" Mary Sue asked, her face grave.

Sara didn't even try to answer. Instead, she clung to her children, taking comfort in the solid reality of them, in their dear faces and healthy bodies.

AND FINALLY it was May.

Not only was the baby due the last week of May, but the month would be a full one with end-of-school activities and the beginning of summer ball practice and weekend rodeos.

Sara tried to find joy when Mary Sue was named class favorite. And when Barry won a trophy for calf roping. After all, this was the life she wanted for them. They were following in their father's footsteps and on their way to becoming hometown heroes.

"For the border, you can crochet these little shells," Sara explained to her daughter, demonstrating how to put the finishing touches on the afghan Mary Sue had made her grandmother for Mother's Day.

Chapter Fourteen

"For the border, you can crochet these little shells," Sara explained to her daughter, demonstrating how to put the finishing touches on the afghan Mary Sue had made her grandmother for Mother's Day.

Mother's Day. Almost a year since Julian had come to dinner and touched her heart.

After getting Mary Sue started on the afghan border, Sara proofread the theme Barry had written for his English class on how he planned to spend his summer vacation. Rodeo and baseball took up most of his theme. But the last paragraph explained that his mother was having a baby, and he planned to help out with the baby and housework. "At first, I didn't want my mom to have this baby," he wrote. "But now that it's almost time for it to be born, I think about it a lot. The baby isn't going to have a father, so it's really going to need a big brother. And I want to be a good big brother."

Sara felt a rush of pride. Her son was growing up to be a fine young man.

He'd apparently done a lot of growing up those four days he was locked in the boxcar. Now, he voluntarily helped his sister with her math. He fussed after his mother to stay off her feet and drink lots of milk. And he took a great deal of pride in the tender green sprouts of wheat that were coming up in the field he had plowed and planted.

She handed Barry's paper to Jim to read. Bea was at a meeting of the church deacons, and Jim had come over to pass the evening with them. As soon as Barry finished his homework, he and his grandfather were going over the junior rodeo circuit schedule and plan Barry's summer season. Jim was encouraging him to try some of the Texas rodeos this summer, and show the folks in Dallas and Lubbock just how well an Oklahoma boy can rope.

Jim read the theme and nodded his approval. "That's good writing, Barry. And that's a right pretty afghan you're making there," Jim told his granddaughter. "Your grandma's going to be mighty proud."

"Did you give your mother and grandmothers presents on Mother's Day?" Mary Sue asked.

"I always made them a card, and I'd buy my mom some little present at the dime store. Money was scarce, so I never could buy her anything nice. But one year, when your daddy was just a baby, I had a bumper wheat crop and bought my mom a string of real pearls. I'll never forget the look on her face when she opened that box. She had never had anything so fine in her whole life. Of course, the only time she ever wore them was for church and funerals—with those same old dresses. I tried to buy her some new dresses, but she wouldn't hear of it. She said the pearls made her feel grand enough—that I should spend my money on my Bea and Ben."

Jim stopped to take out his handkerchief and blow his nose. "I'll tell you, that woman was a saint. She never wanted anything for herself and was always there for her children and husband. She was like a Madonna on a pedestal."

"A pedestal is an awfully small place, Jim," Sara said. "There's not much room to stretch and grow, is there?"

"But that's all she ever wanted," Jim insisted.

"Maybe so," Sara said. "But how do you know? Maybe she wanted to travel or learn to tap dance or paint pictures. Maybe she wanted to have a meal in a restaurant once in a while instead of cooking three meals a day for a lifetime. Maybe she wanted a new dress more than anything but just said that she didn't because that's what you expected her to say. Women of her generation were raised not to expect much out of life. I want more. And I want more for Mary Sue."

"More what?" Jim asked, puzzled.

"More say in my life than your mother had—and more than I had in my marriage with Ben," Sara said carefully, very aware that her children were listening. "I wanted a home for my children and knew one of those animals was going to hurt him someday, but I let him make the decisions about how we lived our lives. Maybe if I'd spoken up more, he wouldn't have been crippled. Maybe if he hadn't had a bad leg, he could have jumped off that tractor in time. If I ever marry again, I want to be an equal partner in my marriage—like you and Bea. You two have a good marriage, but you'd never accuse Bea of being a saint on a pedestal or of never wanting anything for herself. Admit it, Jim, you'd be bored to death with a saint."

Jim wasn't sure he wanted to make any such admission and turned his attention back to the rodeo schedule.

Bea stopped by on her way home for a cup of coffee and to fetch her husband. She was full of plans for Vacation Bible School and wanted Mary Sue to be her assistant teacher in a class for three-year-olds.

"What's that you're reading, honey?" Bea asked Sara as she sat down next to her on the sofa.

"A catalog from Oklahoma City Community College," Sara said.

"You're not really going to leave Murray, are you?" Jim asked.

"Not for a year or so," Sara said. "But yes. Somehow, I'm going to get an education."

"I can't believe you'd really take these children away from the best home they've ever had," Bea said. "I wish to God that trouble-making Julie Campbell had never come back here."

"His name is *Julian*. And I thank God that he did," Sara said. "Without Julian, I never would have understood that mothers have the right to consider their own needs and ambitions when they are deciding what is right for their family. I know now that being a good mother sometimes means making decisions that are unpopular with children but are ultimately in everyone's best interest."

WHILE BEA WAS TAKING a bath, Jim indulged himself in a piece of apple pie and a glass of milk. Bea may not be a saint, but she made pie good enough to be served in heaven.

As usual, they watched the evening news propped up in bed. Bea had insisted they get a television with a remote control, which Jim thought was a ridiculous extravagance, but he loved sitting in bed, switching back and forth from one newscast to the other, seeing who was saying what about whom, comparing the weather forecasts.

He usually dozed off about half way through the "Tonight Show." They didn't make love as much as they used to, but they always embraced and kissed. He still needed to feel her close to him when he slept.

He was just about asleep when he heard her say in the darkness, "Sara's right, you know."

"'Bout what?" he asked sleepily.

"Mothers have the right to consider their own needs along with their children's. Sara is being buried alive here in Murray, and we're the ones throwing in the dirt. Barry ran away because we came between him and his mother. And that's not right."

Jim offered no comment. He had always held his mother up as the ideal—even more so than his beloved Bea, who took care of her family but had certainly managed to have other interests as well. Sara had been more selfless—like his own mother. And now, Sara implied that his mother had been some sort of victim, with no life or wants of her own. And that just wasn't so, Jim thought angrily.

Or was it?

His mother had talked for years about taking a trip to Georgia. Her parents were from Georgia, but she'd been born in Murray and never been anyplace farther away than Oklahoma City. She wanted to see *Gone-with-the-Wind* country, as she called it. She wanted to see the antebellum mansions of the Old South and smell the magnolia blossoms.

But no one ever paid any attention to her.

Jim remembered finding that worn-out copy of *Gone with the Wind* among her things after she died. Her sister had bought it for her as a birthday present when it first came out. And his mother had read it over and over until it fell apart and she held it together with a rubber band.

Other memories came flooding back. His father hadn't been rich, but they did better than most. But his mother didn't have an electric fan to cool her overheated kitchen. She wore the same tired black hat to church for as long as he could remember. And she never saw the mansions in Georgia.

And why was that?

Because she didn't think she had the right to want anything just for herself, Jim thought, realizing the truth of Sara's words.

He rolled over and embraced his wife. "I think I just fell in love with you all over again, honey. You're quite a woman, you know."

"Of course I am. You wouldn't have married me otherwise," Bea said, returning her husband's embrace. "And you're the dearest, most generous man on the face of the earth. That's why I know you're going to get Julian back here for our Sara."

"You're not serious!"

"As serious as a Baptist sermon."

"But Sara's changed over the past months," he protested. "If Julian came back, she'd probably leave with him and take the children with her."

"We've been awfully selfish—trying to keep her and those kids here with us, making her think she'd be a bad mother if she left. We had no right to do that, Jim. I think in your heart you know that."

"But I can't imagine life without those children," he confessed.

"We would lose them eventually anyway. Children grow up and move away. What did we think would happen then— that we'd just install a third recliner in front of the television in the living room for Sara and turn her into an old woman before her time? And it's a sad testimonial on our marriage that we have to have others around to make us happy. We started out with just the two of us, and it wasn't so bad. As I recall, we had ourselves a right good time.''

"The best," Jim acknowledged.

"Maybe we could go two-stepping again," Bea said. "We could buy that empty space next to the B & J and add a banquet room. Try some new menus. Buy one of those motor homes and try out some new fishing holes. For years, we've been saving for our old age. Well, I think it's here. Maybe we should start spending some of that money.''

"Like on a trip to Germany?"

"Well, folks ought not to live and die without ever settin' foot outside the country," Bea said firmly.

"We went to Juarez, Mexico, back in '77," Jim teased. "Spent the whole afternoon there as I recall.''

"Find Julian," Bea said. "We can have the wedding here in the living room and a reception at the cafe.''

"And how long do I have to accomplish this miracle?"

"The kids and I have been talking about it. Actually it was their idea. They said that Sara sighs a lot. And she forgets to eat. Sometimes she forgets to finish sentences and just looks off in the distance. They're worried about her and thought Julian would be the best Mother's Day present they could give her. But they need our help," Bea said, then began to cry. "God, I'm going to miss our babies. I wish things didn't have to change. But Julian is a good man. Our babies will be with a good man.''

Jim called his congressman the next day. The congressman called the Pentagon. An official at the Pentagon got in touch with Julian. Two days after Bea gave her instructions to Jim, Julian was talking to her on the telephone.

"Can you get some time off?" Bea asked.

"Yes, I've got leave time coming. But what if Sara doesn't want me to come back?" he asked.

"Oh, she wants you all right," Bea said. "Just hurry up and get here." Bea had to bite her tongue not to tell him about the baby. But Sara needed to know that he came back out of love and not out of duty, that he came back because of her and not because she was pregnant.

And Bea wanted to see the look on Julian's face when he saw Sara in all her pregnant glory. Just thinking about it made her cry. Making things right felt better than she thought it would.

Just her and Jim. It was a scary thought.

But kind of exciting.

She wondered if she was too fat for two-stepping.

AFTER CHURCH on Mother's Day, Bea insisted on taking Sara shopping in Lawton. "Jim and the kids want us out of the way while they wrap packages and get ready for tonight," she explained. "I understand the kids are going to cook the dinner all by themselves just to show their mother how helpful they can be."

Sunday afternoon was a busy time at the Lawton shopping mall. People were pouring out of the restaurants after their Mother's Day dinner. A Little Miss Comanche County contest was being conducted on a stage in the center of the mall. An antique car club was exhibiting their cars throughout the mall. And the stores were full of shoppers taking advantage of a special mallwide Mother's Day sale.

Bea bought some towels at Sears. And a cookbook featuring low-calorie, low-fat recipes.

"I thought I'd introduce healthy eating to Murray," she explained. "And try to lose a few pounds myself. Jim says he likes me plump, but I'd like to bring a gleam to his eyes again before we're too old to do anything about it."

They window-shopped a while, until Sara realized Bea was maneuvering her into the drop-in beauty salon, which was also doing a brisk Sunday-afternoon business. "Next thing you know folks'll be going to the dentist on Sunday," Bea observed.

"Why are we going in here?" Sara asked.

"When you trim your own hair, it looks like you've been trimming your own hair," Bea said. "You'll want to look nice at the hospital."

"Bea, this baby is going to like me no matter what I look like."

"Indulge me, dear. It's my Mother's Day gift to you."

"I'm not your mother."

"Well, they don't have a daughter-in-law day yet. Come on, Sara. Jim's going to take everyone's picture when we get home. I want you to look pretty. I think I'll get mine cut, too. Something more youthful."

Bea ended up with very short hair that curled softly all over her head and made her look thinner and rather chic. "Not bad for an old farm woman," she said admiring herself in the mirror.

And Sara had to admit that after a shampoo, haircut and blow dry, her own short hair also looked better.

Bea agreed. "If you just had a little makeup on, you'd look halfway presentable," she announced.

"I have makeup on," Sara protested.

"Can't hardly tell it. You need a brighter lipstick and more blush on your cheeks. Come on, they're doing makeovers in Dillard's cosmetics department. You have an appointment."

"I have an appointment! Bea, they'll expect you to buy something. What little makeup I use, I buy at Wal-Mart. You know that."

"Then I'll buy you a lipstick," Bea said firmly.

And Sara found herself being half-dragged to Dillard's and none too gently shoved onto a high pink stool with a pink-smocked woman hovering nearby, waiting to work her magic.

"Not too heavy," Bea instructed the woman. "I want her to look pretty, but not so different she'll just wipe it off before we get home. And when you finish with her, I want a few pointers myself."

Over Sara's protests, Bea kept telling the saleslady she wanted to buy the various items she was using on Sara.

"But why?" Sara asked. "I sure don't need makeup in the delivery room."

"You do when you come out. There's no call for you to turn into a drab old peahen just 'cause you're nesting."

"There now," Bea said, when Sara's makeup was complete, "don't you look better?"

"Yes," Sara agreed. "Tired, but better. Can we go home now?"

"Not until this pretty young lady shows me how to perk up this old face."

Sara watched while the cosmetologist gave Bea pointers on using foundation and blush. She suggested just a touch of mascara and selected a pale peach lipstick for Bea's lips.

"Why, Bea, you look ravishing. Jim will want to drag you off to the boudoir when he sees you," Sara teased.

"Lordy, I hope so."

"Well, are we ready to go now?" Sara asked hopefully.

Bea glanced at her watch. "After I buy some coffee for Jim. He likes that special stuff from the gourmet store."

"Since when?" Sara demanded, rubbing her back. "I've seen that man use three-day-old grounds to brew a new pot."

Bea sniffed at least a half dozen coffee blends before making her selection.

And finally, they were on their way. Exhausted, Sara dozed on the way home.

The house was dark when they pulled in the driveway. "I wonder what those three are up to," Bea said.

When Sara opened the front door, the lights went on. Jim, Mary Sue and Barry were standing in the entry hall, grinning like three Cheshire cats. "Happy Mother's Day," they called out.

"You want your present first?" Mary Sue asked. She was wearing her best Sunday school dress.

"We always have presents after dinner," Sara replied.

"Not this Mother's Day," Bea informed her. "Open the door, Sara, and see what's—or should I say who's—in the living room."

Who. Sara looked from one grinning face to the other.

Her heart began to pound.

No, it couldn't be!

But suddenly Sara knew why she had a new haircut and a freshly made up face, why everyone was grinning at her like this. She threw open the door.

Julian was standing in the middle of the room, tall and elegant in his uniform, the wide grin on his face changing immediately to stunned surprise at the sight of Sara's pregnant body.

With all the grace she could muster, Sara threw her bulging body in his arms.

"My God, Sara, you're..."

"Pregnant," she finished for him. "But it's all right to kiss me. I won't break."

He kissed her mouth, her throat, her hair, her neck. He was crying now. "Oh God, Sara, I've missed you so. Wanted you so. God, a baby. I didn't know. A baby."

"You mean they didn't tell you? You really didn't know? You're not back here because of it?"

He shook his head in disbelief. "I didn't know. Why didn't *you* tell me?"

"I didn't want to force you into a decision that you didn't want to make."

"Would you have told me eventually that I was a father?"

"I don't know. I was feeling mighty prideful for a long time. You didn't want me enough to take a job pumping gas in Murray and put up with two kids who didn't want you around. And I thought that being a good mother meant never acting on my own needs and desires. But apparently, everyone has done a little growing up in the past year."

"Barry and Mary Sue tell me they are willing to give Army life their best shot. But they both would like to spend summers in Murray, and Barry would like to come back here his senior year. Is that agreeable with you?"

Sara nodded.

"Mary Sue and Barry, come here please," Julian said.

Then with Sara and her children facing him, Julian made his formal request. "Mary Sue, Barry and Sara Cate, would you do me the honor of sharing my home and my life? And Sara, would you do me the honor of becoming my wife?"

Sara couldn't speak, only nod.

And all through dinner, she could hardly speak and only nibbled at a few bites. She was overwhelmed with happiness, with the sight of him, the feel of him, the sight of her children working so hard to make Julian feel comfortable and wanted.

"My goodness, you younguns cooked a fine dinner," Bea said. "I'm as full as a tick. And now, I want to see what's inside those packages."

Bea loved her afghan. Mary Sue had made an identical one for her mother. "You thought I was crocheting on the same one all that time, didn't you?" she teased her mother.

Barry had made both his grandmother and mother footstools in his woodworking class.

And there was one more tiny box. For Sara. Inside was an engagement ring—a large pearl surrounded by diamonds. An elegant ring. Sara couldn't help it. She just had to cry.

"That's an awfully beautiful ring for such a short engagement," she said, sniffling. "You are going to marry me soon, aren't you?" she asked, patting her belly.

"As soon as we can get a license."

The children were spending the night with their grandparents and stood with them on the front porch, waving as Julian and Sara climbed in the old truck for the short drive home.

As they pulled up to the house, Sara was suddenly overcome with shyness. "I'm too far along to make love," she managed to say in the darkness of the cab.

"I figured as much. But I can honestly say that I don't mind a bit. It will be an honor just to hold you—both."

Later, in bed, he reverently lifted her nightgown and kissed her pregnant stomach. "I love you, baby," he said. "And I love your mother—more than life itself."

The next morning, Sara showed Julian his aunt's diary. "Rachel loved you after all," Sara said. "She just didn't know how to tell you. When I read her sad words, I knew what a mistake I had made. I hadn't listened to my heart."

"I can't tell you how much this means to me," Julian said after he'd read the diary. "But I'm sorry I didn't come back here and try to make things right with her before she died."

"I think she left this diary for you to read, Julian. She was an old woman. She knew the farm would pass to you. If she didn't want you to find it, she would have burned it long ago. This was her way of getting you two together again."

Bea insisted on cooking one of her huge country breakfasts, although she herself only ate a piece of toast. "Today's the first day of my diet," she announced. "Next Mother's Day, I want to go dancing."

Barry and Mary Sue ate in a rush and hurried off to school. The adults lingered over a second cup of coffee, as Julian explained to Bea and Jim that he and Sara had worked out a compromise. After he completed twenty years of service Julian was going to retire from the Army and find a civilian hospital job in either Oklahoma City or Dallas.

"We both think it's important for the children to be with their grandparents as much as possible. And we hope that you will feel the new baby is your grandchild, too. He or she is going to need grandparents, and you seem to be the only ones around."

"And the baby can call us 'Grandma' and 'Grandpa'?" Bea asked.

"If that's what you want," Julian said.

"Oh yes, that's what we want," Jim said.

Bea nodded as she dabbed her eyes with the corner of her apron.

As Sara sat there, surrounded by the people she loved the most, she knew how hard it was going to be for her and her children to say goodbye to Bea and Jim. Before she met Julian, Sara would have done everything possible to spare

Barry and Mary Sue tears. But she understood now that smiles have little meaning without an occasional tear for measure.

With only the family present, Brother Carmichael married Sara and Julian the next day in front of the fireplace in Bea and Jim's living room.

But the whole town crowded into the B & J for the reception. The ladies of the church circle brought in an enormous amount of food. And after the meal was cleared away, the men pushed back the tables for some old-fashioned fiddling and two-stepping.

Sara clapped her hands while Mary Sue showed Julian the steps. Barry came to sit beside her. She took his arm and put her head on his shoulder.

"I'm in labor, son. We're going to have a baby tonight."

Barry put an arm around her shoulders and pulled her close. "Know what, Mom? That little kid is the luckiest baby in the world to have you for a mother."

HARLEQUIN
American Romance®

ABOUT THE AUTHOR

Anne Henry had this to say about motherhood:

If I weren't a mother, I'd have a better figure, a cleaner house and more time and money to do the things I want to do. And I probably wouldn't have these worry lines between my eyes.

But would I be a happier person?

No way.

Most of the true joy I have experienced in my life has come from my children. And, yes, a lot of the pain, too. But if I didn't have children I would be living a careful sort of life with few surprises. I would be fussy about schedules and cleanliness. I wouldn't know how it felt to care more about others than I do myself. I wouldn't know the sort of love that makes one vulnerable and fearful but oh so rich.

When my children were little, I used to worry that I wouldn't love them as much when they were grown, when I no longer could nuzzle tender little necks and kiss plump little toes. And I do miss the physical part of mothering. But I feel just as much love now as then. I also feel admiration and pride for the fine people my children have become. Hands down, they are the best part of my life.

AHCOR

Harlequin®

JANELLE TAYLOR

Valley of Fire

HARLEQUIN IS PROUD TO PRESENT *VALLEY OF FIRE* BY JANELLE TAYLOR—AUTHOR OF TWENTY-TWO BOOKS, INCLUDING SIX *NEW YORK TIMES* BESTSELLERS

VALLEY OF FIRE—the warm and passionate story of Kathy Alexander, a famous romance author, and Steven Winngate, entrepreneur and owner of the magazine that intended to expose the real Kathy "Brandy" Alexander to her fans.

Don't miss VALLEY OF FIRE, available in May.

HARLEQUIN
American Romance®

Be a part of American Romance's year-long celebration of love and the holidays of 1992. Celebrate those special times each month with your favorite authors.

Next month, we pay tribute to the *first* man in your life—your father—with a special Father's Day romance:

JUNE

S	M	T				S
	1					
7	8					13
14						20
21	22					27
28	29					

FATHER'S DAY

**#441
DADDY'S GIRL
by Barbara Bretton**

Read all the books in *A Calendar of Romance*, coming to you one per month all year, only in American Romance.

Take 4 bestselling love stories FREE

Plus get a FREE surprise gift!

HARLEQUIN

American Romance®

COMING NEXT MONTH

#441 DADDY'S GIRL by Barbara Bretton

Hunter Phillips used to have a happening career and more female company than he could handle, but when he inherited an eight-month-old niece, the carousing Hunter became a walking zombie.... Until he met Jeannie Ross. Hunter knew she'd make a great lover... or was that "mother"?
Don't miss this Calendar of Romance Father's Day book.

#442 CODY'S LAST STAND by Kathy Clark

He had the wildness of the prairie in his eyes, the gentleness of a lover in his lips. Descended from Sitting Bull, John Cody was as ferociously proud of his Indian heritage as Elizabeth Lawrence was of her ancestor, George Custer. A hundred years after the most famous battle of the West, was there any hope that the descendants of two bitter enemies could at last make peace?

#443 THIS OLD HOUSE by Linda Randall Wisdom

Dev Grant and Megan Abernathy wed in a fever of passion . . . then divorced in a fit of fury. Nothing could bring them together again—except for an inherited house with a scandalous history. Seeing each other flamed the fires of temptation again, and when they were banked, neither Dev nor Meg could guess how the reunion would end.

#444 SILVER WAVES by Vella Munn

Was Joseph Cox trying to play Cupid from beyond the grave? As father figure to Kara Hunter he had been the soul of paternal love—but not for his estranged son Dan. In spite of Joseph's attempt to bring them together, Dan and Kara found they had nothing in common . . . except a powerful attraction. But was it strong enough to withstand the truth about Dan's family secret?

FREE GIFT OFFER

To receive your free gift, send us the specified number of proofs-of-purchase from any specially marked Free Gift Offer Harlequin or Silhouette book with the Free Gift Certificate properly completed, plus a check or money order (do not send cash) to cover postage and handling payable to Harlequin/Silhouette Free Gift Promotion Offer. We will send you the specified gift.

FREE GIFT CERTIFICATE

ITEM	A. GOLD TONE EARRINGS	B. GOLD TONE BRACELET	C. GOLD TONE NECKLACE
# of proofs-of-purchase required	3	6	9
Postage and Handling	$2.25	$2.75	$3.25
Check one	☐	☐	☐

Name: _____

Address: _____

City: _____ Province: _____ Postal Code: _____

Mail this certificate, specified number of proofs-of-purchase and a check or money order for postage and handling to: HARLEQUIN/SILHOUETTE FREE GIFT OFFER 1992, P.O. Box 622, Fort Erie, Ontario L2A 5X3. Requests must be received by July 31, 1992.

PLUS—Every time you submit a completed certificate with the correct number of proofs-of-purchase, you are automatically entered in our MILLION DOLLAR SWEEPSTAKES! No purchase or obligation necessary to enter. See below for alternate means of entry and how to obtain complete sweepstakes rules.

✂ HA2C

ONE PROOF-OF-PURCHASE
To collect your fabulous FREE GIFT you must include the necessary FREE GIFT proofs-of-purchase with a properly completed offer certificate.

(See inside back cover for offer details)